# SPECIAL MESSAGE TO READERS

## THE ULVERSCROFT FOUNDATION

( )
w r
rese ses.

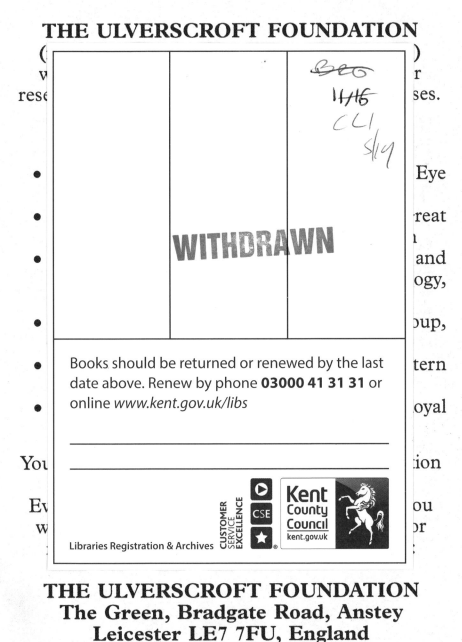

*BEO*
*11/16*
*CLI*
*5/19*

WITHDRAWN

Eye

reat

and

ogy,

up,

Books should be returned or renewed by the last
date above. Renew by phone **03000 41 31 31** or
online *www.kent.gov.uk/libs*

tern

oyal

———————————————————

———————————————————

You tion

Libraries Registration & Archives    CUSTOMER SERVICE EXCELLENCE    Kent County Council kent.gov.uk

Ev ou
w or

## THE ULVERSCROFT FOUNDATION
### The Green, Bradgate Road, Anstey
### Leicester LE7 7FU, England
### Tel: (0116) 236 4325

websit oft.com

A writer of short stories for French periodicals, Maurice Leblanc was the brother of the soprano, actor and author Georgette Leblanc. When he was commissioned in 1905 to write a crime story for *Je Sais Tout*, gentleman burglar Arsène Lupin was born — bringing Leblanc critical and commercial success. In addition to this acclaimed series, Leblanc was a prolific writer of other works — including science fiction and adventure tales — and a recipient of the *Légion d'Honneur* for his services to literature.

## ARSÈNE LUPIN VERSUS
## HOLMLOCK SHEARS

Minutes after M. Gerbois, an unassuming professor of mathematics, purchases a small mahogany writing-desk for his daughter, he is swiftly approached by a young man offering him three times the price for it. Impatiently, he refuses. That evening, the desk is stolen — and, with it, the winning ticket for the latest Press-Association Lottery, worth one million francs! So begins an adventure which will see Arsène Lupin engaged in a battle of wits with his nemesis — the famed English detective Holmlock Shears . . .

*Books by Maurice Leblanc*
*Published by Ulverscroft:*


ARSÈNE LUPIN
ARSÈNE LUPIN, GENTLEMAN BURGLAR

MAURICE LEBLANC

◆

# ARSÈNE LUPIN
# VERSUS
# HOLMLOCK SHEARS

Being a Record of the Duel of Wits between
Arsène Lupin and the English Detective

*Translated from the French by*
*Alexander Teixeira de Mattos*

*Complete and Unabridged*

# ULVERSCROFT
*Leicester*

First published in France as *Arsène Lupin vs. Herlock Sholmès* in 1908

This translation first published in Great Britain in 1910

This Large Print Edition
published 2016

*A catalogue record for this book is available from the British Library.*

ISBN 978–1–4448–3049–1

Published by
F. A. Thorpe (Publishing)
Anstey, Leicestershire

Set by Words & Graphics Ltd.
Anstey, Leicestershire
Printed and bound in Great Britain by
T. J. International Ltd., Padstow, Cornwall

This book is printed on acid-free paper

# Contents

# FIRST EPISODE

## The Blonde Lady

# 1

## Number 514, Series 23

On the 8th of December last, M. Gerbois, professor of mathematics at Versailles College, rummaging among the stores at a second-hand dealer's, discovered a small mahogany writing-desk, which took his fancy because of its many drawers.

'That's just what I want for Suzanne's birthday,' he thought.

M. Gerbois' means were limited and, anxious as he was to please his daughter, he felt it his duty to beat the dealer down. He ended by paying sixty-five francs. As he was writing down his address, a well-groomed and well-dressed young man, who had been hunting through the shop in every direction, caught sight of the writing-desk and asked:

'How much for this?'

'It's sold,' replied the dealer.

'Oh . . . to this gentleman?'

M. Gerbois bowed and, feeling all the happier that one of his fellow-men envied him his purchase, left the shop. But he had not taken ten steps in the street before the young man caught him up and, raising his hat, said, very politely:

'I beg a thousand pardons, sir . . . I am going to ask you an indiscreet question . . . Were you looking for this desk rather than anything else?'

'No. I went to the shop to see if I could find a cheap set of scales for my experiments.'

'Therefore, you do not want it very particularly?'

'I want it, that's all.'

'Because it's old I suppose?'

'Because it's useful.'

'In that case, would you mind exchanging it for another desk, quite as useful, but in better condition?'

'This one is in good condition and I see no point in exchanging it.'

'Still . . . '

M. Gerbois was a man easily irritated and quick to take offense. He replied curtly:

'I must ask you to drop the subject, sir.'

The young man placed himself in front of him.

'I don't know how much you paid, sir . . . but I offer you double the price.'

'No, thank you.'

'Three times the price.'

'Oh, that will do,' exclaimed the professor, impatiently. 'The desk belongs to me and is not for sale.'

4

The young man stared at him with a look that remained imprinted on M. Gerbois' memory, then turned on his heel, without a word, and walked away.

★   ★   ★

An hour later, the desk was brought to the little house on the Viroflay Road where the professor lived. He called his daughter:

'This is for you, Suzanne; that is, if you like it.'

Suzanne was a pretty creature, of a demonstrative temperament and easily pleased. She threw her arms round her father's neck and kissed him as rapturously as though he had made her a present fit for a queen.

That evening, assisted by Hortense the maid, she carried up the desk to her room, cleaned out the drawers and neatly put away her papers, her stationery, her correspondence, her picture postcards and a few secret souvenirs of her cousin Philippe.

M. Gerbois went to the college at half-past seven the next morning. At ten o'clock Suzanne, according to her daily custom, went to meet him at the exit; and it was a great pleasure to him to see her graceful, smiling figure waiting on the pavement opposite the gate.

They walked home together.

'And how do you like the desk?'

'Oh, it's lovely! Hortense and I have polished up the brass handles till they shine like gold.'

'So you're pleased with it?'

'I should think so! I don't know how I did without it all this time.'

They walked up the front garden. The professor said:

'Let's go and look at it before lunch.'

'Yes, that's a good idea.'

She went up the stairs first, but, on reaching the door of her room, she gave a cry of dismay.

'What's the matter?' exclaimed M. Gerbois.

He followed her into the room. The writing-desk was gone.

★ ★ ★

What astonished the police was the wonderful simplicity of the means employed. While Suzanne was out and the maid making her purchases for the day, a ticket-porter, wearing his badge, had stopped his cart before the garden, in sight of the neighbours, and rung the bell twice. The neighbours, not knowing that the servant had left the house, suspected nothing, so that the man was able to effect his object absolutely undisturbed.

This fact must be noted: not a cupboard had been broken open, not so much as a clock displaced. Even Suzanne's purse, which she had left on the marble slab of the desk, was found on the adjacent table, with the gold which it contained. The object of the theft was clearly determined, therefore, and this made it the more difficult to understand; for, after all, why should a man run so great a risk to secure so trivial a spoil?

The only clue which the professor could supply was the incident of the day before:

'From the first, that young man displayed a keen annoyance at my refusal; and I have a positive impression that he left me under a threat.'

It was all very vague. The dealer was questioned. He knew neither of the two gentlemen. As for the desk, he had bought it for forty francs at Chevreuse, at the sale of a person deceased, and he considered that he had re-sold it at a fair price. A persistent inquiry revealed nothing further.

But M. Gerbois remained convinced that he had suffered an enormous loss. A fortune must have been concealed in some secret drawer and that was why the young man, knowing of the hiding-place, had acted with such decision.

'Poor father! What should we have done

with the fortune?' Suzanne kept saying.

'What! Why, with that for your dowry, you could have made the finest match going!'

Suzanne aimed at no one higher than her cousin Philippe, who had not a penny to bless himself with, and she gave a bitter sigh. And life in the little house at Versailles went on gaily, less carelessly than before, shadowed over as it now was with regret and disappointment.

* * *

Two months elapsed. And suddenly, one after the other, came a sequence of the most serious events, forming a surprising run of alternate luck and misfortune.

On the 1st of February, at half-past five, M. Gerbois, who had just come home, with an evening paper in his hand, sat down, put on his spectacles and began to read. The political news was uninteresting. He turned the page and a paragraph at once caught his eye, headed:

### THIRD DRAWING OF THE PRESS-ASSOCIATION LOTTERY

*First prize, 1,000,000 francs: No. 514, Series 23.*

The paper dropped from his hands. The walls swam before his eyes and his heart stopped beating. Number 514, series 23, was the number of his ticket! He had bought it by accident, to oblige one of his friends, for he did not believe in luck; and now he had won!

He took out his memorandum-book, quick! He was quite right: *number 514, series 23,* was jotted down on the fly-leaf. But where was the ticket?

He flew to his study to fetch the box of stationery in which he had put the precious ticket away; and he stopped short as he entered and staggered back, with a pain at his heart: the box was not there and — what an awful thing! — he suddenly realized that the box had not been there for weeks.

'Suzanne! Suzanne!'

She had just come in and ran up the stairs hurriedly. He stammered, in a choking voice:

'Suzanne . . . the box . . . the box of stationery . . . '

'Which one?'

'The one I bought at Louvre . . . on a Thursday . . . it used to stand at the end of the table.'

'But don't you remember, father? . . . We put it away together . . . '

'When?'

'That evening . . . you know, the day before . . . '

'But where? . . . Quick, tell me . . . it's more than I can bear . . . '

'Where? . . . In the writing-desk.'

'In the desk that was stolen?'

'Yes.'

'In the desk that was stolen!'

He repeated the words in a whisper, with a sort of terror. Then he took her hand, and lower still:

'It contained a million, Suzanne . . . '

'Oh, father, why didn't you tell me?' she murmured innocently.

'A million!' he repeated. 'It was the winning number in the press lottery.'

The hugeness of the disaster crushed them and, for a long time, they maintained a silence which they had not the courage to break. At last Suzanne said:

'But, father, they will pay you all the same.'

'Why? On what evidence?'

'Does it require evidence?'

'Of course!'

'And have you none?'

'Yes, I have.'

'Well?'

'It was in the box.'

'In the box that has disappeared?'

'Yes. And the other man will get the money.'

'Why, that would be outrageous! Surely,

father, you can stop the payment?'

'Who knows? Who knows? That man must be extraordinarily clever! He has such wonderful resources . . . Remember . . . think how he got hold of the desk . . . '

His energy revived; he sprang up and, stamping his foot on the floor.

'No, no, no,' he shouted, 'he shan't have that million, he shan't! Why should he? After all, sharp as he may be, he can do nothing, either. If he calls for the money, they'll lock him up! Ah, we shall see, my friend!'

'Have you thought of something, father?'

'I shall defend our rights to the bitter end, come what may! And we shall succeed! . . . The million belongs to me and I mean to have it!'

A few minutes later, he dispatched this telegram:

*Governor,*
*Crédit Foncier,*
*Rue Capucines,*
*Paris.*

*Am owner number 514, series 23; oppose by every legal method payment to any other person.*

*Gerbois*

At almost the same time, the Crédit Foncier received another telegram:

*Number 514, series 23, is in my possession.*
*Arsène Lupin.*

Whenever I sit down to tell one of the numberless adventures which compose the life of Arsène Lupin, I feel a genuine embarrassment, because it is quite clear to me that even the least important of these adventures is known to every one of my readers. As a matter of fact, there is not a move on the part of 'our national thief,' as he has been happily called, but has been described all over the country, not an exploit but has been studied from every point of view, not an action but has been commented upon with an abundance of detail generally reserved for stories of heroic deeds.

Who, for instance, does not know that strange case of the blonde lady, with the curious episodes which were reported under flaring headlines as 'NUMBER 514, SERIES 23!' . . . 'THE MURDER IN THE AVENUE HENRI-MARTIN!' . . . and 'THE BLUE DIAMOND!' . . . What an excitement there was about the intervention of Holmlock Shears, the famous English detective! What an effervescence surrounded the varying fortunes that marked the struggle between those two great artists! And what a din along the boulevards on the day when the newsboys shouted:

'Arrest of Arsène Lupin!'

My excuse is that I can supply something new: I can furnish the key to the puzzle. There is always a certain mystery about these adventures: I can dispel it. I reprint articles that have been read over and over again; I copy out old interviews: but all these things I rearrange and classify and put to the exact test of truth. My collaborator in this work is Arsène Lupin himself, whose kindness to me is inexhaustible. I am also under an occasional obligation to the unspeakable Wilson, the friend and confidant of Holmlock Shears.

★ ★ ★

My readers will remember the Homeric laughter that greeted the publication of the two telegrams. The name of Arsène Lupin alone was a guarantee of originality, a promise of amusement for the gallery. And the gallery, in this case, was the whole world.

An inquiry was immediately set on foot by the Crédit Foncier and it was ascertained that number 514, series 23, had been sold by the

Versailles branch of the Crédit Lyonnais to Major Bressy of the artillery. Now the major had died of a fall from his horse; and it appeared that he told his brother officers, some time before his death, that he had been obliged to part with his ticket to a friend.

'That friend was myself,' declared M. Gerbois.

'Prove it,' objected the governor of the Crédit Foncier.

'Prove it? That's quite easy. Twenty people will tell you that I kept up constant relations with the major and that we used to meet at the café on the Place d'Armes. It was there that, one day, to oblige him in a moment of financial embarrassment, I took his ticket off him and gave him twenty francs for it.'

'Have you any witnesses to the transaction?'

'No.'

'Then upon what do you base your claim?'

'Upon the letter which he wrote me on the subject.'

'What letter?'

'A letter pinned to the ticket.'

'Produce it.'

'But it was in the stolen writing-desk!'

'Find it.'

★ ★ ★

The letter was communicated to the press by Arsène Lupin. A paragraph inserted in the *Écho de France* — which has the honour of being his official organ and in which he seems to be one of the principal shareholders — announced that he was placing in the hands of Maître Detinan, his counsel, the letter which Major Bressy had written to him, Lupin, personally.

There was a burst of delight: Arsène Lupin was represented by counsel! Arsène Lupin, respecting established customs, had appointed a member of the bar to act for him!

The reporters rushed to interview Maître Detinan, an influential radical deputy, a man endowed with the highest integrity and a mind of uncommon shrewdness, which was, at the same time, somewhat skeptical and given to paradox.

Maître Detinan was exceedingly sorry to say that he had never had the pleasure of meeting Arsène Lupin, but he had, in point of fact, received his instructions, was greatly flattered at being selected, keenly alive to the honour shown him and determined to defend his client's rights to the utmost. He opened his brief and without hesitation showed the major's letter. It proved the sale of the ticket, but did not mention the purchaser's name. It began, 'My dear friend,' simply.

' 'My dear friend' means me,' added Arsène Lupin, in a note enclosing the major's letter. 'And the best proof is that I have the letter.'

The bevy of reporters at once flew off to M. Gerbois, who could do nothing but repeat: ' 'My dear friend' is no one but myself. Arsène Lupin stole the major's letter with the lottery-ticket.'

'Tell him to prove it,' was Lupin's rejoinder to the journalists.

'But he stole the desk!' exclaimed M. Gerbois in front of the same journalists.

'Tell him to prove it!' retorted Lupin once again.

And a delightful entertainment was provided for the public by this duel between the two owners of number 514, series 23, by the constant coming and going of the journalists and by the coolness of Arsène Lupin as opposed to the frenzy of poor M. Gerbois.

Unhappy man! The press was full of his lamentations! He confessed the full extent of his misfortunes in a touchingly ingenuous way:

'It's Suzanne's dowry, gentlemen, that the villain has stolen! . . . For myself, personally, I don't care; but for Suzanne! Just think, a million! Ten hundred thousand francs! Ah, I always said the desk contained a treasure!'

He was told in vain that his adversary,

when taking away the desk, knew nothing of the existence of the lottery-ticket and that, in any case, no one could have foreseen that this particular ticket would win the first prize. All he did was to moan:

'Don't talk to me; of course he knew! . . . If not, why should he have taken the trouble to steal that wretched desk?'

'For unknown reasons, but certainly not to get hold of a scrap of paper which, at that time, was worth the modest sum of twenty francs.'

'The sum of a million! He knew it . . . He knows everything! . . . Ah, you don't know the sort of a man he is, the ruffian! . . . He hasn't defrauded you of a million, you see! . . . '

This talk could have gone on a long time yet. But, twelve days later, M. Gerbois received a letter from Arsène Lupin, marked 'Private and confidential,' which worried him not a little:

*Dear Sir*

*The gallery is amusing itself at our expense. Do you not think that the time has come to be serious? I, for my part, have quite made up my mind.*

*The position is clear: I hold a ticket which I am not entitled to cash and you are entitled* to cash a ticket which you do not hold. Therefore neither of us can do anything without the other.

Now you would not consent to surrender your rights to me nor I to give up my ticket to you.

What are we to do?

I see only one way out of the difficulty: let us divide. Half a million for you, half a million for me. Is not that fair? And would not this judgment of Solomon satisfy the sense of justice in each of us?

I propose this as an equitable solution, but also an immediate solution. It is not an offer which you have time to discuss, but a necessity before which circumstances compel you to bow. I give you three days for reflection. I hope that, on Friday morning, I may have the pleasure of seeing a discreet advertisement in the agony-column of the Écho de France, addressed to 'M. Ars. Lup.' and containing, in veiled terms, your unreserved assent to the compact which I am suggesting to you. In that event, you will at once recover possession of the ticket and receive the million, on the understanding that you will hand me five hundred thousand francs in a way which I will indicate hereafter.

Should you refuse, I have taken measures that will produce exactly the same result;

*but, apart from the very serious trouble which your obstinacy would bring upon you, you would be the poorer by twenty-five thousand francs, which I should have to deduct for additional expenses.*

*I am, dear sir,*
*Very respectfully yours,*
*Arsène Lupin.*

M. Gerbois, in his exasperation, was guilty of the colossal blunder of showing this letter and allowing it to be copied. His indignation drove him to every sort of folly:

'Not a penny! He shall not have a penny!' he shouted before the assembled reporters. 'Share what belongs to me? Never! Let him tear up his ticket if he likes!'

'Still, half a million francs is better than nothing.'

'It's not a question of that, but of my rights; and those rights I shall establish in a court of law.'

'Go to law with Arsène Lupin? That would be funny!'

'No, but the Crédit Foncier. They are bound to hand me the million.'

'Against the ticket or at least against evidence that you bought it?'

'The evidence exists, seeing that Arsène Lupin admits that he stole the desk.'

'What judge is going to take Arsène Lupin's word?'

'I don't care, I shall go to law!'

The gallery was delighted. Bets were made, some people being certain that Lupin would bring M. Gerbois to terms, others that he would not go beyond threats. And the people felt a sort of apprehension; for the adversaries were unevenly matched, the one being so fierce in his attacks, while the other was as frightened as a hunted deer.

On Friday, there was a rush for the *Écho de France* and the agony-column on the fifth page was scanned with feverish eyes. There was not a line addressed to 'M. Ars. Lup.' M. Gerbois had replied to Arsène Lupin's demands with silence. It was a declaration of war.

That evening the papers contained the news that Mlle. Gerbois had been kidnapped.

\* \* \*

The most delightful factor in what I may call the Arsène Lupin entertainment is the eminently ludicrous part played by the police. Everything passes outside their knowledge. Lupin speaks, writes, warns, orders, threatens, carries out his plans, as though there were no police, no detectives, no magistrates, no impediment of any kind in existence. They seem of no account to him whatever. No obstacle enters into his calculations.

And yet the police struggle to do their best. The moment the name of Arsène Lupin is mentioned, the whole force, from top to bottom, takes fire, boils and foams with rage. He is the enemy, the enemy who mocks you, provokes you, despises you, or, even worse, ignores you. And what can one do against an enemy like that?

According to the evidence of the servant, Suzanne went out at twenty minutes to ten. At five minutes past ten, her father, on leaving the college, failed to see her on the pavement where she usually waited for him. Everything, therefore, must have taken place in the course of the short twenty minutes' walk which brought Suzanne from her door to the college, or at least quite close to the college.

Two neighbours declared that they had passed her about three hundred yards from the house. A lady had seen a girl walking along the avenue whose description corresponded with Suzanne's. After that, all was blank.

Inquiries were made on every side. The officials at the railway-stations and the customs-barriers were questioned. They had seen nothing on that day which could relate to the kidnapping of a young girl. However, a grocer at Ville-d'Avray stated that he had supplied a closed motor-car, coming from Paris, with petrol. There was a chauffeur on the front seat and a lady with fair hair — exceedingly fair hair, the witness said — inside. The car returned from Versailles an hour later. A block in the traffic compelled it to slacken speed and the grocer was able to perceive that there was now another lady seated beside the blonde lady whom he had seen first. This second lady was wrapped up in veils and shawls. No doubt it was Suzanne Gerbois.

Consequently, the abduction must have taken place in broad daylight, on a busy road, in the very heart of the town! How? At what spot? Not a cry had been heard, not a suspicious movement observed.

The grocer described the car, a Peugeot limousine, 24 horse-power, with a dark blue body. Inquiries were made, on chance, of Mme. Bob-Walthour, the manageress of the Grand Garage, who used to make a specialty of motor-car elopements. She had, in fact, on Friday morning, hired out a Peugeot limousine for the day to a fair-haired lady, whom she had not seen since.

'But the driver?'

'He was a man called Ernest, whom I engaged the day before on the strength of his excellent testimonials.'

'Is he here?'

'No, he brought back the car and has not been here since.'

'Can't we get hold of him?'

'Certainly, by applying to the people who recommended him. I will give you the addresses.'

The police called on these persons. None of them knew the man called Ernest.

And every trail which they followed to find their way out of the darkness led only to greater darkness and denser fogs.

M. Gerbois was not the man to maintain a contest which had opened in so disastrous a fashion for him. Inconsolable at the disappearance of his daughter and pricked with remorse, he capitulated. An advertisement which appeared in the *Écho de France* and aroused general comment proclaimed his absolute and unreserved surrender. It was a complete defeat: the war was over in four times twenty-four hours.

Two days later, M. Gerbois walked across the courtyard of the Crédit Foncier. He was shown in to the governor and handed him number 514, series 23. The governor gave a start:

'Oh, so you have it? Did they give it back to you?'

'I mislaid it and here it is,' replied M. Gerbois.

'But you said . . . There was a question . . .'

'That's all lies and tittle-tattle.'

'But nevertheless we should require some corroborative document.'

'Will the major's letter do?'

'Certainly.'

'Here it is.'

'Very well. Please leave these papers with us. We are allowed a fortnight in which to verify them. I will let you know when you can call for the money. In the meanwhile, I think that you would be well-advised to say nothing and to complete this business in the most absolute silence.'

'That is what I intend to do.'

M. Gerbois did not speak, nor the governor either. But there are certain secrets which leak out without any indiscretion having been committed, and the public suddenly learnt that Arsène Lupin had had the pluck to send number 514, series 23, back to M. Gerbois! The news was received with a sort of stupefied admiration. What a bold player he must be, to fling so important a trump as the precious ticket upon the table! True, he had parted with it wittingly, in exchange for a card which equalized the chances. But suppose the girl escaped? Suppose they succeeded in recapturing his hostage?

The police perceived the enemy's weak point and redoubled their efforts. With Arsène Lupin disarmed and despoiled by himself, caught in his own toils, receiving not a single sou of the coveted million . . . the laugh would at once be on the other side.

But the question was to find Suzanne. And they did not find her, nor did she escape!

'Very well,' people said, 'that's settled: Arsène has won the first game. But the difficult part is still to come! Mlle. Gerbois is in his hands, we admit, and he will not hand her over without the five hundred thousand francs. But how and where is the exchange to take place? For the exchange to take place, there must be a meeting; and what is to prevent M. Gerbois from informing the police and thus both recovering his daughter and keeping the money?'

The professor was interviewed. Greatly cast down, longing only for silence, he remained impenetrable:

'I have nothing to say; I am waiting.'

'And Mlle. Gerbois?'

'The search is being continued.'

'But Arsène Lupin has written to you?'

'No.'

'Do you swear that?'

'No.'

'That means yes. What are his instructions?'

'I have nothing to say.'

Maître Detinan was next besieged and showed the same discretion.

'M. Lupin is my client,' he replied, with an affectation of gravity. 'You will understand that I am bound to maintain the most absolute reserve.'

All these mysteries annoyed the gallery. Plots were evidently hatching in the dark. Arsène Lupin was arranging and tightening the meshes of his nets, while the police were keeping up a watch by day and night round M. Gerbois. And people discussed the only three possible endings: arrest, triumph, or grotesque and pitiful failure.

But, as it happened, public curiosity was destined to be only partially satisfied; and the exact truth is revealed for the first time in these pages.

On Thursday, the 12th of March, M. Gerbois received the notice from the Crédit Foncier, in an ordinary envelope.

At one o'clock on Friday, he took the train for Paris. A thousand notes of a thousand francs each were handed to him at two.

While he was counting them over, one by one, with trembling hands — for was this money not Suzanne's ransom? — two men sat talking in a cab drawn up at a short distance from the main entrance. One of these men had grizzled hair and a powerful face, which contrasted oddly with his dress and bearing, which was that of a small clerk. It was Chief-Inspector Ganimard, old Ganimard, Lupin's implacable enemy. And Ganimard said to Detective-Sergeant Folenfant:

'The old chap won't be long . . . we shall see him come out in five minutes. Is everything ready?'

'Quite.'

'How many are we?'

'Eight, including two on bicycles.'

'And myself, who count as three. It's enough, but not too many. That Gerbois must not escape us at any price . . . if he does, we're diddled: he'll meet Lupin at the place they have agreed upon; he'll swap the young lady for the half-million; and the trick's done.'

'But why on earth won't the old chap act with us? It would be so simple! By giving us a hand in the game, he could keep the whole million.'

'Yes, but he's afraid. If he tries to jockey the other, he won't get his daughter back.'

'What other?'

'Him.'

Ganimard pronounced this word 'him' in a grave and rather awe-struck tone, as though he were speaking of a supernatural being who had already played him a nasty trick or two.

'It's very strange,' said Sergeant Folenfant, judiciously, 'that we should be reduced to protecting that gentleman against himself.'

'With Lupin, everything is upside down,' sighed Ganimard.

A minute elapsed.

'Look out!' he said.

M. Gerbois was leaving the bank. When he came to the end of the Rue des Capucines, he turned down the boulevard, keeping to the left-hand side. He walked away slowly, along the shops, and looked into the windows.

'Our friend's too quiet,' said Ganimard. 'A fellow with a million in his pocket does not keep so quiet as all that.'

'What can he do?'

'Oh, nothing, of course . . . No matter, I mistrust him. It's Lupin, Lupin . . . '

At that moment M. Gerbois went to a kiosk, bought some newspapers, took his change, unfolded one of the sheets and, with outstretched arms, began to read, while walking on with short steps. And, suddenly, with a bound, he jumped into a motor-cab which was waiting beside the curb. The power must have been on, for the car drove off rapidly, turned the corner of the Madeleine and disappeared.

'By Jupiter!' cried Ganimard. 'Another of his inventions!'

He darted forward and other men, at the same time as himself, ran round the Madeleine. But he burst out laughing. The motor-car had broken down at the beginning of the Boulevard Malesherbes and M. Gerbois was getting out.

'Quick, Folenfant . . . the driver . . . perhaps it's the man called Ernest.'

Folenfant tackled the chauffeur. It was a man called Gaston, one of the motor-cab company's drivers; a gentleman had engaged him ten minutes before and had told him to wait by the newspaper-kiosk, 'with steam up,' until another gentleman came.

'And what address did the second fare give?' asked Folenfant.

'He gave me no address . . . 'Boulevard Malesherbes . . . Avenue de Messine . . . give you an extra tip': that's all he said.'

★  ★  ★

During this time, however, M. Gerbois, without losing a minute, had sprung into the first passing cab:

'Drive to the Concorde tube-station!'

The professor left the tube at the Place du Palais-Royal, hurried into another cab and drove to the Place de la Bourse. Here he went by tube again, as far as the Avenue de Villiers, where he took a third cab:

'25, Rue Clapeyron!'

No. 25, Rue Clapeyron, is separated from the Boulevard des Batignolles by the house at the corner. The professor went up to the first floor and rang. A gentleman opened the door.

'Does Maître Detinan live here?'

'I am Maître Detinan. M. Gerbois, I presume?'

'That's it.'

'I was expecting you. Pray come in.'

When M. Gerbois entered the lawyer's office, the clock was striking three and he at once said:

'This is the time he appointed. Isn't he here?'

'Not yet.'

M. Gerbois sat down, wiped his forehead, looked at his watch as though he did not know the time and continued, anxiously:

'Will he come?'

The lawyer replied:

'You are asking me something, sir, which I myself am most curious to know. I have never felt so impatient in my life. In any case, if he comes, he is taking a big risk, for the house has been closely watched for the past fortnight . . . They suspect me.'

'And me even more,' said the professor. 'I am not at all sure that the detectives set to watch me have been thrown off my track.'

'But then . . . '

'It would not be my fault,' cried the professor, vehemently, 'and he can have nothing to reproach me with. What did I promise to do? To obey his orders. Well, I have obeyed his orders blindly: I cashed the ticket at the time which he fixed and came on to you in the manner which he ordered. I am responsible for my daughter's misfortune and I have kept my engagements in all good faith. It is for him to keep his.' And he added, in an anxious voice, 'He will bring back my daughter, won't he?'

'I hope so.'

'Still . . . you've seen him?'

'I? No. He simply wrote asking me to receive you both, to send away my servants before three o'clock and to let no one into my flat between the time of your arrival and his departure. If I did not consent to this proposal, he begged me to let him know by means of two lines in the *Écho de France*. But I am only too pleased to do Arsène Lupin a service and I consent to everything.'

M. Gerbois moaned:

'Oh, dear, how will it all end?'

He took the bank-notes from his pocket, spread them on the table and divided them into two bundles of five hundred each. Then the two men sat silent. From time to time, M. Gerbois pricked up his ears: wasn't that a ring at the door-bell? . . . His anguish increased with every minute that passed. And Maître Detinan also experienced an impression that was almost painful.

For a moment, in fact, the advocate lost all his composure. He rose abruptly from his seat:

'We shan't see him . . . How can we expect to? . . . It would be madness on his part! He trusts us, no doubt: we are honest men, incapable of betraying him. But the danger lies elsewhere.'

And M. Gerbois, shattered, with his hands on the notes, stammered:

'If he would only come, oh, if he would only come! I would give all this to have Suzanne back.'

The door opened.

'Half will do, M. Gerbois.'

Some one was standing on the threshold — a young man, fashionably dressed — and M. Gerbois at once recognized the person who had accosted him outside the curiosity-shop. He leapt toward him:

'And Suzanne? Where is my daughter?'

Arsène Lupin closed the door carefully and, quietly unbuttoning his gloves, said to the lawyer:

'My dear maître, I can never thank you sufficiently for your kindness in consenting to defend my rights. I shall not forget it.'

Maître Detinan could only murmur:

'But you never rang . . . I did not hear the door . . .'

'Bells and doors are things that have to do their work without ever being heard. I am here all the same; and that is the great thing.'

'My daughter! Suzanne! What have you done with her?' repeated the professor.

'Heavens, sir,' said Lupin, 'what a hurry you're in! Come, calm yourself; your daughter will be in your arms in a moment.'

He walked up and down the room and then, in the tone of a magnate distributing praises:

'I congratulate you, M. Gerbois, on the skilful way in which you acted just now. If the motor hadn't had that ridiculous accident we should simply have met at the Étoile and saved Maître Detinan the annoyance of this visit . . . However, it was destined otherwise!'

He caught sight of the two bundles of bank-notes and cried:

'Ah, that's right! The million is there!

. . . Let us waste no time . . . Will you allow me?'

'But,' said Maître Detinan, placing himself in front of the table, 'Mlle. Gerbois is not here yet.'

'Well?'

'Well, isn't her presence indispensable?'

'I see, I see! Arsène Lupin inspires only a partial confidence. He pockets his half-million, without restoring the hostage. Ah, my dear maître, I am sadly misunderstood! Because fate has obliged me to perform acts of a rather . . . special character, doubts are cast upon my good faith . . . mine! I, a man all scruples and delicacy! . . . However, my dear maître, if you're afraid, open your window and call out. There are quite a dozen detectives in the street.'

'Do you think so?'

Arsène Lupin raised the blind:

'I doubt if M. Gerbois is capable of throwing Ganimard off the scent . . . What did I tell you? There he is, the dear old chap!'

'Impossible!' cried the professor. 'I swear to you, though . . . '

'That you have not betrayed me? . . . I don't doubt it, but the fellows are clever. Look, there's Folenfant! . . . And Gréaume! . . . And Dieuzy! . . . All my best pals, what?'

Maître Detinan looked at him in surprise.

What calmness! He was laughing with a happy laugh, as though he were amusing himself at some child's game, with no danger threatening him.

This carelessness did even more than the sight of the detectives to reassure the lawyer. He moved away from the table on which the bank-notes lay.

Arsène Lupin took up the two bundles one after the other, counted twenty-five notes from each of them and, handing the lawyer the fifty bank-notes thus obtained, said:

'M. Gerbois' share of your fee, my dear maître, and Arsène Lupin's. We owe you that.'

'You owe me nothing,' said Maître Detinan.

'What! After all the trouble we've given you!'

'You forget the pleasure it has been to me to take that trouble.'

'You mean to say, my dear maître, that you refuse to accept anything from Arsène Lupin. That's the worst,' he sighed, 'of having a bad reputation.' He held out the fifty thousand francs to the professor. 'Monsieur, let me give you this in memory of our pleasant meeting: it will be my wedding-present to Mlle. Gerbois.'

M. Gerbois snatched at the notes, but protested:

'My daughter is not being married.'

'She can't be married if you refuse your consent. But she is dying to be married.'

'What do you know about it?'

'I know that young ladies often cherish dreams without Papa's consent. Fortunately, there are good geniuses, called Arsène Lupin, who discover the secret of those charming souls hidden away in their writing-desks.'

'Did you discover nothing else?' asked Maître Detinan. 'I confess that I am very curious to know why that desk was the object of your attentions.'

'Historical reasons, my dear maître. Although, contrary to M. Gerbois' opinion, it contained no treasure beyond the lottery-ticket, of which I did not know, I wanted it and had been looking for it for some time. The desk, which is made of yew and mahogany, decorated with acanthus-leaf capitals, was found in Marie Walewska's discreet little house at Boulogne-sur-Seine and has an inscription on one of the drawers: '*Dedicated to Napoleon I., Emperor of the French, by his most faithful servant, Mancion.*' Underneath are these words, carved with the point of a knife: '*Thine, Marie.*' Napoleon had it copied afterward for the Empress Josephine, so that the writing-desk which people used to admire at the Malmaison and which they still admire at the Garde-Meuble is only an imperfect copy of the one which now forms part of my collection.'

M. Gerbois sighed:

'Oh, dear! If I had only known this at the shop, how willingly I would have let you have it!'

Arsène Lupin laughed:

'Yes; and you would, besides, have had the appreciable advantage of keeping the whole of number 514, series 23, for yourself.'

'And you would not have thought of kidnapping my daughter, whom all this business must needs have upset.'

'All what business?'

'The abduction . . . '

'But, my dear sir, you are quite mistaken. Mlle. Gerbois was not abducted.'

'My daughter was not abducted!'

'Not at all. Kidnapping, abduction implies violence. Now Mlle. Gerbois acted as a hostage of her own free will.'

'Of her own free will!' repeated the professor, in confusion.

'And almost at her own request! Why, a quick-witted young lady like Mlle. Gerbois, who, moreover, harbours a secret passion at the bottom of her heart, was hardly likely to refuse the opportunity of securing her dowry. Oh, I assure you it was easy enough to make her understand that there was no other way of overcoming your resistance!'

Maître Detanin was greatly amused. He put in:

'You must have found a difficulty in coming to terms. I can't believe that Mlle. Gerbois allowed you to speak to her.'

'I didn't. I have not even the honour of knowing her. A lady of my acquaintance was good enough to undertake the negotiations.'

'The blonde lady in the motor-car, I suppose?' said Maître Detinan.

'Just so. Everything was settled at the first interview near the college. Since then, Mlle. Gerbois and her new friend have been abroad, have visited Belgium and Holland in the most agreeable and instructive manner for a young girl. However, she will tell you everything herself . . . '

The hall-door bell rang: three rings in quick succession, then a single ring, then another single ring.

'There she is,' said Lupin. 'My dear maître, if you would not mind . . . '

The lawyer ran to open the door.

★ ★ ★

Two young women entered. One of them flung herself into M. Gerbois' arms. The other went up to Lupin. She was tall and shapely, with a very pale face, and her fair hair, which glittered like gold, was parted into two loosely waved bandeaux. Dressed in black, wearing no ornament beyond a five-fold jet necklace, she nevertheless struck a note of elegance and refinement.

Arsène Lupin spoke a few words to her and then, bowing to Mlle. Gerbois, said:

'I must apologize to you, mademoiselle, for all this annoyance; but I hope, nevertheless, that you have not been too unhappy . . . '

'Unhappy! I should even have been very happy, if it had not been for my poor father.'

'Then all is for the best. Embrace him once more and take the opportunity — you will never have a better — of speaking to him about your cousin.'

'My cousin? . . . What do you mean? . . . I don't understand . . . '

'Oh, I think you understand . . . Your cousin Philippe . . . the young man whose letters you kept so preciously . . . '

Suzanne blushed, lost countenance and then, taking Lupin's advice, threw herself once more into her father's arms.

Lupin looked at them both with a melting eye:

'Ah, we are always rewarded for doing good! What a touching sight! Happy father! Happy daughter! And to think that this happiness is your work, Lupin! Those two beings will bless you later . . . Your name will be piously handed down to their children and their children's children . . . Oh, family life! . . . Family life! . . . ' He turned to the window. 'Is our dear Ganimard there still? . . . How he would love to witness this charming display of affection! . . . But no, he is not there . . . There is nobody . . . they're all gone . . . By Jove, the position is growing serious! . . . I shouldn't wonder if they were in the gateway by now . . . or by the porter's lodge . . . or even on the stairs!'

M. Gerbois made an involuntary movement. Now that his daughter was restored to him, he began to see things in their true light. The arrest of his adversary meant half a million to him. Instinctively, he took a step toward the door . . . Lupin barred his way, as though by accident:

'Where are you going, M. Gerbois? To defend me against them? You are too kind! Pray don't trouble. Besides, I assure you they are more perplexed than I.' And he continued, reflectively: 'What do they know, when all is said? That you are here . . . and, perhaps, that Mlle. Gerbois is here too, for they must have seen her come with an unknown lady. But they have no idea that I am here. How could I have entered a house which they searched this morning from cellar to garret? No, in all probability they are waiting for me to catch me on the wing . . . poor fellows! . . . Unless they have guessed that the unknown lady was sent by me and presume that she has been commissioned to effect the exchange . . . In that case, they are preparing to arrest her when she leaves . . . '

The bell rang.

Lupin stopped M. Gerbois with an abrupt gesture and, in a harsh and peremptory voice, said:

'Stay where you are, sir! Think of your daughter and be reasonable; if not . . . As for you, Maître Detinan, I have your word.'

M. Gerbois stood rooted to the floor. The lawyer did not move.

Lupin took up his hat without the least show of haste. There was a little dust on it; he brushed it with the back of his coat-sleeve:

'My dear maître, if I can ever be of use to you . . . My best wishes, Mlle. Suzanne, and kind regards to M. Philippe.' He took a heavy gold hunter from his pocket. 'M. Gerbois, it is now eighteen minutes to four: I authorize you to leave this room at fourteen minutes to four . . . Not a moment before fourteen minutes to four . . . Is it understood?'

'But they'll enter by force!' Maître Detinan could not help saying.

'You forget the law, my dear maître! Ganimard would never dare to violate the sanctity of a Frenchman's home. We should have time for a pleasant rubber. But forgive me, you all three seem a little upset and I would not for the world abuse . . . '

He placed the watch on the table, opened the door of the room and, addressing the fair-haired lady, said:

'Shall we go, dear?'

He stood back for her to pass, made a parting and very respectful bow to Mlle. Gerbois, walked out and closed the door after him. And they heard him, in the hall, saying aloud:

'Good-afternoon, Ganimard, how are you? Remember me very kindly to Mme. Ganimard . . . I must drop in on her to lunch one of these days . . . Good-bye, Ganimard!'

The bell rang again, sharply, violently, followed by repeated knocks and by the sound of voices on the landing . . .

'A quarter to four,' stammered M. Gerbois.

After a few seconds, he stepped boldly into the hall. Arsène Lupin and the fair-haired lady were not there.

'Father! . . . You mustn't! . . . Wait!' cried Suzanne.

'Wait? You're mad! . . . Show consideration to that scoundrel! . . . And what about the half-million? . . . '

He opened the door.

Ganimard rushed in:

42

'Where's that lady? . . . And Lupin?'

'He was there . . . he is there now.'

Ganimard gave a shout of triumph:

'We've got him! . . . The house is surrounded.'

Maître Detinan objected:

'But the servants' staircase?'

'The servants' staircase leads to the court-yard and there's only one outlet, the front door: I have ten men watching it.'

'But he did not come in by the front door . . . He won't go out that way either . . . '

'Which way, then?' jeered Ganimard. 'Through the air?'

He drew back a curtain. A long passage was revealed, leading to the kitchen. Ganimard ran down it and found that the door of the servants' staircase was double-locked.

Opening the window, he called to one of the detectives:

'Seen any one?'

'No, sir.'

'Then,' he exclaimed, 'they are in the flat! . . . They are hiding in one of the rooms! . . . It is physically impossible for them to have escaped . . . Ah, Lupin, my lad, you did me once, but I'm having my revenge this time! . . . '

★　★　★

At seven o'clock in the evening, astonished at receiving no news, the head of the detective-service, M. Dudouis, called at the Rue Clapeyron in person. He put a few questions to the men who were watching the house and then went up to Maître Detinan, who took him to his room. There he saw a man, or rather a man's two legs struggling on the carpet, while the body to which they belonged was stuffed up the chimney.

'Hi! . . . Hi! . . . ' yelped a stifled voice.

And a more distant voice, from right above, echoed:

'Hi! . . . Hi! . . . '

M. Dudouis laughed and exclaimed:

'Well, Ganimard, what are you playing sweep for?'

The inspector withdrew his body from the chimney. He was unrecognizable, with his black face, his sooty clothes and his eyes glowing with fever.

'I'm looking for him,' he growled.

'For whom?'

'Arsène Lupin . . . Arsène Lupin and his lady friend.'

'But what next? You surely don't imagine they're hiding up the chimney?'

Ganimard rose to his feet, put his five soot-covered fingers on the sleeve of his superior's coat and, in a hollow, angry voice, said:

'Where would you have them be, chief? They must be somewhere. They are beings of flesh and blood, like you and me; they can't vanish into thin air.'

'No; but they vanish for all that.'

'Where? Where? The house is surrounded! There are men on the roof!'

'What about the next house?'

'There's no communication.'

'The flats on the other floors?'

'I know all the tenants. They have seen nobody. They have heard nobody.'

'Are you sure you know them all?'

'Every one. The porter answers for them. Besides, as an additional precaution, I have posted a man in each flat.'

'We must find them, you know.'

'That's what I say, chief, that's what I say. We must and we shall, because they are both here . . . they can't be anywhere else. Be easy, chief; if I don't catch them to-night, I shall to-morrow . . . I shall spend the night here! . . . I shall spend the night here! . . . '

He did, in fact, spend the night there and the next night and the night after that. And, when three whole days and three nights had elapsed, not only had he failed to discover the elusive Lupin and his no less elusive companion, but he had not even observed the slightest clue upon which to found the slightest supposition.

And that is why he refused to budge from his first opinion:

'Once there's no trace of their flight, they must be here!'

It is possible that, in the depths of his mind, he was less firmly convinced. But he refused to admit as much to himself. No, a thousand times no: a man and a woman do not vanish into space like the wicked genii in the fairy-tales! And, without losing courage, he continued his searchings and investigations, as though he hoped to discover them hidden in some impenetrable retreat, bricked up in the walls of the house.

# 2

## The Blue Diamond

In the evening of the twenty-seventh of March, old General Baron d'Hautrec, who had been French Ambassador in Berlin under the Second Empire, was sleeping comfortably in an easy-chair in the house which his brother had left him six months before, at 134, Avenue Henri-Martin. His lady companion continued to read aloud to him, while Sœur Auguste warmed the bed and prepared the night-light.

As an exceptional case, the sister was returning to her convent that evening, to spend the night with the Mother Superior, and, at eleven o'clock, she said:

'I'm finished now, Mlle. Antoinette, and I'm going.'

'Very well, sister.'

'And don't forget that the cook is sleeping out to-night and that you are alone in the house with the man-servant.'

'You need have no fear for monsieur le baron: I shall sleep in the next room, as arranged, and leave the door open.'

The nun went away. A minute later, Charles, the man servant, came in for his orders. The baron had woke up. He replied himself:

'Just the same as usual, Charles. Try the electric bell, to see if it rings in your bedroom properly, and, if you hear it during the night, run down at once and go straight to the doctor.'

'Are you still anxious, general?'

'I don't feel well . . . I don't feel at all well. Come, Mlle. Antoinette, where were we in your book?'

'Aren't you going to bed, monsieur le baron?'

'No, no, I don't care to go to bed till very late; besides, I can do without help.'

Twenty minutes later, the old man dozed off again and Antoinette moved away on tiptoe.

At that moment, Charles was carefully closing the shutters on the ground floor, as usual. In the kitchen, he pushed the bolt of the door that led to the garden and, in the front hall, he not only locked the double door, but put up the chain fastening the two leaves. Then he went up to his attic on the third floor, got into bed and fell asleep.

Perhaps an hour had elapsed when, suddenly, he jumped out of bed: the bell was ringing. It went on for quite a long time, seven or eight seconds, perhaps, and in a steady, uninterrupted way.

'That's all right,' said Charles, recovering his wits. 'Some fresh whim of the baron's, I suppose.'

He huddled on his clothes, ran down the stairs, stopped before the door and, from habit, knocked. No answer. He entered the room:

'Hullo!' he muttered. 'No light . . . What on earth have they put the light out for?' And he called, in a whisper, 'Mademoiselle! . . . '

No reply.

'Are you there, mademoiselle? . . . What's the matter? Is monsieur le baron ill?'

The same silence continued around him, a heavy silence that ended by impressing him. He took two steps forward: his foot knocked against a chair and, on touching it, he perceived that it was overturned. And thereupon his hand came upon other objects on the floor: a small table, a fire-screen. Greatly alarmed, he went back to the wall and felt for the electric switch. He found it and turned on the light.

In the middle of the room, between the table and the looking-glass wardrobe, lay the body of his master, the Baron d'Hautrec.

'What!' he stammered. 'Is it possible?'

He did not know what to do and, without moving, with his eyes starting from his head, he stood gazing at the general disorder of the room: the chairs upset, a great crystal candle-stick smashed into a thousand pieces, the clock lying on the marble hearth-stone, all signs of a fierce and hideous struggle. The handle of a little steel dagger gleamed near the body. The blade was dripping with blood. A handkerchief stained with red marks hung down from the mattress.

Charles gave a yell of horror: the body had suddenly stretched itself in one last effort and then shrunk up again . . . Two or three convulsions; and that was all.

He stooped forward. Blood was trickling from a tiny wound in the neck and spotting the carpet with dark stains. The face still wore an expression of mad terror.

'They've killed him,' he stammered, 'they've killed him!'

And he shuddered at the thought of another probable crime: was not the companion sleeping in the next room? And would not the baron's murderer have killed her too?

He pushed open the door: the room was empty. He concluded that either Antoinette had been carried off or that she had gone before the crime.

He returned to the baron's room and, his

eyes falling upon the writing-desk, he observed that it had not been broken open. More remarkable still, he saw a handful of louis d'or on the table, beside the bunch of keys and the pocketbook which the baron placed there every evening. Charles took up the pocketbook and went through it. One of the compartments contained bank-notes. He counted them: there were thirteen notes of a hundred francs each.

Then the temptation became too strong for him: instinctively, mechanically, while his thoughts did not even take part in the movement of his hand, he took the thirteen notes, hid them in his jacket, rushed down the stairs, drew the bolt, unhooked the chain, closed the door after him and fled through the garden.

⋆   ⋆   ⋆

Charles was an honest man at heart. He had no sooner pushed back the gate than, under the influence of the fresh air, with his face cooled by the rain, he stopped. The deed of which he had been guilty appeared to him in its true light and struck him with sudden horror.

A cab passed. He hailed the driver:

'Hi, mate! Go to the police-station and

bring back the commissary ... Gallop! There's murder been done!'

The driver whipped up his horse. But, when Charles tried to go in again, he could not: he had closed the gate himself and the gate could not be opened from the outside.

On the other hand, it was of no use ringing, for there was no one in the house. He therefore walked up and down along the gardens which, at the La Muette end, line the avenue with a pleasant border of trim green shrubs. And it was not until he had waited for nearly an hour that he was at last able to tell the commissary the details of the crime and hand him the thirteen bank-notes.

During this time, a locksmith was sent for who, with great difficulty, succeeded in forcing the gate of the garden and the front door. The commissary went upstairs and, at once, at the first glance, said to the servant:

'Why, you told me that the room was in the greatest disorder!'

He turned round. Charles seemed pinned to the threshold, hypnotized: all the furniture had resumed its usual place! The little table was standing between the two windows, the chairs were on their legs and the clock in the middle of the mantelpiece. The shivers of the smashed candlestick had disappeared.

Gaping with stupor, he articulated:

'The body . . . Monsieur le baron . . . '

'Yes,' cried the commissary, 'where is the victim?'

He walked up to the bed. Under a large sheet, which he drew aside, lay General the Baron d'Hautrec, late French Ambassador in Berlin. His body was covered with his general's cloak, decorated with the cross of the Legion of Honour. The face was calm. The eyes were closed.

The servant stammered:

'Someone must have come.'

'Which way?'

'I can't say, but someone has been here during my absence . . . Look, there was a very thin steel dagger there, on the floor . . . And then, on the table, a blood-stained handkerchief . . . That's all gone . . . They've taken everything away . . . They've arranged everything . . . '

'But who?'

'The murderer!'

'We found all the doors closed.'

'He must have remained in the house.'

'Then he would be here still, as you never left the pavement.'

The man reflected and said, slowly:

'That's so . . . that's so . . . and I did not go far from the gate either . . . Still . . . '

'Let us see, who was the last person you saw with the baron?'

'Mlle. Antoinette, the companion.'

'What has become of her?'

'I should say that, as her bed was not even touched, she must have taken advantage of Sœur Auguste's absence to go out also. It would only half surprise me if she had: she is young . . . and pretty . . . '

'But how could she have got out?'

'Through the door.'

'You pushed the bolt and fastened the chain!'

'A good deal later! By that time, she must have left the house.'

'And the crime was committed, you think, after she went?'

'Of course.'

They searched the house from top to bottom, from the garrets to the cellars; but the murderer had fled. How? When? Was it he or an accomplice who had thought proper to return to the scene of the crime and do away with anything that might have betrayed him? Those were the questions that suggested themselves to the police.

★ ★ ★

The divisional surgeon came upon the scene at seven o'clock, the head of the detective-service at eight. Next came the turn of the public prosecutor and the examining magistrate. In addition, the house was filled with policemen, inspectors, journalists, Baron d'Hautrec's nephew and other members of the family.

They rummaged about, they studied the position of the body, according to Charles's recollection, they questioned Sœur Auguste the moment she arrived. They discovered nothing. At most, Sœur Auguste was surprised at the disappearance of Antoinette Bréhat. She had engaged the girl twelve days before, on the strength of excellent references, and refused to believe that she could have abandoned the sick man confided to her care, to go running about at night alone.

'All the more so,' the examining magistrate insisted, 'as, in that case, she would have been in before now. We therefore come back to the same point: what has become of her?'

'If you ask me,' said Charles, 'she has been carried off by the murderer.'

The suggestion was plausible enough and fitted in with certain details. The head of the detective service said:

'Carried off? Upon my word, it's quite likely.'

'It's not only unlikely,' said a voice, 'but absolutely opposed to the facts, to the results of the investigation, in short, to the evidence itself.'

The voice was harsh, the accent gruff and

no one was surprised to recognize Ganimard. He alone, besides, would be forgiven that rather free and easy way of expressing himself.

'Hullo, is that you, Ganimard?' cried M. Dudouis. 'I hadn't seen you.'

'I have been here for two hours.'

'So you do take an interest in something besides number 514, series 23, the Rue Clapeyron mystery, the blonde lady and Arsène Lupin?'

'Hee, hee!' grinned the old inspector. 'I won't go so far as to declare that Lupin has nothing to do with the case we're engaged on ... But let us dismiss the story of the lottery-ticket from our minds, until further orders, and look into this matter.'

★ ★ ★

Ganimard is not one of those mighty detectives whose proceedings form a school, as it were, and whose names will always remain inscribed on the judicial annals of Europe. He lacks the flashes of genius that illumine a Dupin, a Lecoq or a Holmlock Shears. But he possesses first-rate average qualities: perspicacity, sagacity, perseverance and even a certain amount of intuition. His greatest merit lies in the fact that he is absolutely independent of outside influences. Short of a kind of fascination which Arsène Lupin wields over him, he works without allowing himself to be biased or disturbed.

At any rate, the part which he played that morning did not lack brilliancy and his assistance was of the sort which a magistrate is able to appreciate.

'To start with,' he began, 'I will ask Charles here to be very definite on one point: were all the objects which, on the first occasion, he saw upset or disturbed put back, on the second, exactly in their usual places?'

'Exactly.'

'It is obvious, therefore, that they can only have been put back by a person to whom the place of each of those objects was familiar.'

The remark impressed the bystanders. Ganimard resumed:

'Another question, Mr. Charles . . . You were woke by a ring . . . Who was it, according to you, that called you?'

'Monsieur le baron, of course.'

'Very well. But at what moment do you take it that he rang?'

'After the struggle . . . at the moment of dying.'

'Impossible, because you found him lying, lifeless, at a spot more than four yards removed from the bell-push.'

'Then he rang during the struggle.'

'Impossible, because the bell, you told us, rang steadily, without interruption, and went on for seven or eight seconds. Do you think that his assailant would have given him time to ring like that?'

'Then it was before, at the moment when he was attacked.'

'Impossible. You told us that, between the ring of the bell and the instant when you entered the room, three minutes elapsed, at most. If, therefore, the baron had rung before, it would be necessary for the struggle, the murder, the dying agony and the flight to have taken place within that short space of three minutes. I repeat, it is impossible.'

'And yet,' said the examining magistrate, 'some one rang. If it was not the baron, who was it?'

'The murderer.'

'With what object?'

'I can't tell his object. But at least the fact that he rang proves that he must have known that the bell communicated with a servant's bedroom. Now who could have known this detail except a person belonging to the house?'

The circle of suppositions was becoming narrower. In a few quick, clear, logical sentences, Ganimard placed the question in its true light; and, as the old inspector allowed his thoughts to appear quite plainly, it seemed only natural that the examining magistrate should conclude:

'In short, in two words, you suspect Antoinette Bréhat.'

'I don't suspect her; I accuse her.'

'You accuse her of being the accomplice?'

'I accuse her of killing General Baron d'Hautrec.'

'Come, come! And what proof . . . ?'

'This handful of hair, which I found in the victim's right hand, dug into his flesh by the points of his nails.'

He showed the hair; it was hair of a brilliant fairness, gleaming like so many threads of gold; and Charles muttered:

'That is certainly Mlle. Antoinette's hair. There is no mistaking it.' And he added, 'Besides . . . there's something more . . . I believe the knife . . . the one I didn't see the second time . . . belonged to her . . . She used it to cut the pages of the books.'

The silence that followed was long and painful, as though the crime increased in horror through having been committed by a woman. The examining magistrate argued:

'Let us admit, until further information is obtained, that the baron was murdered by Antoinette Bréhat. We should still have to explain what way she can have taken to go out after committing the crime, to return after Charles's departure and to go out again before the arrival of the commissary. Have you any opinion on this subject, M. Ganimard?'

'No.'

'Then . . . ?'

Ganimard wore an air of embarrassment. At last, he spoke, not without a visible effort:

'All that I can say is that I find in this the same way of setting to work as in the ticket 514–23 case, the same phenomenon which one might call the faculty of disappearance. Antoinette Bréhat appears and disappears in this house as mysteriously as Arsène Lupin made his way into Maître Detinan's and escaped from there in the company of the blonde lady.'

'Which means . . . ?'

'Which means that I cannot help thinking of these two coincidences, which, to say the least, are very odd: first, Antoinette Bréhat was engaged by Sœur Auguste twelve days ago, that is to say, on the day after that on which the blonde lady slipped through my fingers. In the second place, the hair of the blonde lady has precisely the same violent colouring, the metallic brilliancy with a golden sheen, which we find in this.'

'So that, according to you, Antoinette Bréhat . . . '

'Is none other than the blonde lady.'

'And Lupin, consequently, plotted both cases?'

'I think so.'

There was a loud burst of laughter. It was the chief of the detective-service indulging his merriment:

'Lupin! Always Lupin! Lupin is in everything; Lupin is everywhere!'

'He is just where he is,' said Ganimard, angrily.

'And then he must have his reasons for being in any particular place,' remarked M. Dudouis, 'and, in this case, his reasons seem to me obscure. The writing-desk has not been broken open nor the pocketbook stolen. There is even gold left lying on the table.'

'Yes,' cried Ganimard, 'but what about the famous diamond?'

'What diamond?'

'The blue diamond! The celebrated diamond which formed part of the royal crown of France and which was presented by the Duc d' Alais to Léonide Latouche and, on her death, was bought by Baron d'Hautrec in memory of the brilliant actress whom he had passionately loved. This is one of those recollections which an old Parisian like myself never forgets.'

'It is obvious,' said the examining magistrate, 'that, if the blue diamond is not found, the thing explains itself. But where are we to look?'

'On monsieur le baron's finger,' replied Charles. 'The blue diamond was never off his left hand.'

'I have looked at that hand,' declared Ganimard, going up to the corpse, 'and, as you can see for yourselves, there is only a plain gold ring.'

'Look inside the palm,' said the servant.

Ganimard unfolded the clenched fingers. The bezel was turned inward and, contained within the bezel, glittered the blue diamond.

'The devil!' muttered Ganimard, absolutely nonplussed. 'This is beyond me!'

'And I hope that you will now give up suspecting that unfortunate Arsène Lupin?' said M. Dudouis, with a grin.

Ganimard took his time, reflected and retorted, in a sententious tone:

'It is just when a thing gets beyond me that I suspect Arsène Lupin most.'

These were the first discoveries effected by the police on the day following upon that strange murder, vague, inconsistent discoveries to which the subsequent inquiry imparted neither consistency nor certainty. The movements of Antoinette Bréhat remained as absolutely inexplicable as those of the blonde lady, nor was any light thrown upon the identity of that mysterious creature with the golden hair who had killed Baron d'Hautrec without taking from his finger the fabulous diamond from the royal crown of France.

Moreover and especially, the curiosity which it inspired raised the murder above the level of a sordid crime to that of a mighty, if heinous trespass, the mystery of which irritated the public mind.

★　★　★

Baron d'Hautrec's heirs were obliged to benefit by this great advertisement. They arranged an exhibition of the furniture and personal effects in the Avenue Henri-Martin, in the house itself, on the scene of the crime, prior to the sale at the Salle Drouot. The furniture was modern and in indifferent taste, the knicknacks had no artistic value . . . but, in the middle of the bedroom, on a stand covered with ruby velvet, the ring with the blue diamond sparkled under a glass shade, closely watched by two detectives.

It was a magnificent diamond of enormous size and incomparable purity and of that undefined blue which clear water takes from the sky which it reflects, the blue which we can just suspect in newly-washed linen. People admired it, went into raptures over it . . . and cast terrified glances round the victim's room, at the spot where the corpse had lain, at the floor stripped of its blood-stained carpet and especially at the walls, those solid walls through which the criminal had passed. They felt to make sure that the marble chimney-piece did not swing on a pivot, that there was no secret spring in the mouldings of the mirrors. They pictured yawning cavities, tunnels communicating with the sewers, with the catacombs . . .

★  ★  ★

The blue diamond was sold at the Hôtel Drouot on the thirtieth of January. The auction-room was crammed and the bidding proceeded madly.

All Paris, the Paris of the first nights and great public functions, was there, all those who buy and all those who like others to think that they are in a position to buy: stock-brokers, artists, ladies in every class of society, two members of the Government, an Italian tenor, a king in exile who, in order to reëstablish his credit, with great self-possession and in a resounding voice, permitted himself the luxury of running up the price to a hundred thousand francs. A hundred thousand francs! His Majesty was quite safe in making the bid. The Italian tenor was soon offering a hundred and fifty thousand, an actress at the Français a hundred and seventy-five.

At two hundred thousand francs, however, the competition became less brisk. At two hundred and fifty thousand, only two bidders remained: Herschmann, the financial magnate, known as the Gold-mine King; and a wealthy American lady, the Comtesse de Crozon, whose collection of diamonds and other precious stones enjoys a world-wide fame.

'Two hundred and sixty thousand . . . two hundred and seventy thousand . . . seventy-five . . . eighty,' said the auctioneer, with a questioning glance at either competitor in turn. 'Two hundred and eighty thousand for madame . . . No advance on two hundred and eighty thousand . . . ?'

'Three hundred thousand,' muttered Herschmann.

A pause followed. All eyes were turned on the Comtesse de Crozon. Smiling, but with a pallor that betrayed her excitement, she stood leaning over the back of the chair before her. In reality, she knew and everybody present knew that there was no doubt about the finish of the duel: it was logically and fatally bound to end in favour of the financier, whose whims were served by a fortune of over five hundred millions. Nevertheless, she said:

'Three hundred and five thousand.'

There was a further pause. Every glance was now turned on the Gold-mine King, in expectation of the inevitable advance. It was sure to come, in all its brutal and crushing strength.

It did not come. Herschmann remained impassive, with his eyes fixed on a sheet of paper which he held in his right hand, while the other crumpled up the pieces of a torn envelope.

'Three hundred and five thousand,' repeated the auctioneer. 'Going . . . going . . . No further bid . . . ?'

No one spoke.

'Once more: going . . . going . . . '

Herschmann did not move. A last pause. The hammer fell.

'Four hundred thousand!' shouted Herschmann, starting up, as though the tap of the hammer had roused him from his torpor.

Too late. The diamond was sold.

Herschmann's acquaintances crowded round him. What had happened? Why had he not spoken sooner?

He gave a laugh:

'What happened? Upon my word, I don't know. My thoughts wandered for a second.'

'You don't mean that!'

'Yes, some one brought me a letter.'

'And was that enough . . . ?'

'To put me off? Yes, for the moment.'

Ganimard was there. He had watched the sale of the ring. He went up to one of the porters:

'Did you hand M. Herschmann a letter?'

'Yes.'

'Who gave it you?'

'A lady.'

'Where is she?'

'Where is she? . . . Why, sir, there she is . . . the lady over there, in a thick veil.'

'Just going out?'

'Yes.'

Ganimard rushed to the door and saw the lady going down the staircase. He ran after her. A stream of people stopped him at the entrance. When he came outside, he had lost sight of her.

He went back to the room, spoke to Herschmann, introduced himself and asked him about the letter. Herschmann gave it to him. It contained the following simple words, scribbled in pencil and in a handwriting unknown to the financier:

'The blue diamond brings ill-luck. Remember Baron d'Hautrec.'

* * *

The tribulations of the blue diamond were not over. Already famous through the murder of Baron d'Hautrec and the incidents at the Hôtel Drouot, it attained the height of its celebrity six months later. In the summer, the precious jewel which the Comtesse de Crozon had been at such pains to acquire was stolen.

Let me sum up this curious case, marked by so many stirring, dramatic and exciting episodes, upon which I am at last permitted to throw some light.

On the evening of the tenth of August, M. and Madame de Crozon's guests were gathered in the drawing-room of the magnificent château overlooking the Bay of Somme. There was a request for some music. The countess sat down to the piano, took off her rings, which included Baron d'Hautrec's, and laid them on a little table that stood beside the piano.

An hour later, the count went to bed, as did his two cousins, the d'Andelles, and Madame de Réal, an intimate friend of the Comtesse de Crozon, who remained behind with Herr Bleichen, the Austrian consul, and his wife.

They sat and talked and then the countess turned down the big lamp which stood on the drawing-room table. At the same moment,

Herr Bleichen put out the two lamps on the piano. There was a second's darkness and groping; then the consul lit a candle and they all three went to their rooms. But, the instant the countess reached hers, she remembered her jewels and told her maid to go and fetch them. The woman returned and placed them on the mantelpiece. Madame de Crozon did not examine them; but, the next morning, she noticed that one of the rings was missing, the ring with the blue diamond.

She told her husband. Both immediately came to the same conclusion: the maid being above suspicion, the thief could be none but Herr Bleichen.

The count informed the central commissary of police at Amiens, who opened an inquiry and arranged discreetly for the house to be constantly watched, so as to prevent the Austrian consul from selling or sending away the ring. The château was surrounded by detectives night and day.

A fortnight elapsed without the least incident. Then Herr Bleichen announced his intention of leaving. On the same day, a formal accusation was laid against him. The commissary made an official visit and ordered the luggage to be examined. In a small bag of which the consul always carried the key, they found a flask containing tooth-powder; and, inside the flask, the ring!

Mrs. Bleichen fainted. Her husband was arrested.

My readers will remember the defense set up by the accused. He was unable, he said, to explain the presence of the ring, unless it was there as the result of an act of revenge on the part of M. de Crozon:

'The count ill-treats his wife,' he declared, 'and makes her life a misery. I had a long conversation with her and warmly urged her to sue for a divorce. The count must have heard of this and revenged himself by taking the ring and slipping it into my dressing-bag when I was about to leave.'

The count and countess persisted in their charge. It was an even choice between their explanation and the consul's: both were equally probable. No new fact came to weigh down either scale. A month of gossip, of guess-work and investigations, failed to produce a single element of certainty.

Annoyed by all this worry and unable to bring forward a definite proof of guilt to justify their accusation, M. and Madame de Crozon wrote to Paris for a detective capable of unravelling the threads of the skein. The police sent Ganimard.

For four days the old inspector rummaged and hunted about, strolled in the park, had long talks with the maids, the chauffeur, the gardeners, the people of the nearest post-offices, and examined the rooms occupied by the Bleichen couple, the d'Andelle cousins and Madame de Réal. Then, one morning, he disappeared without taking leave of his hosts.

But, a week later, they received this telegram:

'Please meet me five o'clock to-morrow, Friday afternoon at Thé Japonais, Rue Boissy-d'Anglas.

'Ganimard.'

*  *  *

At five o'clock to the minute, on the Friday, their motor-car drew up in front of 9, Rue Boissy-d' Anglas. The old inspector was waiting for them on the pavement and, without a word of explanation, led them up to the first-floor of the Thé Japonais.

In one of the rooms they found two persons, whom Ganimard introduced to them.

'M. Gerbois, professor at Versailles College, whom, you will remember, Arsène Lupin robbed of half a million . . . M. Léonce d'Hautrec, nephew and residuary legatee of the late Baron d'Hautrec.'

The four sat down. A few minutes later, a fifth arrived. It was the chief of the detective-service.

M. Dudouis appeared to be in a rather bad temper. He bowed and said:

'Well, what is it, Ganimard? They gave me your telephone message at headquarters. Is it serious?'

'Very serious, chief. In less than an hour, the last adventures in which I have assisted will come to an issue here. I considered that your presence was indispensable.'

'And does this apply also to the presence of Dieuzy and Folenfant, whom I see below, hanging round the door?'

'Yes, chief.'

'And what for? Is somebody to be arrested? What a melodramatic display! Well, Ganimard, say what you have to say.'

Ganimard hesitated for a few moments and then, with the evident intention of impressing his hearers, said:

'First of all, I wish to state that Herr Bleichen had nothing to do with the theft of the ring.'

'Oh,' said M. Dudouis, 'that's a mere statement . . . and a serious one!'

And the count asked:

'Is this . . . discovery the only thing that has come of your exertions?'

'No, sir. Two days after the theft, three of your guests happened to be at Crécy, in the course of a motor-trip. Two of them went on to visit the famous battlefield, while the third hurried to the post-office and sent off a little parcel, packed up and sealed according to the regulations and insured to the value of one hundred francs.'

M. de Crozon objected:

'There is nothing out of the way in that.'

'Perhaps you will think it less natural when I tell you that, instead of the real name, the sender gave the name of Rousseau and that the addressee, a M. Beloux, residing in Paris, changed his lodgings on the very evening of the day on which he received the parcel, that is to say, the ring.'

'Was it one of my d' Andelle cousins, by any chance?' asked the count.

'No, it was neither of those gentlemen.'

'Then it was Mme. de Réal?'

'Yes.'

The countess, in amazement, exclaimed:

'Do you accuse my friend Mme. de Réal?'

'A simple question, madame,' replied Ganimard. 'Was Mme. de Réal present at the sale of the blue diamond?'

'Yes, but in a different part of the room. We were not together.'

'Did she advise you to buy the ring?'

The countess collected her memory:

'Yes . . . as a matter of fact . . . I think she was the first to mention it to me.'

'I note your answer, madame,' said Ganimard. 'So it is quite certain that it was Mme. de Réal who first spoke to you of the ring and advised you to buy it.'

'Still . . . my friend is incapable . . . '

'I beg your pardon, I beg your pardon, Mme. de Réal is only your chance acquaintance and not an intimate friend, as the newspapers stated, thus diverting suspicion from her. You have only known her since last winter. Now I can undertake to prove to you that all that she has told you about herself, her past, her connections is absolutely false; that Mme. Blanche de Réal did not exist before she met you; and that she has ceased to exist at this present moment.'

'Well?' said M. Dudouis, 'what next?'

'What next?' echoed Ganimard.

'Yes, what next? . . . This is all very interesting; but what has it to do with the case? If Mme. de Réal took the ring, why was it found in Herr Bleichen's tooth-powder? Come, Ganimard! A person who takes the trouble to steal the blue diamond keeps it. What have you to answer to that?'

'I, nothing. But Mme. de Réal will answer.'

'Then she exists?'

'She exists . . . without existing. In a few words, here it is: three days ago, reading the paper which I read every day, I saw at the head of the list of arrivals at Trouville, 'Hôtel Beaurivage, Mme. de Réal,' and so on . . . You can imagine that I was at Trouville that same evening, questioning the manager of the Beaurivage. According to the description and certain clues which I gathered, this Mme. de Réal was indeed the person whom I was looking for, but she had gone from the hotel, leaving her address in Paris, 3, Rue du Colisée. On Wednesday, I called at that address and learnt that there was no Madame de Réal, but just a woman called Réal, who lived on the second floor, followed the occupation of a diamond-broker and was often away. Only the day before, she had come back from a journey. Yesterday, I rang at her door and, under a false name, offered my services to Mme. de Réal as an intermediary to introduce her to people who were in a position to buy valuable stones. We made an appointment to meet here to-day for a first transaction.'

'Oh, so you expect her?'

'At half-past five.'

'And are you sure? . . . '

'That it is Mme. de Réal of the Château de Crozon? I have indisputable proofs. But . . . hark! . . . Folenfant's signal! . . . '

A whistle had sounded. Ganimard rose briskly:

'We have not a moment to lose. M. and Madame de Crozon, go into the next room,

75

please. You too, M. d'Hautrec . . . and you also, M. Gerbois . . . The door will remain open and, at the first sign, I will ask you to intervene. Do you stay, chief, please.'

'And, if anyone else comes in?' asked M. Dudouis.

'No one will. This is a new establishment and the proprietor, who is a friend of mine, will not let a living soul come up the stairs . . . except the blonde lady.'

'The blonde lady? What do you mean?'

'The blonde lady herself, chief, the friend and accomplice of Arsène Lupin, the mysterious blonde lady, against whom I have positive proofs, but against whom I want, over and above those and in your presence, to collect the evidence of all the people whom she has robbed.'

He leant out of the window:

'She is coming . . . She has gone in . . . She can't escape now: Folenfant and Dieuzy are guarding the door . . . The blonde lady is ours, chief; we've got her!'

★ ★ ★

Almost at that moment, a woman appeared upon the threshold, a tall, thin woman, with a very pale face and violent golden hair.

Ganimard was stifled by such emotion that

he stood dumb, incapable of articulating the least word. She was there, in front of him, at his disposal! What a victory over Arsène Lupin! And what a revenge! And, at the same time, that victory seemed to him to have been won with such ease that he wondered whether the blonde lady was not going to slip through his fingers, thanks to one of those miracles which Lupin was in the habit of performing.

She stood waiting, meanwhile, surprised at the silence, and looked around her without disguising her uneasiness.

'She will go! She will disappear!' thought Ganimard, in dismay.

Suddenly, he placed himself between her and the door. She turned and tried to go out.

'No, no,' he said. 'Why go?'

'But, monsieur, I don't understand your ways. Let me pass ... '

'There is no reason for you to go, madame, and every reason, on the contrary, why you should stay.'

'But ... '

'It's no use, you are not going.'

Turning very pale, she sank into a chair and stammered:

'What do you want?'

Ganimard triumphed. He had got the blonde lady. Mastering himself, he said:

'Let me introduce the friend of whom I

spoke to you, the one who would like to buy some jewels . . . especially diamonds. Did you obtain the one you promised me?'

'No . . . no . . . I don't know . . . I forget . . .'

'Oh, yes . . . Just try . . . Someone you knew was to bring you a coloured diamond . . . 'Something like the blue diamond,' I said, laughing, and you answered, 'Exactly. I may have what you want.' Do you remember?'

She was silent. A little wristbag which she was holding in her hand fell to the ground. She picked it up quickly and pressed it to her. Her fingers trembled a little.

'Come,' said Ganimard. 'I see that you do not trust us, Madame de Réal. I will set you a good example and let you see what I have got to show.'

He took a piece of paper from his pocketbook and unfolded it:

'Here, first of all, is some of the hair of Antoinette Bréhat, torn out by the baron and found clutched in the dead man's hand. I have seen Mlle. de Gerbois: she has most positively recognized the colour of the hair of the blonde lady . . . the same colour as yours, for that matter . . . exactly the same colour.'

Mme. de Réal watched him with a stupid expression, as though she really did not grasp the sense of his words. He continued:

'And now here are two bottles of scent. They are empty, it is true, and have no labels; but enough of the scent still clings to them to have enabled Mlle. Gerbois, this very morning, to recognize the perfume of the blonde lady who accompanied her on her fortnight's excursion. Now, one of these bottles comes from the room which Mme. de Réal occupied at the Château de Crozon and the other from the room which you occupied at the Hôtel Beaurivage.'

'What are you talking about? . . . The blonde lady . . . the Château de Crozon . . . '

The inspector, without replying, spread four sheets of paper on the table.

'Lastly,' he said, 'here, on these four sheets, we have a specimen of the handwriting of Antoinette Bréhat, another of the lady who sent a note to Baron Herschmann during the sale of the blue diamond, another of Mme. de Réal, at the time of her stay at Crozon, and the fourth . . . your own, madame . . . your name and address given by yourself to the hall-porter of the Hôtel Beaurivage at Trouville. Now, please compare these four handwritings. They are one and the same.'

'But you are mad, sir, you are mad! What does all this mean?'

'It means, madame,' cried Ganimard, with a great outburst, 'that the blonde lady, the friend and accomplice of Arsène Lupin, is none other than yourself.'

He pushed open the door of the next room, rushed at M. Gerbois, shoved him along by the shoulders and, planting him in front of Mme. Réal:

'M. Gerbois, do you recognize the person who took away your daughter and whom you saw at Maître Detinan's?'

'No.'

There was a commotion of which every one felt the shock. Ganimard staggered back:

'No? . . . Is it possible? . . . Come, just think . . . '

'I have thought . . . Madame is fair, like the blonde lady . . . and pale, like her . . . but she doesn't resemble her in the least.'

'I can't believe it . . . a mistake like that is inconceivable . . . M. d'Hautrec, do you recognize Antoinette Bréhat?'

'I have seen Antoinette Bréhat at my uncle's . . . this is not she.'

'And madame is not Mme. de Réal, either,' declared the Comte de Crozon.

This was the finishing stroke. It stunned Ganimard, who stood motionless, with hanging head and shifting eyes. Of all his contrivances, nothing remained. The whole edifice was tumbling about his shoulders.

M. Dudouis rose:

'I must beg you to forgive us, madame. There has been a regrettable confusion of identities, which I will ask you to forget. But what I cannot well understand is your agitation . . . the strangeness of your manner since you arrived . . .'

'Why, monsieur, I was frightened . . . there is over a hundred thousand francs' worth of jewels in my bag . . . and your friend's attitude was not very reassuring.'

'But your continual absences? . . .'

'Surely my occupation demands them?'

M. Dudouis had no reply to make. He turned to his subordinate:

'You have made your inquiries with a deplorable want of thoroughness, Ganimard, and your behaviour toward madame just now was uncouth. You shall give me an explanation in my office.'

The interview was over and the chief of the detective service was about to take his leave, when a really disconcerting thing happened. Mme. Réal went up to the inspector and said:

'Do I understand your name to be M. Ganimard? . . . Did I catch the name right?'

'Yes.'

'In that case, this letter must be for you. I received it this morning, addressed as you see: 'M. Justin Ganimard, care of Mme. Réal.' I thought it was a joke, as I did not know you under that name, but I have no doubt the writer, whoever he is, knew of your appointment.'

By a singular intuition, Justin Ganimard was very nearly seizing the letter and destroying it. He dared not do so, however, before his superior and he tore open the envelope. The letter contained the following words, which he uttered in a hardly intelligible voice:

*There was once a Blonde Lady, a Lupin and a Ganimard. Now the naughty Ganimard wanted to harm the pretty Blonde Lady and the good Lupin did not wish it. So the good Lupin, who was anxious for the Blonde Lady to become friends with the Comtesse de Crozon, made her take the name of Mme. de Réal, which is the same — or nearly — as that of an honest tradeswoman whose hair is golden and her features pale. And the good Lupin said to himself, 'If ever the naughty Ganimard is on the track of the Blonde Lady, how useful it will be for me to shunt him on to the track of the honest tradeswoman!' A wise precaution, which has borne fruit. A little note sent to the naughty Ganimard's newspaper, a bottle of scent forgotten on purpose at the Hôtel Beaurivage by the real Blonde Lady, Mme. Réal's name and address written by the real Blonde Lady in the visitors' book at the hotel, and the trick is done. What do you say to it, Ganimard? I wanted to tell you the story in detail, knowing that, with your sense of humour, you would be the first to laugh at it. It is, indeed, a pretty story and I confess that, for my part, it has diverted me vastly.*

*My best thanks to you, then, my dear friend, and kind regards to that capital M. Douois.*

Arsène Lupin.

'But he knows everything!' moaned Ganimard, who did not think of laughing. 'He knows things that I have not told to a soul! How could he know that I would ask you to come, chief? How could he know that I had discovered the first scent-bottle? . . . How could he know? . . . '

He stamped about, tore his hair, a prey to the most tragic distress.

M. Dudouis took pity on him:

'Come, Ganimard, console yourself. We must try to do better next time.'

And the chief detective went away, accompanied by Mme. Réal.

★ ★ ★

Ten minutes elapsed, while Ganimard read Lupin's letter over and over again and M. and

Mme. de Crozon, M. d'Hautrec and M. Gerbois sustained an animated conversation in a corner. At last, the count crossed over to the inspector and said:

'The upshot of all this, my dear sir, is that we are no further than we were.'

'Pardon me. My inquiry has established the fact that the blonde lady is the undoubted heroine of these adventures and that Lupin is directing her. That is a huge step forward.'

'And not the smallest use to us. If anything, it makes the mystery darker still. The blonde lady commits murder to steal the blue diamond and does not steal it. She steals it and does so to get rid of it for another's benefit.'

'What can I do?'

'Nothing, but some one else might . . . '

'What do you mean?'

The count hesitated, but the countess said, point blank:

'There is one man, one man only, in my opinion, besides yourself, who would be capable of fighting Lupin and reducing him to cry for mercy. M. Ganimard, would you very much mind if we called in the assistance of Holmlock Shears?'

He was taken aback:

'No . . . no . . . only . . . I don't exactly understand . . . '

'Well, it's like this: all this mystery is making

me quite ill. I want to know where I am. M. Gerbois and M. d'Hautrec have the same wish and we have come to an agreement to apply to the famous English detective.'

'You are right, madame,' said the inspector, with a loyalty that did him credit; 'you are right. Old Ganimard is not clever enough to fight against Arsène Lupin. The question is, will Holmlock Shears be more successful? I hope so, for I have the greatest admiration for him . . . Still . . . it's hardly likely . . . '

'It's hardly likely that he will succeed?'

'That's what I think. I consider that a duel between Holmlock Shears and Arsène Lupin can only end in one way. The Englishman will be beaten.'

'In any case, can he rely on you?'

'Certainly, madame. I will assist him to the very best of my power.'

'Do you know his address?'

'Yes; 219, Parker Street.'

★   ★   ★

That evening, the Comte and Comtesse de Crozon withdrew the charge against Herr Bleichen and a collective letter was addressed to Holmlock Shears.

# 3

## Holmlock Shears Opens Hostilities

'What can I get you, gentlemen?'

'Anything you please,' replied Arsène Lupin, in the voice of a man who takes no interest in his food. 'Anything you please, but no meat or wine.'

The waiter walked away, with a scornful air.

I exclaimed:

'Do you mean to say that you are still a vegetarian?'

'Yes, more than ever,' said Lupin.

'From taste? Conviction? Habit?'

'For reasons of health.'

'And do you never break your rule?'

'Oh, yes . . . when I go out to dinner, so as not to appear eccentric.'

We were dining near the Gare du Nord, inside a little restaurant where Arsène Lupin had invited me to join him. He is rather fond of telegraphing to me, occasionally, in the morning and arranging a meeting of this kind in some corner or other of Paris. He always arrives in the highest spirits, rejoicing in life, unaffectedly and good-humouredly, and always has some surprising anecdote to tell me, some memory, the story of some adventure that I have not heard before.

That evening, he seemed to me to let himself go even more than usual. He laughed and chatted with a singular animation and with that delicate irony which is all his own, an irony devoid of bitterness, light and spontaneous. It was a pleasure to see him like that, and I could not help expressing my satisfaction.

'Oh, yes,' he cried, 'I have days when everything seems delightful, when life bubbles in me like an infinite treasure which I can never exhaust. And yet goodness knows that I live without counting!'

'Too much so, perhaps.'

'The treasure is infinite, I tell you! I can spend myself and squander myself, I can fling my strength and my youth to the four winds of heaven and I am only making room for greater and more youthful strength . . . And then, really, my life is so beautiful! . . . I need only have the wish — isn't it so? — to become, from one day to the next, anything: an orator, a great manufacturer, a politician . . . Well, I swear to you, the idea would never enter my head! Arsène Lupin I am, Arsène Lupin I remain. And I search history in vain for a destiny to compare with mine, fuller, more intense . . . Napoleon? Yes, perhaps . . . But then it is Napoleon at the end of his imperial career, during the campaign in France, when Europe was crushing him and when he was wondering whether each battle was not the last which he would fight.'

Was he serious? Was he jesting? The tone of his voice had grown more eager and he continued:

'Everything's there, you see: danger! The uninterrupted impression of danger! Oh, to breathe it like the air one breathes, to feel it around one, blowing, roaring, lying in wait, approaching! . . . And, in the midst of the storm, to remain calm . . . not to flinch! . . . If you do, you are lost . . . There is only one sensation to equal it, that of the chauffeur driving his car. But that drive lasts for a morning, whereas mine lasts all through life!'

'How lyrical we are!' I cried. 'And you would have me believe that you have no special reason for excitement!'

He smiled.

'You're a shrewd enough psychologist,' he replied. 'There is something more, as you say.'

He poured out a tumbler of water, drank it down and asked:

'Have you seen the *Temps* to-day?'

'No.'

'Holmlock Shears was to have crossed the Channel this afternoon; he arrived in Paris at six.'

'The devil he did! And why?'

'He's taking a little trip at the expense of the Crozons, Hautrec's nephew and the Gerbois fellow. They all met at the Gare du Nord and went on to see Ganimard. The six of them are in conference at this moment.'

Notwithstanding the immense curiosity with which he inspires me, I never venture to question Arsène Lupin as to the acts of his private life until he has spoken of them to me himself. It is a matter of discretion on my part, with which I never compound. Besides, at that time, his name had not yet been mentioned, at least not publicly, in connection with the blue diamond. I waited patiently, therefore. He continued:

'The *Temps* also prints an interview with that excellent Ganimard, according to which a certain blonde lady, said to be my friend, is supposed to have murdered Baron d'Hautrec and tried to steal his famous ring from Madame de Crozon. And it goes without saying that he accuses me of being the instigator of both these crimes.'

A slight shiver passed through me. Could it be true? Was I to believe that the habit of theft, his mode of life, the sheer logic of events had driven this man to murder? I looked at him. He seemed so calm! His eyes met mine so frankly!

I examined his hands: they were modelled with infinite daintiness, were really inoffensive hands, the hands of an artist.

'Ganimard is a lunatic,' I muttered.

He protested:

'Not a bit of it, not a bit of it! Ganimard is shrewd enough ... sometimes he's even quick-witted.'

'Quick-witted!'

'Yes, yes. For instance, this interview is a masterstroke. First, he announces the coming of his English rival, so as to put me on my guard and make Shears's task more difficult. Secondly, he specifies the exact point to which he has carried the case, so that Shears may enjoy only the benefit of his own discoveries. That's fair fighting.'

'Still you have two adversaries to deal with now; and such adversaries!'

'Oh, one of them doesn't count.'

'And the other?'

'Shears? Oh, I admit that he's more of a match for me; but that's just what I love and why you see me in such good spirits. To begin with, there's the question of my vanity: they consider that I'm worth asking the famous

Englishman to meet. Next, think of the pleasure which a fighter like myself must take in the prospect of a duel with Holmlock Shears. Well, I shall have to exert myself to the utmost. For I know the fellow: he won't retreat a step.'

'He's a clever man.'

'A very clever man. As a detective, I doubt if his equal exists, or has ever existed. Only, I have one advantage over him, which is that he's attacking, while I'm on the defensive. Mine is the easier game to play. Besides . . .' He gave an imperceptible smile before completing his phrase. 'Besides, I know his way of fighting, and he does not know mine. And I have a few sly thrusts in store for him which will give him something to think about . . .'

He tapped the table lightly with his fingers and flung out little sentences with a delighted air:

'Arsène Lupin versus Holmlock Shears! France versus England . . . Revenge for Trafalgar at last! . . . Ah, the poor wretch . . . he little thinks that I am prepared . . . and a Lupin armed . . .'

He stopped suddenly, seized with a fit of coughing, and hid his face in his napkin, as though something had gone down the wrong way.

'What is it?' I asked. 'A crumb? . . . Why don't you take some water?'

'No, it's not that,' he gasped.

'What, then?'

'I want air.'

'Shall I open the window?'

'No, I shall go out . . . Quick, give me my hat and coat . . . I'm off!'

'But what does it all mean?'

'You see the taller of those two men who have just come in? Well, I want you to keep on my left as we go out, to prevent his seeing me.'

'The one sitting behind you? . . . '

'Yes . . . For personal reasons, I prefer . . . I'll tell you why outside . . . '

'But who is it?'

'Holmlock Shears.'

He made a violent effort to overcome his agitation, as though he felt ashamed of it, put down his napkin, drank a glass of water and then, quite recovered, said, with a smile:

'It's funny, isn't it? I'm not easily excited but this unexpected meeting . . . '

'What are you afraid of, seeing that no one can recognize you under all your transformations? I myself, each time I see you, feel as if I were with a new person.'

'*He* will recognize me,' said Arsène Lupin. '*He* saw me only once, but I felt that he saw me for life and that what he saw was not my appearance, which I can always alter, but the very being that I am . . . And then . . . and then . . . I wasn't prepared . . . What a curious meeting! . . . In this little restaurant! . . . '

'Well,' said I, 'shall we go?'

'No . . . no . . . '

'What do you propose to do?'

'The best thing will be to act frankly . . . to trust him.'

'You can't be serious?'

'Oh, but I am . . . Besides, it would be a good thing to question him, to know what he knows . . . Ah, there, I feel that his eyes are fixed on my neck, on my shoulders . . . He's trying to think . . . to remember . . . '

He reflected. I noticed a mischievous smile on his lips; and then, obeying, I believe, some whim of his frivolous nature rather than the needs of the position itself, he rose abruptly, spun round on his heels and, with a bow, said, gaily:

'What a stroke of luck! Who would have thought it? . . . Allow me to introduce my friend.'

For a second or two, the Englishman was taken aback. Then he made an instinctive movement, as though he were ready to fling himself upon Arsène Lupin. Lupin shook his head:

'That would be a mistake ... to say nothing of the bad taste of it ... and the uselessness!'

The Englishman turned his head from side to side, as though looking for assistance.

'That's no better ... And also, are you quite sure that you are entitled to lay hands upon me? Come, be a sportsman!'

The display of sportsmanlike qualities was not particularly tempting on this occasion. Nevertheless, it probably appeared to Shears to be the wisest course; for he half rose and coldly introduced his companion:

'Mr. Wilson, my friend and assistant ... M. Arsène Lupin.'

Wilson's stupefaction made us all laugh. His eyes and mouth, both wide open, drew two streaks across his expansive face, with its skin gleaming and tight-stretched like an apple's, while his bristly hair stood up like so many thick-set, hardy blades of grass.

'Wilson, you don't seem able to conceal your bewilderment at one of the most natural incidents in the world,' grinned Holmlock Shears, with a touch of sarcasm in his voice.

Wilson stammered:

'Why ... why don't you arrest him?'

'Don't you see, Wilson, that the gentleman is standing between the door and myself and at two steps from the door. Before I moved a

94

finger, he would be outside.'

'Don't let that stand in your way,' said Lupin.

He walked round the table and sat down so that the Englishman was between him and the door, thus placing himself at his mercy. Wilson looked at Shears to see if he might admire this piece of pluck. Shears remained impenetrable. But, after a moment, he called.

'Waiter!'

The waiter came up.

'Four whiskeys and sodas.'

Peace was signed . . . until further orders. Soon after, seated all four round one table, we were quietly chatting.

Holmlock Shears is a man . . . of the sort one meets every day. He is about fifty years of age and looks like a decent City clerk who has spent his life keeping books at a desk. He has nothing to distinguish him from the ordinary respectable Londoner, with his clean-shaven face and his somewhat heavy appearance, nothing except his terribly keen, bright, penetrating eyes.

And then, of course, he is Holmlock Shears, that is to say, a sort of miracle of intuition, of insight, of perspicacity, of shrewdness. It is as though nature had amused herself by taking the two most extraordinary types of detective that fiction had invented, Poe's Dupin and

Gaboriau's Lecoq, in order to build up one in her own fashion, more extraordinary yet and more unreal. And, upon my word, any one hearing of the adventures which have made the name of Holmlock Shears famous all over the world must feel inclined to ask if he is not a legendary person, a hero who has stepped straight from the brain of some great novel-writer, of a Conan Doyle, for instance.

He at once, when Arsène Lupin asked him how long he meant to stay, led the conversation into its right channel and replied:

'That depends upon yourself, M. Lupin.'

'Oh,' exclaimed the other, laughing, 'if it depended on me, I should ask you to take to-night's boat back.'

'To-night is rather early. But I hope in a week or ten days . . . '

'Are you in such a hurry?'

'I am very busy. There's the robbery at the Anglo-Chinese Bank; and Lady Eccleston has been kidnapped, as you know . . . Tell me, M. Lupin, do you think a week will do?'

'Amply, if you confine yourself to the two cases connected with the blue diamond. It will just give me time to take my precautions, supposing the solution of those two mysteries to give you certain advantages over me that might endanger my safety.'

'Yes,' said the Englishman, 'I expect to have gained those advantages in a week or ten days.'

'And to have me arrested on the eleventh?'

'On the tenth, at the very latest.'

Lupin reflected and, shaking his head:

'It will be difficult ... it will be difficult ... '

'Difficult, yes, but possible and, therefore, certain ... '

'Absolutely certain,' said Wilson, as though he himself had clearly perceived the long series of operations which would lead his friend to the result announced.

Holmlock Shears smiled:

'Wilson, who knows what he is talking about, is there to confirm what I say.' And he went on, 'Of course, I have not all the cards in my hands, because the case is already a good many months old. I have not the factors, the clues upon which I am accustomed to base my inquiries.'

'Such as mud-stains and cigarette-ashes,' said Wilson, with an air of importance.

'But, in addition to the remarkable conclusions arrived at by M. Ganimard, I have at my service all the articles written on the subject, all the evidence collected and, consequently, a few ideas of my own regarding the mystery.'

'A few views suggested to us either by

analysis or hypothesis,' added Wilson, sententiously.

'Would it be indiscreet,' said Arsène Lupin, in the deferential tone which he adopted toward Shears, 'would it be indiscreet to ask what general opinion you have been able to form?'

It was really most stimulating to see those two men seated together, with their elbows on the table, arguing solemnly and dispassionately, as though they were trying to solve a steep problem or to come to an agreement on some controversial point. And this was coupled with a very delicate irony, which both of them, as experts and artists, thoroughly enjoyed. As for Wilson, he was in the seventh heaven.

Shears slowly filled his pipe, lit it and said:

'I consider that this case is infinitely less complicated than it appears at first sight.'

'Very much less,' echoed Wilson, faithfully.

'I say the case, for, in my opinion, there is but one case. The death of Baron d'Hautrec, the story of the ring and — don't let us forget that — the mystery of number 514, series 23, are only the different aspects of what we may call the puzzle of the blonde lady. Now, in my opinion, what lies before me is simply to discover the link which connects these three phases of the same story, the particular fact which proves the uniformity of the three methods. Ganimard, who is a little superficial in his judgments, sees this uniformity in the faculty of disappearing, in the power of coming and going unseen. This intervention of miracles does not satisfy me.'

'Well?'

'Well, according to me,' said Shears, decidedly, 'the characteristic shared by the three incidents lies in your manifest and evident, although hitherto unperceived intention to have the affair performed on a stage which you have previously selected. This points to something more than a plan on your part: a necessity rather, a *sine quâ non* of success.'

'Could you give a few particulars?'

'Easily. For instance, from the commencement of your contest with M. Gerbois, it was *evident* that Maître Detinan's flat was the place selected by you, the inevitable place at which you were all to meet. No place seemed quite as safe to you, so much so that you made what one might almost call a public appointment there with the blonde lady and Mlle. Gerbois.'

'The daughter of the professor,' explained Wilson.

'Let us now speak of the blue diamond. Did you try to get hold of it during all the years that Baron d'Hautrec had it in his possession? No. But the baron moves into his brother's house: six months later, Antoinette

Bréhat appears upon the scene and the first attempt is made ... You fall to secure the diamond and the sale takes place, amid great excitement, at the Hôtel Drouot. Is the sale free? Is the richest bidder sure of getting the diamond? Not at all. At the moment when Herschmann is about to become the owner, a lady has a threatening letter thrust into his hand and the diamond goes to the Comtesse de Crozon, who has been worked upon and influenced by the same lady. Does it vanish at once? No: you lack the facilities. So an interval ensues. But the countess moves to her country-house. This is what you were waiting for. The ring disappears.'

'To reappear in the tooth-powder of Bleichen, the consul,' objected Lupin. 'How odd!'

'Come, come!' said Shears, striking the table with his fist. 'Tell that to the marines. You can take in fools with that, but not an old fox like me.'

'What do you mean?'

Shears took his time, as though he wished to save up his effect. Then he said:

'The blue diamond found in the tooth-powder is an imitation diamond. The real one you kept.'

Arsène Lupin was silent for a moment and then, with his eyes fixed on the Englishman, said very simply:

'You're a great man, sir.'

'Isn't he?' said Wilson, emphatically and gaping with admiration.

'Yes,' said Lupin, 'everything becomes cleared up and appears in its true sense. Not one of the examining magistrates, not one of the special reporters who have been exciting themselves about these cases has come half as near the truth. I look upon you as a marvel of insight and logic.'

'Pooh!' said the Englishman, flattered at the compliment paid him by so great an expert. 'It only needed a little thought.'

'It needed to know how to use one's thought; and there are so few who do know. But, now that the field of surmise has been narrowed and the ground swept clear . . . '

'Well, now, all that I have to do is to discover why the three cases were enacted at 25, Rue Clapeyron, at 134, Avenue Henri-Martin and within the walls of the Château de Crozon. The whole case lies there. The rest is mere talk and child's play. Don't you agree?'

'I agree.'

'In that case, M. Lupin, am I not right in saying that I shall have finished my business in ten days?'

'In ten days, yes, the whole truth will be known.'

'And you will be arrested.'

'No.'

'No?'

'For me to be arrested there would have to be a conjunction of such unlikely circumstances, a series of such stupefying pieces of ill-luck, that I cannot admit the possibility.'

'What neither circumstances nor luck may be able to effect, M. Lupin, can be brought about by one man's will and persistence.'

'If the will and persistence of another man do not oppose an invincible obstacle to that plan, Mr. Shears.'

'There is no such thing as an invincible obstacle, M. Lupin.'

The two exchanged a penetrating glance, free from provocation on either side, but calm and fearless. It was the clash of two swords about to open the combat. It sounded clear and frank.

'Joy!' cried Lupin. 'Here's a man at last! An adversary is a *rara avis* at any time; and this one is Holmlock Shears! We shall have some sport.'

'You're not afraid?' asked Wilson.

'Very nearly, Mr. Wilson,' said Lupin, rising, 'and the proof is that I am going to hurry to make good my retreat . . . else I might risk being caught napping. Ten days, we said, Mr. Shears?'

'Ten days. This is Sunday. It will all be over by Wednesday week.'

'And I shall be under lock and key?'

'Without the slightest doubt.'

'By Jove! And I was congratulating myself on my quiet life! No bothers, a good, steady little business, the police sent to the right about and a comforting sense of the general sympathy that surrounds me ... We shall have to change all this! It is the reverse of the medal . . . After sunshine comes rain . . . This is no time for laughing! Good-bye.'

'Look sharp!' said Wilson, full of solicitude on behalf of a person whom Shears inspired with such obvious respect. 'Don't lose a minute.'

'Not a minute, Mr. Wilson, except to tell you how pleased I have been to meet you and how I envy the leader who has an assistant so valuable as yourself.'

Courteous bows were exchanged, as between two adversaries on the fencing-ground who bear each other no hatred, but who are constrained by fate to fight to the death. And Lupin took my arm and dragged me outside:

'What do you say to that, old fellow? There's a dinner that will be worth describing in your memoirs of me!'

He closed the door of the restaurant and,

stopping a little way off:

'Do you smoke?'

'No, but no more do you, surely.'

'No more do I.'

He lit a cigarette with a wax match which he waved several times to put it out. But he at once flung away the cigarette, ran across the road and joined two men who had emerged from the shadow, as though summoned by a signal. He talked to them for a few minutes on the opposite pavement and then returned to me:

'I beg your pardon; but I shall have my work cut out with that confounded Shears. I swear, however, that he has not done with Lupin yet . . . By Jupiter, I'll show the fellow the stuff I'm made of! . . . Good night . . . The unspeakable Wilson is right: I have not a minute to lose.'

He walked rapidly away.

Thus ended that strange evening, or, at least that part of it with which I had to do. For many other incidents occurred during the hours that followed, events which the confidences of the others who were present at that dinner have fortunately enabled me to reconstruct in detail.

★ ★ ★

At the very moment when Lupin left me, Holmlock Shears took out his watch and rose in his turn:

'Twenty to nine. At nine o'clock, I am to meet the count and countess at the railway station.'

'Let's go!' cried Wilson, tossing off two glasses of whiskey in succession.

They went out.

'Wilson, don't turn your head . . . We may be followed: if so, let us act as though we don't care whether we are or not . . . Tell me, Wilson, what's your opinion: why was Lupin in that restaurant?'

Wilson, without hesitation, replied:

'To get some dinner.'

'Wilson, the longer we work together, the more clearly I perceive the constant progress you are making. Upon my word, you're becoming amazing.'

Wilson blushed with satisfaction in the dark; and Shears resumed:

'Yes, he went to get some dinner and then, most likely, to make sure if I am really going to Crozon, as Ganimard says I am, in his interview. I shall leave, therefore, so as not to disappoint him. But, as it is a question of gaining time upon him, I shall not leave.'

'Ah!' said Wilson, nonplussed.

'I want you, old chap, to go down this

street. Take a cab, take two cabs, three cabs. Come back later to fetch the bags which we left in the cloak room and then drive as fast as you can to the Elysée-Palace.'

'And what am I to do at the Élysée-Palace?'

'Ask for a room, go to bed, sleep the sleep of the just and await my instructions.'

★ ★ ★

Wilson, proud of the important task allotted to him, went off. Holmlock Shears took his ticket at the railway station and entered the Amiens express, in which the Comte and Comtesse de Crozon had already taken their seats.

He merely bowed to them, lit a second pipe and smoked it placidly, standing, in the corridor.

The train started. Ten minutes later, he came and sat down beside the countess and asked:

'Have you the ring on you, madame?'

'Yes.'

'Please let me look at it.'

He took it and examined it:

'As I thought: it is a faked diamond.'

'Faked?'

'Yes, by a new process which consists in subjecting diamond-dust to enormous heat until it melts . . . whereupon it is simply reformed into a single diamond.'

'Why, but my diamond is real!'

'Yes, yours; but this is not yours.'

'Where is mine, then?'

'In the hands of Arsène Lupin.'

'And this one?'

'This one was put in its place and slipped into Herr Bleichen's tooth-powder flask, where you found it.'

'Then it's an imitation?'

'Absolutely.'

Nonplussed and overwhelmed, the countess said nothing more, while her husband, refusing to believe the statement, turned the jewel over and over in his fingers. She finished by stammering out:

'But it's impossible! Why didn't they just simply take it? And how did they get it?'

'That's just what I mean to try to discover.'

'At Crozon?'

'No, I shall get out at Creil and return to Paris. That's where the game between Arsène Lupin and myself must be played out. The tricks will count the same, wherever we make them; but it is better that Lupin should think that I am out of town.'

'Still . . .'

'What difference can it make to you, madame? The main object is your diamond, is it not?'

'Yes.'

'Well, set your mind at rest. Only a little while ago, I gave an undertaking which will be much more difficult to keep. On the word of Holmlock Shears, you shall have the real diamond back.'

The train slowed down. He put the imitation diamond in his pocket and opened the carriage-door. The count cried:

'Take care; that's the wrong side!'

'Lupin will lose my tracks this way, if he's having me shadowed. Good-bye.'

A porter protested. The Englishman made for the station-master's office. Fifty minutes later, he jumped into a train which brought him back to Paris a little before midnight.

He ran across the station into the refreshment room, went out by the other door and sprang into a cab:

'Drive to the Rue Clapeyron.'

After making sure that he was not being followed, he stopped the cab at the commencement of the street and began to make a careful examination of the house in which Maître Detinan lived and of the two adjoining houses. He paced off certain distances and noted the measurements in his memorandum book:

'Now drive to the Avenue Henri-Martin.'

He dismissed his cab at the corner of the avenue and the Rue de la Pompe, walked along the pavement to No. 134 and went through the same performance in front of the house which Baron d'Hautrec had occupied and the two houses by which it was hemmed in on either side, measuring the width of their respective frontages and calculating the depth of the little gardens in front of the houses.

The avenue was deserted and very dark under its four rows of trees, amid which an occasional gas-jet seemed to struggle vainly against the thickness of the gloom. One of these lamps threw a pale light upon a part of the house and Shears saw the notice 'To Let' hanging on the railings, saw the two neglected walks that encircled the miniature lawn and the great empty windows of the uninhabited house.

'That's true,' he thought. 'There has been no tenant since the baron's death . . . Ah, if I could just get in and make a preliminary visit!'

The idea no sooner passed through his mind than he wanted to put it into execution. But how to manage? The height of the gate made it impossible for him to climb it. He took an electric lantern from his pocket, as well as a skeleton key which he always carried. To his great surprise, he found that one of the doors of the gate was standing ajar. He, therefore, slipped into the garden, taking care not to close the gate behind him. He had not gone three steps, when he stopped. A glimmer of light had passed along one of the windows on the second floor.

And the glimmer passed along a second window and a third, while he was able to see nothing but a shadow outlined against the walls of the rooms. And the glimmer descended from the second floor to the first and, for a long time, wandered from room to room.

'Who on earth can be walking about, at one in the morning, in the house where Baron d'Hautrec was murdered?' thought Shears, feeling immensely interested.

There was only one way of finding out, which was to enter the house himself. He did not hesitate. But the man must have seen him as he crossed the belt of light cast by the gas-jet and made his way to the steps, for the glimmer suddenly went out and Shears did not see it again.

He softly tried the door at the top of the steps. It was open also. Hearing no sound, he ventured to penetrate the darkness, felt for the knob of the baluster, found it and went up one floor. The same silence, the same darkness continued to reign.

On reaching the landing, he entered one of the rooms and went to the window, which showed white in the dim light of the night outside. Through the window, he caught sight of the man, who had doubtless gone down by another staircase and out by another door and was now slipping along the shrubs, on the left, that lined the wall separating the two gardens:

'Dash it!' exclaimed Shears. 'He'll escape me!'

He rushed downstairs and leapt into the garden, with a view to cutting off the man's retreat. At first, he saw no one; and it was some seconds before he distinguished, among the confused heap of shrubs, a darker form which was not quite stationary.

The Englishman paused to reflect. Why had the fellow not tried to run away when he could easily have done so? Was he staying there to spy, in his turn, upon the intruder who had disturbed him in his mysterious errand?

'In any case,' thought Shears, 'it is not Lupin. Lupin would be cleverer. It must be one of his gang.'

Long minutes passed. Shears stood motionless, with his eyes fixed upon the adversary who was watching him. But, as the adversary was motionless too and as the Englishman was not the man to hang about doing nothing, he felt to see if the cylinder of his revolver worked, loosened his dagger in its sheath and walked straight up to the enemy, with the cool daring and the contempt of danger which make him so formidable.

A sharp sound: the man was cocking his revolver. Shears rushed into the shrubbery. The other had no time to turn: the Englishman was upon him. There was a violent and desperate struggle, amid which Shears was aware that the man was making every effort to draw his knife. But Shears, stimulated by the thought of his coming victory and by the fierce longing to lay hold at once of this accomplice of Arsène Lupin's, felt an irresistible strength welling up within himself. He threw his adversary, bore upon him with all his weight and, holding him down with his five fingers clutching at his throat like so many claws, he felt for his electric lantern with the hand that was free, pressed the button and threw the light upon his prisoner's face:

'Wilson!' he shouted, in terror.

'Holmlock Shears!' gasped a hollow, stifled voice.

★ ★ ★

They remained long staring at each other, without exchanging a word, dumbfounded, stupefied. The air was torn by the horn of a motor-car. A breath of wind rustled through the leaves. And Shears did not stir, his fingers still fixed in Wilson's throat, which continued to emit an ever fainter rattle.

And, suddenly, Shears, overcome with rage, let go his friend, but only to seize him by the shoulders and shake him frantically:

'What are you doing here? Answer me! . . . What are you here for? . . . Who told you to hide in the shrubbery and watch me?'

'Watch you?' groaned Wilson. 'But I didn't know it was you.'

'Then what? Why are you here? I told you to go to bed.'

'I did go to bed.'

'I told you to go to sleep.'

'I did.'

'You had no business to wake up.'

'Your letter . . . '

'What letter?'

'The letter from you which a commissionaire brought me at the hotel.'

'A letter from me? You're mad!'

'I assure you.'

'Where is the letter?'

Wilson produced a sheet of note-paper and, by the light of his lantern, Shears read, in amazement:

*Get up at once, Wilson, and go to the Avenue Henri-Martin as fast as you can.*

*The house is empty. Go in, inspect it, make out an exact plan and go back to bed.*
*Holmlock Shears.*

'I was busy measuring the rooms,' said Wilson, 'when I saw a shadow in the garden. I had only one idea . . . '

'To catch the shadow . . . The idea was excellent . . . Only, look here, Wilson,' said Shears, helping his friend up and leading him away, 'next time you get a letter from me, make sure first that it's not a forgery.'

'Then the letter was not from you?' asked Wilson, who began to have a glimmering of the truth.

'No, worse luck!'

'Who wrote it, then?'

'Arsène Lupin.'

'But with what object?'

'I don't know, and that's just what bothers me. Why the deuce should he take the trouble to disturb your night's rest? If it were myself, I could understand, but you . . . I can't see what interest . . . '

'I am anxious to get back to the hotel.'

'So am I, Wilson.'

They reached the gate. Wilson, who was in front, took hold of one of the bars and pulled it:

'Hullo!' he said. 'Did you shut it?'

'Certainly not: I left the gate ajar.'

'But . . .'

Shears pulled in his turn and then frantically flung himself upon the lock. An oath escaped him:

'Damn it all! It's locked! . . . The gate's locked!'

He shook the gate with all his might, but, soon realizing the hopelessness of his exertions, let his arms fall to his sides in discouragement and jerked out:

'I understand the whole thing now: it's his doing! He foresaw that I should get out at Creil and he laid a pretty little trap for me, in case I should come to start my inquiry to-night. In addition, he had the kindness to send you to keep me company in my captivity. All this to make me lose a day and also, no doubt, to show me that I would do much better to mind my own business . . .'

'That is to say that we are his prisoners.'

'You speak like a book. Holmlock Shears and Wilson are the prisoners of Arsène Lupin. The adventure is beginning splendidly . . . But no, no, I refuse to believe . . .'

A hand touched his shoulder. It was Wilson's hand.

'Look,' he said. 'Up there . . . a light . . .'

It was true: there was a light visible through one of the windows on the first floor.

They both raced up, each by his own staircase, and reached the door of the lighted room at the same time. A candle-end was burning in the middle of the floor. Beside it stood a basket, from which protruded the neck of a bottle, the legs of a chicken and half a loaf of bread.

Shears roared with laughter:

'Splendid! He gives us our supper. It's an enchanted palace, a regular fairy-land! Come, Wilson, throw off that dismal face. This is all very amusing.'

'Are you sure it's very amusing?' moaned Wilson, dolefully.

'Sure?' cried Shears, with a gaiety that was too boisterous to be quite natural. 'Of course I'm sure! I never saw anything more amusing in my life. It's first-rate farce . . . What a master of chaff this Arsène Lupin is! . . . He tricks you, but he does it so gracefully! . . . I wouldn't give my seat at this banquet for all the gold in the world . . . Wilson, old chap, you disappoint me. Can I have been mistaken in you? Are you really deficient in that nobility of character which makes a man bear up under misfortune? What have you to complain of? At this moment, you might be lying with my dagger in your throat . . . or I with yours in mine . . . for that was what you were trying for, you faithless friend!'

He succeeded, by dint of humour and

sarcasm, in cheering up the wretched Wilson and forcing him to swallow a leg of the chicken and a glass of wine. But, when the candle had gone out and they had to stretch themselves on the floor to sleep, with the wall for a pillow, the painful and ridiculous side of the situation became apparent to them. And their slumbers were sad.

In the morning, Wilson woke aching in every bone and shivering with cold. A slight sound caught his ear: Holmlock Shears, on his knees, bent in two, was examining grains of dust through his lens and inspecting certain hardly perceptible chalk-marks, which formed figures which he put down in his note-book.

Escorted by Wilson, who seemed to take a particular interest in this work, he studied each room and found similar chalk-marks in two of the others. He also observed two circles on some oak panels, an arrow on a wainscoting and four figures on four steps of the staircase.

After an hour spent in this way, Wilson asked:

'The figures are correct, are they not?'

'I don't know if they're correct,' replied Shears, whose good temper had been restored by these discoveries, 'but, at any rate, they mean something.'

'Something very obvious,' said Wilson. 'They represent the number of planks in the floor.'

'Oh!'

'Yes. As for the two circles, they indicate that the panels sound hollow, as you can see by trying, and the arrow points to show the direction of the dinner-lift.'

Holmlock Shears looked at him in admiration:

'Why, my dear chap, how do you know all this? Your perspicacity almost makes me ashamed of myself.'

'Oh, it's very simple,' said Wilson, bursting with delight. 'I made those marks myself last night, in consequence of your instructions . . . or rather Lupin's instructions, as the letter I received from you came from him.'

I have little doubt that, at that moment, Wilson was in greater danger than during his struggle with Shears in the shrubbery. Shears felt a fierce longing to wring his neck. Mastering himself with an effort, he gave a grin that pretended to be a smile and said:

'Well done, well done, that's an excellent piece of work; most useful. Have your wonderful powers of analysis and observation been exercised in any other direction? I may as well make use of the results obtained.'

'No; that's all I did.'

'What a pity! The start was so promising! Well, as things are, there is nothing left for us to do but go.'

'Go? But how?'

'The way respectable people usually go: through the gate.'

'It's locked.'

'We must get it opened.'

'Whom by?'

'Would you mind calling those two policemen walking down the avenue?'

'But . . .'

'But what?'

'It's very humiliating . . . What will people say, when they learn that you, Holmlock Shears, and I, Wilson, have been locked up by Arsène Lupin?'

'It can't be helped, my dear fellow; they will laugh like anything,' replied Shears, angrily, with a frowning face. 'But we can't go on living here forever, can we?'

'And you don't propose to try anything?'

'Not I!'

'Still, the man who brought the basket of provisions did not cross the garden either in coming or going. There must, therefore, be another outlet. Let us look for it, instead of troubling the police.'

'Ably argued. Only you forget that the whole police of Paris have been hunting for

119

this outlet for the past six months and that I myself, while you were asleep, examined the house from top to bottom. Ah, my dear Wilson, Arsène Lupin is a sort of game we are not accustomed to hunt: he leaves nothing behind him, you see . . . '

★   ★   ★

Holmlock Shears and Wilson were let out at eleven o'clock and . . . taken to the nearest police-station, where the commissary, after cross-questioning them severely, released them with the most exasperating pretences of courtesy:

'Gentlemen, I am grieved beyond measure at your mishap. You will have a poor opinion of our French hospitality. Lord, what a night you must have spent! Upon my word, Lupin might have shown you more consideration!'

They took a cab to the Élysée-Palace. Wilson went to the office and asked for the key of his room.

The clerk looked through the visitors' book and replied, in great surprise:

'But you gave up your room this morning, sir!'

'What do you mean? How did I give up my room?'

'You sent us a letter by your friend.'

'What friend?'

'Why, the gentleman who brought us your letter . . . Here it is, with your card enclosed.'

Wilson took the letter and the enclosure. It was certainly one of his visiting-cards and the letter was in his writing:

'Good Lord!' he muttered. 'Here's another nasty trick.' And he added, anxiously, 'What about the luggage?'

'Why, your friend took it with him.'

'Oh! . . . So you gave it to him?'

'Certainly, on the authority of your card.'

'Just so . . . just so . . . '

They both went out and wandered down the Champs-Élysèes, slowly and silently. A fine autumn sun filled the avenue. The air was mild and light.

At the Rond-Point, Shears lit his pipe and resumed his walk. Wilson cried:

'I can't understand you, Shears; you take it so calmly! The man laughs at you, plays with you as a cat plays with a mouse . . . and you don't utter a word!'

Shears stopped and said:

'I'm thinking of your visiting-card, Wilson.'

'Well?'

'Well, here is a man, who, by way of preparing for a possible struggle with us, obtains specimens of your handwriting and mine and has one of your cards ready in his pocketbook. Have you thought of the amount of precaution, of perspicacity, of determination, of method, of organization that all this represents?'

'You mean to say . . . '

'I mean to say, Wilson, that, to fight an enemy so formidably armed, so wonderfully equipped — and to beat him — takes . . . a man like myself. And, even then, Wilson,' he added, laughing, 'one does not succeed at the first attempt, as you see!'

\* \* \*

At six o'clock, the *Écho de France* published the following paragraph in its special edition:

'This morning, M. Thénard, the commissary of police of the 16th division, released Messrs. Holmlock Shears and Wilson, who had been confined, by order of Arsène Lupin, in the late Baron d'Hautrec's house, where they spent an excellent night.

'They were also relieved of their luggage and have laid an information against Arsène Lupin.

'Arsène Lupin has been satisfied with giving them a little lesson this time; but he earnestly begs them not to compel him to adopt more serious measures.'

'Pooh!' said Holmlock Shears, crumpling

up the paper. 'Schoolboy tricks! That's the only fault I have to find with Lupin . . . he's too childish, too fond of playing to the gallery . . . He's a street arab at heart!'

'So you continue to take it calmly, Shears?'

'Quite calmly,' replied Shears, in a voice shaking with rage. 'What's the use of being angry? *I am so certain of having the last word!*'

# 4

## A Glimmer in the Darkness

However impervious to outside influences a man's character may be — and Shears is one of those men upon whom ill-luck takes hardly any hold — there are yet circumstances in which the most undaunted feel the need to collect their forces before again facing the chances of a battle.

'I shall take a holiday to-day,' said Shears.

'And I?'

'You, Wilson, must go and buy clothes and shirts and things to replenish our wardrobe. During that time, I shall rest.'

'Yes, rest, Shears. I shall watch.'

Wilson uttered those three words with all the importance of a sentry placed on outpost duty and therefore exposed to the worst dangers. He threw out his chest and stiffened his muscles. With a sharp eye, he glanced round the little hotel bedroom where they had taken up their quarters.

'That's right, Wilson: watch. I shall employ the interval in preparing a plan of campaign better suited to the adversary whom we have to deal with. You see, Wilson, we were wrong about Lupin. We must start again from the beginning.'

'Even earlier, if we can. But have we time?'

'Nine days, old chap: five days more than we want.'

★  ★  ★

The Englishman spent the whole afternoon smoking and dozing. He did not begin operations until the following morning:

'I'm ready now, Wilson. We can go ahead.'

'Let's go ahead,' cried Wilson, full of martial ardour. 'My legs are twitching to start.'

Shears had three long interviews: first, with Maître Detinan, whose flat he inspected through and through; next, with Suzanne Gerbois, to whom he telegraphed to come and whom he questioned about the blonde lady; lastly with Sœur Auguste, who had returned to the Visitation Convent after the murder of Baron d'Hautrec.

At each visit, Wilson waited outside and, after each visit, asked:

'Satisfied?'

'Quite.'

'I was sure of it. We're on the right track now. Let's go ahead.'

They did a great deal of going. They called

125

at the two mansions on either side of the house in the Avenue Henri-Martin. From there they went on to the Rue Clapeyron and, while he was examining the front of No. 25, Shears continued:

'It is quite obvious that there are secret passages between all these houses . . . But what I cannot make out . . . '

For the first time and in his inmost heart, Wilson doubted the omnipotence of his talented chief. Why was he talking so much and doing so little?

'Why?' cried Shears, replying to Wilson's unspoken thoughts. 'Because, with that confounded Lupin, one has nothing to go upon; one works at random. Instead of deriving the truth from exact facts, one has to get at it by intuition and verify it afterward to see if it fits in.'

'But the secret passages . . . ?'

'What then? Even if I knew them, if I knew the one which admitted Lupin to his lawyer's study or the one taken by the blonde lady after the murder of Baron d'Hautrec, how much further should I be? Would that give me a weapon to go for him with?'

'Let's go for him, in any case,' said Wilson.

He had not finished speaking, when he jumped back with a cry. Something had fallen at their feet: a bag half-filled with sand, which might have hurt them seriously.

Shears looked up: some men were working in a cradle hooked on to the balcony of the fifth floor.

'Upon my word,' he said, 'we've had a lucky escape! The clumsy beggars! Another yard and we should have caught that bag on our heads. One would really think . . . '

He stopped, darted into the house, rushed up the staircase, rang the bell on the fifth landing, burst into the flat, to the great alarm of the footman who opened the door, and went out on the balcony. There was no one there.

'Where are the workmen who were here a moment ago?' he asked the footman.

'They have just gone.'

'Which way?'

'Why, down the servants' staircase.'

Shears leant over. He saw two men leaving the house, leading their bicycles. They mounted and rode away.

'Have they been working on this cradle long?'

'No, only since this morning. They were new men.'

Shears joined Wilson down below.

They went home in a depressed mood; and this second day ended in silent gloom.

★　★　★

127

They followed a similar programme on the following day. They sat down on a bench in the Avenue Henri-Martin. Wilson, who was thoroughly bored by this interminable wait opposite the three houses, felt driven to desperation:

'What do you expect, Shears? To see Lupin come out?'

'No.'

'Or the blonde lady?'

'No.'

'What, then?'

'I expect some little thing to happen, some little tiny thing which I can use as a starting-point.'

'And, if nothing happens?'

'In that case, something will happen inside myself: a spark that will set us going.'

The only incident that broke the monotony of the morning was a rather disagreeable one. A gentleman was coming down the riding-path that separates the two roadways of the avenue, when his horse swerved, struck the bench on which they were sitting and backed against Shears's shoulder.

'Tut, tut!' snarled Shears. 'A shade more and I should have had my shoulder smashed.'

The rider was struggling with his horse. The Englishman drew his revolver and took aim. But Wilson seized his arm smartly:

'You're mad, Holmlock! Why . . . look here . . . you'll kill that gentleman!'

'Let go, Wilson . . . do let go!'

A wrestle ensued, during which the horseman got his mount under control and galloped away.

'Now you can fire!' exclaimed Wilson, triumphantly, when the man was at some distance.

'But, you confounded fool, don't you understand that that was a confederate of Arsène Lupin's?'

Shears was trembling with rage. Wilson stammered, piteously:

'What do you mean? That gentleman . . . ?'

'Was a confederate of Lupin's, like the workmen who flung that bag at our heads.'

'It's not credible!'

'Credible or not, there was a means handy of obtaining a proof.'

'By killing that gentleman?'

'By simply bringing down his horse. But for you, I should have got one of Lupin's pals. Do you see now what a fool you've been?'

The afternoon was passed in a very sullen fashion. Shears and Wilson did not exchange a word. At five o'clock, as they were pacing up and down the Rue Clapeyron, taking care, however, to keep away from the houses, three young workingmen came along the pavement singing, arm-in-arm, knocked up against them and tried to continue their road without separating. Shears, who was in a bad temper, pushed them back. There was a short scuffle. Shears put up his fists, struck one of the men in the chest and gave another a blow in the face, whereupon the men desisted and walked away with the third.

'Ah,' cried Shears, 'I feel all the better for that! . . . My nerves were a bit strained . . . Good business! . . . '

But he saw Wilson leaning against the wall:

'Hullo, old chap,' he said, 'what's up? You look quite pale.'

Old chap pointed to his arm, which was hanging lifeless by his side, and stammered:

'I don't know . . . my arm's hurting me . . . '

'Your arm? . . . Badly?'

'Yes . . . rather . . . it's my right arm . . . '

He tried to lift it, but could not. Shears felt it, gently at first and then more roughly, 'to see exactly,' he said, 'how much it hurts.' It hurt exactly so much that Wilson, on being led to a neighbouring chemist's shop, experienced an immediate need to fall into a dead faint.

The chemist and his assistant did what they could. They discovered that the arm was broken and that it was a case for a surgeon, an operation and a hospital. Meanwhile, the patient was undressed and began to relieve his sufferings by roaring with pain.

'That's all right, that's all right,' said Shears, who was holding Wilson's arm. 'Just a little patience, old chap . . . in five or six weeks, you won't know that you've been hurt . . . But I'll make them pay for it, the scoundrels! . . . You understand . . . I mean him especially . . . for it's that wretched Lupin who's responsible for this . . . Oh, I swear to you that if ever . . . '

He interrupted himself suddenly, dropped the arm, which gave Wilson such a shock of pain that the poor wretch fainted once more, and, striking his forehead, shouted:

'Wilson, I have an idea . . . Could it possibly . . . ?'

He stood motionless, with his eyes fixed before him, and muttered in short sentences:

'Yes, that's it . . . It's all clear now . . . the explanation staring us in the face . . . Why, of course, I knew it only needed a little thought! . . . Ah, my dear Wilson, this will rejoice your heart!'

And, leaving old chap where he was, he rushed into the street and ran to No. 25.

One of the stones above the door, on the right, bore the inscription: 'Destange, architect, 1875.'

The same inscription appeared on No. 23.

So far, this was quite natural. But what would he find down there, in the Avenue Henri-Martin?

He hailed a passing cab:

'Drive to 134, Avenue Henri-Martin. Go as fast as you can.'

Standing up in the cab, he urged on the horse, promising the driver tip after tip:

'Faster! . . . Faster still!'

He was in an agony as he turned the corner of the Rue de la Pompe. Had he caught a glimpse of the truth?

On one of the stones of the house, he read the words: '*Destange, architect, 1874.*' And he found the same inscription — '*Destange, architect, 1874*' — on each of the adjoining blocks of flats.

★ ★ ★

The reaction after this excitement was so great that he sank back into the cab for a few minutes, all trembling with delight. At last a tiny glimmer flickered in the darkness! Amid the thousand intersecting paths in the great, gloomy forest, he had found the first sign of a trail followed by the enemy!

He entered a telephone-office and asked to be put on to the Château de Crozon. The countess herself answered.

'Hullo! . . . Is that you, madame?'

'Is that Mr. Shears? How are things going?'

'Very well. But tell me, quickly . . . Hullo! Are you there? . . . '

'Yes . . . '

'When was the Château de Crozon built?'

'It was burnt down thirty years ago and rebuilt.'

'By whom? And in what year?'

'There's an inscription over the front door: '*Lucien Destange, architect, 1877.*''

'Thank you, madame. Good-bye.'

'Good-bye.'

He went away, muttering:

'Destange . . . Lucien Destange . . . I seem to know the name . . . '

He found a public library, consulted a modern biographical dictionary and copied out the reference to 'Lucien Destange, born 1840, Grand-Prix de Rome, officer of the Legion of Honour, author of several valuable works on architecture,' etc.

He next went to the chemist's and, from there, to the hospital to which Wilson had been moved. Old chap was lying on his bed of pain, with his arm in splints, shivering with fever and slightly delirious.

'Victory! Victory!' cried Shears. 'I have one end of the clue.'

'What clue?'

'The clue that will lead me to success. I am now treading firm soil, where I shall find marks and indications . . . '

'Cigarette-ashes?' asked Wilson, whom the interest of the situation was reviving.

'And plenty of other things! Just think, Wilson, I have discovered the mysterious link that connects the three adventures of the blonde lady. Why were the three houses in which the three adventures took place selected by Arsène Lupin?'

'Yes, why?'

'Because those three houses, Wilson, were built by the same architect. It was easy to guess that, you say? Certainly it was . . . And that's why nobody thought of it.'

'Nobody except yourself.'

'Just so! And I now understand how the same architect, by contriving similar plans, enabled three actions to be performed which appeared to be miraculous, though they were really quite easy and simple.'

'What luck!'

'It was high time, old chap, for I was beginning to lose patience . . . This is the fourth day.'

'Out of ten.'

'Oh, but from now onward . . . '

He could no longer keep his seat, exulting in his gladness beyond his wont:

'Oh, when I think that, just now, in the street, those ruffians might have broken my arm as well as yours! What do you say to that, Wilson?'

Wilson simply shuddered at the horrid thought.

And Shears continued:

'Let this be a lesson to us! You see, Wilson, our great mistake has been to fight Lupin in the open and to expose ourselves, in the most obliging way, to his attacks. The thing is not as bad as it might be, because he only got at you . . . '

'And I came off with a broken arm,' moaned Wilson.

'Whereas it might have been both of us. But no more swaggering. Watched, in broad daylight, I am beaten. Working freely, in the shade, I have the advantage, whatever the enemy's strength may be.'

'Ganimard might be able to help you.'

'Never! On the day when I can say, 'Arsène Lupin is there; that is his hiding-place; this is how you must set to work to catch him,' I shall hunt up Ganimard at one of the two addresses he gave me, his flat in the Rue Pergolèse, or the Taverne Suisse, on the Place du Châtelet. But till then I shall act alone.'

He went up to the bed, put his hand on Wilson's shoulder — the bad shoulder, of course — and said, in a very affectionate voice:

'Take care of yourself, old chap. Your task, henceforth, will consist in keeping two or three of Lupin's men busy. They will waste their time waiting for me to come and inquire after you. It's a confidential task.'

'Thank you ever so much,' replied Wilson, gratefully. 'I shall do my best to perform it conscientiously. So you are not coming back?'

'Why should I?' asked Shears, coldly.

'No . . . you're quite right . . . you're quite right . . . I'm going on as well as can be expected. You might do one thing for me, Holmlock: give me a drink.'

'A drink?'

'Yes, I'm parched with thirst; and this fever of mine . . . '

'Why, of course! Wait a minute.'

He fumbled about among some bottles, came upon a packet of tobacco, filled and lit his pipe and, suddenly, as though he had not even heard his friend's request, walked away, while old chap cast longing glances at the water-bottle beyond his reach.

★  ★  ★

'Is M. Destange at home?'

The butler eyed the person to whom he

had opened the door of the house — the magnificent house at the corner of the Place Malesherbes and the Rue Montchanin — and, at the sight of the little gray-haired, ill-shaven man, whose long and far from immaculate frock-coat matched the oddity of a figure to which nature had been anything but kind, replied, with due scorn:

'M. Destange may be at home or he may be out. It depends. Has monsieur a card?'

Monsieur had no card, but he carried a letter of introduction and the butler had to take it to M. Destange, whereupon M. Destange ordered the newcomer to be shown in.

He was ushered into a large circular room, which occupied one of the wings of the house and which was lined with books all round the walls.

'Are you M. Stickmann?' asked the architect.

'Yes, sir.'

'My secretary writes that he is ill and sends you to continue the general catalogue of my books, which he began under my direction, and of the German books in particular. Have you any experience of this sort of work?'

'Yes, sir, a long experience,' replied Stickmann, in a strong Teutonic accent.

In these conditions, the matter was soon settled; and M. Destange set to work with his new secretary without further delay.

Holmlock Shears had carried the citadel.

In order to escape Lupin's observation and to obtain an entrance into the house which Lucien Destange occupied with his daughter Clotilde, the illustrious detective had been obliged to take a leap in the dark, to resort to untold stratagems, to win the favour and confidence of a host of people under endless different names, in short, to lead forty-eight hours of the most complex life.

The particulars which he had gathered were these: M. Destange, who was in failing health and anxious for rest, had retired from business and was living among the architectural books which it had been his hobby to collect. He had no interest left in life beyond the handling and examining of those old dusty volumes.

As for his daughter Clotilde, she was looked upon as eccentric. She spent her days, like her father, in the house, but in another part of it, and never went out.

'This is all,' thought Shears, as he wrote down the titles of the books in his catalogue, to M. Destange's dictation, 'this is all more or less indefinite; but it is a good step forward. I am bound to discover the solution of one at least of these exciting problems: is M. Destange an accomplice of Arsène Lupin's? Does he see him now? Are there any papers relating to the building of the three houses? Will these papers supply me with the address of other properties, similarly faked, which Lupin may have reserved for his own use and that of his gang?'

M. Destange an accomplice of Arsène Lupin's! This venerable man, an officer of the Legion of Honour, working hand in hand with a burglar! The presumption was hardly tenable. Besides, supposing that they were accomplices, how did M. Destange come to provide for Arsène Lupin's various escapes thirty years before they occurred, at a time when Arsène was in his cradle?

No matter, the Englishman stuck to his guns. With his prodigious intuition, with that instinct which is all his own, he felt a mystery surrounding him. This was perceptible by small signs, which he could not have described with precision, but which impressed him from the moment when he first set foot in the house.

On the morning of the second day, he had as yet discovered nothing of interest. He first saw Clotilde Destange at two o'clock, when she came to fetch a book from the library. She was a woman of thirty, dark, with slow and silent movements; and her features bore the look of indifference of those who live much within themselves. She exchanged a few words with M. Destange and left the room without so much as glancing at Shears.

The afternoon dragged on monotonously. At five o'clock, M. Destange stated that he was going out. Shears remained alone in the circular gallery that ran round the library, half-way between floor and ceiling. It was growing dark and he was preparing to leave, in his turn, when he heard a creaking sound and, at the same time, felt that there was some one in the room. Minute followed slowly upon minute. And, suddenly, he started: a shadow had emerged from the semidarkness, quite close to him, on the balcony. Was it credible? How long had this unseen person been keeping him company? And where did he come from?

And the man went down the steps and turned in the direction of a large oak cupboard. Crouching on his knees behind the tapestry that covered the rail of the gallery, Shears watched and saw the man rummage among the papers with which the cupboard was crammed. What was he looking for?

And, suddenly, the door opened and Mlle. Destange entered quickly, saying to some one behind her:

'So you have quite changed your mind about going out, father? . . . In that case, I'll turn on the light . . . Wait a minute . . . don't move.'

*   *   *

The man closed the doors of the cupboard and hid himself in the embrasure of a broad window, drawing the curtains in front of him. How was it that Mlle. Destange did not see him! How was it that she did not hear him? She calmly switched on the electric light and stood back for her father to pass.

They sat down side by side. Mlle. Destange opened a book which she had brought with her and began to read.

'Has your secretary gone?' she said, presently.

'Yes . . . so it seems . . . '

'Are you still satisfied with him?' she continued, as if in ignorance of the real secretary's illness and of the arrival of Stickmann in his stead.

'Quite . . . quite . . . '

M. Destange's head dropped on his chest. He fell asleep.

A moment elapsed. The girl went on reading. But one of the window curtains was moved aside and the man slipped along the wall, toward the door, an action which made him pass behind M. Destange, but right in front of Clotilde and in such a way that Shears was able to see him plainly. It was Arsène Lupin!

The Englishman quivered with delight. His

calculations were correct, he had penetrated to the very heart of the mystery and Lupin was where he had expected to find him.

Clotilde, however, did not stir, although it was impossible that a single movement of that man had escaped her. And Lupin was close to the door and had his arm stretched toward the handle, when his clothes grazed a table and something fell to the ground. M. Destange woke with a start. In a moment, Arsène Lupin was standing before him, smiling, hat in hand.

'Maxime Bermond!' cried M. Destange, in delight. 'My dear Maxime! . . . What stroke of good luck brings you here to-day?'

'The wish to see you and Mlle. Destange.'

'When did you come back?'

'Yesterday.'

'Are you staying to dinner?'

'Thank you, no, I am dining out with some friends.'

'Come to-morrow, then. Clotilde, make him come to-morrow. My dear Maxime! . . . I was thinking of you only the other day.'

'Really?'

'Yes, I was arranging my old papers, in that cupboard, and I came across our last account.'

'Which one?'

'The Avenue Henri-Martin account.'

'Do you mean to say you keep all that

waste paper? What for?'

The three moved into a little drawing-room which was connected with the round library by a wide recess.

'Is it Lupin?' thought Shears, seized with a sudden doubt.

All the evidence pointed to him, but it was another man as well; a man who resembled Arsène Lupin in certain respects and who, nevertheless, preserved his distinct individuality, his own features, look and complexion.

Dressed for the evening, with a white tie and a soft-fronted shirt following the lines of his body, he talked gaily, telling stories which made M. Destange laugh aloud and which brought a smile to Clotilde's lips. And each of these smiles seemed a reward which Arsène Lupin coveted and which he rejoiced at having won. His spirits and gaiety increased and, imperceptibly, at the sound of his clear and happy voice, Clotilde's face brightened up and lost the look of coldness that tended to spoil it.

'They are in love,' thought Shears. 'But what on earth can Clotilde Destange and Maxime Bermond have in common? Does she know that Maxime is Arsène Lupin?'

He listened anxiously until seven o'clock, making the most of every word spoken. Then, with infinite precautions, he came down and crossed the side of the room where there was no danger of his being seen from the drawing-room.

\* \* \*

Once outside, after assuring himself that there was no motor-car or cab waiting, he limped away along the Boulevard Malesherbes. Then he turned down a side street, put on the overcoat which he carried over his arm, changed the shape of his hat, drew himself up and, thus transformed, returned to the square, where he waited, with his eyes fixed on the door of the Maison Destange.

Arsène Lupin came out almost at once and walked, down the Rue de Constantinople and the Rue de Londres, toward the centre of the town. Shears followed him at a hundred yards' distance.

It was a delicious moment for the Englishman. He sniffed the air greedily, like a good hound scenting a fresh trail. It really seemed infinitely sweet to him to be following his adversary. It was no longer he that was watched, but Arsène Lupin, the invisible Arsène Lupin. He kept him, so to speak, fastened at the end of his eyes, as though with unbreakable bonds. And he revelled in contemplating, among the other pedestrians, this prey which belonged to him.

But a curious incident soon struck him: in the centre of the space that separated Arsène Lupin and himself, other people were going in the same direction, notably two tall fellows in bowler hats on the left pavement, while two others, in caps, were following on the right pavement, smoking cigarettes as they went.

This might be only a coincidence. But Shears was more surprised when the four men stopped as Lupin entered a tobacconist's shop; and still more when they started again as he came out, but separately, each keeping to his own side of the Chaussèe d'Antin.

'Confound it!' thought Shears. 'He's being shadowed!'

The idea that others were on Arsène Lupin's track, that others might rob him not of the glory — he cared little for that — but of the huge pleasure, the intense delight of conquering unaided the most formidable enemy that he had ever encountered: this idea exasperated him. And yet there was no possibility of a mistake: the men wore that look of detachment, that too-natural look which distinguishes persons who, while regulating their gait by another's, endeavour to remain unobserved.

'Does Ganimard know more than he pretends?' muttered Shears. 'Is he making game of me?'

He felt inclined to accost one of the four men, with a view to acting in concert with him. But as they approached the boulevard, the crowd became denser: he was afraid of losing Lupin and quickened his pace. He turned into the boulevard just as Lupin had his foot on the step of the Restaurant Hongrois, at the corner of the Rue du Helder. The door was open and Shears, sitting on a bench on the boulevard, on the opposite side of the road, saw him take his seat at a table laid with the greatest luxury and decorated with flowers, where he was warmly welcomed by three men in evening clothes and two beautifully-dressed ladies who had been waiting for him.

Shears looked for the four rough fellows and saw them scattered among the groups of people who were listening to the Bohemian band of the neighbouring café. Strange to say, they appeared to be not nearly so much interested in Arsène Lupin as in the people surrounding them.

Suddenly, one of them took a cigarette from his case and addressed a gentleman in a frock-coat and tall hat. The gentleman offered a light from his cigar and Shears received the impression that they were talking at greater length than the mere lighting of a cigarette demanded. At last the gentleman went up the steps and glanced into the restaurant. Seeing Lupin, he walked up to him, exchanged a few words with him and selected a table close at hand; and Shears realized that he was none other than the horseman of the Avenue Henri-Martin.

Now he understood. Not only was Arsène not being shadowed, but these men were members of his gang! These men were watching over his safety! They were his bodyguard, his satellites, his vigilant escort. Wherever the master ran any danger, there his accomplices were, ready to warn him, ready to defend him. The four men were accomplices! The gentleman in the frock-coat was an accomplice!

A thrill passed through the Englishman's frame. Would he ever succeed in laying hands on that inaccessible person? The power represented by an association of this kind, ruled by such a chief, seemed boundless.

He tore a leaf from his note-book, wrote a few lines in pencil, put the note in an envelope and gave it to a boy of fifteen who had lain down on the bench beside him:

'Here, my lad, take a cab and give this letter to the young lady behind the bar at the Taverne Suisse on the Place du Châtelet. Be as quick as you can.'

He handed him a five-franc piece. The boy went off.

Half an hour elapsed. The crowd had increased and Shears but occasionally caught sight of Lupin's followers. Then some one grazed against him and a voice said in his ear:

'Well, Mr. Shears, what can I do for you?'

'Is that you, M. Ganimard?'

'Yes; I got your note. What is it?'

'He's there.'

'What's that you say?'

'Over there . . . inside the restaurant . . . Move a little to the right . . . Do you see him?'

'No.'

'He is filling the glass of the lady on his left.'

'But that's not Lupin.'

'Yes, it is.'

'I assure you . . . And yet . . . Well, it may be . . . Oh, the rascal, *how like himself he is!*' muttered Ganimard, innocently. 'And who are the others? Accomplices?'

'No, the lady beside him is Lady Cliveden. The other is the Duchess of Cleath; and, opposite her, is the Spanish Ambassador in London.'

Ganimard took a step toward the road. But Shears held him back:

'Don't be so reckless: you are alone.'

'So is he.'

'No, there are men on the boulevard mounting guard . . . Not to mention that gentleman inside the restaurant . . . '

'But I have only to take him by the collar and shout his name to have the whole restaurant on my side, all the waiters . . . '

'I would rather have a few detectives.'

'That would set Lupin's friends off . . . No, Mr. Shears, we have no choice, you see.'

He was right and Shears felt it. It was better to make the attempt and take advantage of the exceptional circumstances. He contented himself with saying to Ganimard:

'Do your best not to be recognized before you can help it.'

He himself slipped behind a newspaper-kiosk, without losing sight of Arsène Lupin who was leaning over Lady Cliveden, smiling.

The inspector crossed the street, looking straight before him, with his hands in his pockets. But, the moment he reached the opposite pavement, he veered briskly round and sprang up the steps.

A shrill whistle sounded . . . Ganimard knocked up against the head-waiter, who suddenly blocked the entrance and pushed him back with indignation, as he might push back any intruder whose doubtful attire would have disgraced the luxury of the establishment. Ganimard staggered. At the same moment, the gentleman in the frock-coat came out. He took the part of the inspector and began a violent discussion with the head-waiter. Both of them had hold of Ganimard, one pushing him forward, the other back, until, in spite of all his efforts and angry protests, the unhappy man was hustled to the bottom of the steps.

A crowd gathered at once. Two policemen, attracted by the excitement, tried to make their way through; but they encountered an incomprehensible resistance and were unable to get clear of the shoulders that pushed against them, the backs that barred their progress.

And, suddenly, as though by enchantment, the way was opened! . . . The head-waiter, realizing his mistake, made the most abject apologies; the gentleman in the frock-coat withdrew his assistance; the crowd parted, the policemen passed in; and Ganimard rushed toward the table with the six guests . . . There were only five left! He looked round: there was no way out except the door.

'Where is the person who was sitting here?' he shouted to the five bewildered guests. 'Yes, there were six of you . . . Where is the sixth?'

'M. Destro?'

'No, no: Arsène Lupin!'

A waiter stepped up:

'The gentleman has just gone up to the mezzanine floor.'

Ganimard flew upstairs. The mezzanine floor consisted of private rooms and had a separate exit to the boulevard!

'It's no use now,' groaned Ganimard. 'He's far away by this time!'

★　★　★

He was not so very far away, two hundred yards at most, in the omnibus running between the Bastille and the Madeleine, which lumbered peacefully along behind its three horses, crossing the Place de l'Opéra and going down the Boulevard des Capucines. Two tall fellows in bowler hats stood talking on the conductor's platform. On the top, near the steps, a little old man sat dozing: it was Holmlock Shears.

And, with his head swaying from side to side, rocked by the movement of the omnibus, the Englishman soliloquized:

'Ah, if dear old Wilson could see me now, how proud he would be of his chief! . . . Pooh, it was easy to foresee, from the moment when the whistle sounded that the game was up and that there was nothing serious to be done, except to keep a watch around the restaurant! But that devil of a man adds a zest to life, and no mistake!'

On reaching the end of the journey, Shears

leant over, saw Arsène Lupin pass out in front of his guards and heard him mutter:

'At the Étoile.'

'The Étoile, just so: an assignation. I shall be there. I'll let him go ahead in that motor-cab, while I follow his two pals in a four-wheeler.'

The two pals went off on foot, made for the Étoile and rang at the door of No 40, Rue Chalgrin, a house with a narrow frontage. Shears found a hiding place in the shadow of a recess formed by the angle of that unfrequented little street.

One of the two windows on the ground floor opened and a man in a bowler hat closed the shutters. The window space above the shutters was lit up.

In ten minutes' time, a gentleman came and rang at the same door; and, immediately afterward, another person. And, at last, a motor-cab drew up and Shears saw two people get out: Arsène Lupin and a lady wrapped in a cloak and a thick veil.

'The blonde lady, I presume,' thought Shears, as the cab drove away.

He waited for a moment, went up to the house, climbed on to the window-ledge and, by standing on tip-toe, succeeded in peering into the room through that part of the window which the shutters failed to cover.

Arsène Lupin was leaning against the chimney and talking in an animated fashion. The others stood round and listened attentively. Shears recognized the gentleman in the frock-coat and thought he recognized the head-waiter of the restaurant. As for the blonde lady, she was sitting in a chair, with her back turned toward him.

'They are holding a council,' he thought. 'This evening's occurrences have alarmed them and they feel a need to discuss things . . . Oh, if I could only catch them all at one swoop!'

One of the accomplices moved and Shears leapt down and fell back into the shadow. The gentleman in the frock-coat and the head-waiter left the house. Then the first floor was lit up and some one closed the window-shutters. It was now dark above and below.

'He and she have remained on the ground floor,' said Holmlock to himself. 'The two accomplices live on the first story.'

He waited during a part of the night without stirring from his place, fearing lest Arsène Lupin should go away during his absence. At four o'clock in the morning, seeing two policemen at the end of the street, he went up to them, explained the position and left them to watch the house.

Then he went to Ganimard's flat in the

Rue Pergolèse and told the servant to wake him.

'I've got him again.'

'Arsène Lupin?'

'Yes.'

'If you haven't got him any better than you did just now, I may as well go back to bed. However, let's go and see the commissary.'

They went to the Rue Mesnil and, from there, to the house of the commissary, M. Decointre. Next, accompanied by half a dozen men, they returned to the Rue Chalgrin.

'Any news?' asked Shears of the two policemen watching the house.

'No, sir; none.'

The daylight was beginning to show in the sky when the commissary, after disposing his men, rang and entered the lodge of the concierge. Terrified by this intrusion, the woman, all trembling, said that there was no tenant on the ground floor.

'What do you mean; no tenant?' cried Ganimard.

'No, it's the people on the first floor, two gentlemen called Leroux ... They have furnished the apartment below for some relations from the country ... '

'A lady and gentleman?'

'Yes.'

'Did they come with them last night?'

'They may have ... I was asleep ... I

don't think so, though, for here's the key — they didn't ask for it.'

With this key, the commissary opened the door on the other side of the passage. The ground floor flat contained only two rooms: they were empty.

'Impossible!' said Shears. 'I saw them both here.'

The commissary grinned:

'I dare say; but they are not here now.'

'Let us go to the first floor. They must be there.'

'The first floor is occupied by two gentlemen called Leroux.'

'We will question the two gentleman called Leroux.'

They all went upstairs and the commissary rang. At the second ring, a man, who was none other than one of the bodyguards, appeared in his shirt-sleeves and, with a furious air:

'Well, what is it? What's all this noise about; what do you come waking people up for?'

But he stopped in confusion:

'Lord bless my soul! . . . Am I dreaming? Why, it's M. Decointre! . . . And you too, M. Ganimard? What can I do for you?'

There was a roar of laughter. Ganimard was splitting with a fit of merriment which doubled him up and seemed to threaten an apoplectic fit:

'It's you, Leroux!' he spluttered out. 'Oh, that's the best thing I ever heard: Leroux, Arsène Lupin's accomplice! . . . It'll be the death of me, I know it will! . . . And where's your brother, Leroux? Is he visible?'

'Are you there, Edmond? It's M. Ganimard come to pay us a visit.'

Another man came forward, at the sight of whom Ganimard's hilarity increased still further:

'Well, I never! Dear, dear me! Ah, my friends, you're in a nice pickle . . . Who would have suspected it? It's a good thing that old Ganimard keeps his eyes open and still better that he has friends to help him . . . friends who have come all the way from England!'

And, turning to Shears, he said:

'Mr. Shears, let me introduce Victor Leroux, detective-inspector, one of the best in the iron brigade . . . And Edmond Leroux, head-clerk in the Finger-print Department . . . '

# 5

## Kidnapped

Holmlock Shears restrained his feelings. What was the use of protesting, of accusing those two men? Short of proofs, which he did not possess and which he would not waste time in looking for, no one would take his word.

With nerves on edge and fists tight-clenched, he had but one thought, that of not betraying his rage and disappointment before the triumphant Ganimard. He bowed politely to those two mainstays of society, the brothers Leroux, and went downstairs.

In the hall he turned toward a small, low door, which marked the entrance to the cellar, and picked up a small red stone: it was a garnet.

Outside, he looked up and read, close to the number of the house, the inscription: 'Lucien Destange, architect, 1877.' He saw the same inscription on No. 42.

'Always that double outlet,' he thought. 'Nos. 40 and 42 communicate. Why did I not think of it before? I ought to have stayed with the policemen all night.'

And, addressing them, he said, pointing to

the door of the next house:

'Did two people go out by that door while I was away?'

'Yes, sir; a lady and gentleman.'

He took the arm of the chief-inspector and led him along:

'M. Ganimard, you have enjoyed too hearty a laugh to be very angry with me for disturbing you like this . . . '

'Oh, I'm not angry with you at all.'

'That's right. But the best jokes can't go on forever and I think we must put an end to this one.'

'I am with you.'

'This is our seventh day. It is absolutely necessary that I should be in London in three days hence.'

'I say! I say!'

'I shall be there, though, and I beg you to hold yourself in readiness on Tuesday night.'

'For an expedition of the same kind?' asked Ganimard, chaffingly.

'Yes, of the same kind.'

'And how will this one end?'

'In Lupin's capture.'

'You think so.'

'I swear it, on my honour.'

Shears took his leave and went to seek a short rest in the nearest hotel, after which, refreshed and full of confidence, he returned to the Rue Chalgrin, slipped two louis into the hand of the concierge, made sure that the brothers Leroux were out, learned that the house belonged to a certain M. Harmingeat and, carrying a candle, found his way down to the cellar through the little door near which he had picked up the garnet.

At the foot of the stairs, he picked up another of exactly the same shape.

'I was right,' he thought. 'This forms the communication . . . Let's see if my skeleton-key opens the door of the cellar that belongs to the ground-floor tenant . . .Yes, capital . . . Now let's examine these wine-bins . . . Aha, here are places where the dust has been removed . . . and footprints on the floor! . . . '

A slight sound made him prick up his ears. He quickly closed the door, blew out his candle and hid behind a stack of empty wine-cases. After a few seconds, he noticed that one of the iron bins was turning slowly on a pivot, carrying with it the whole of the piece of wall to which it was fastened. The light of a lantern was thrown into the cellar. An arm appeared. A man entered.

He was bent in two, like a man looking for something. He fumbled in the dust with his finger-tips, and, several times, he straightened himself and threw something into a card-board box which he carried in his left hand.

Next, he removed the marks of his footsteps, as well as those left by Lupin and the blonde lady, and went back to the wine-bin.

He gave a hoarse cry and fell. Shears had leapt upon him. It was the matter of a moment and, in the simplest way possible, the man found himself stretched on the floor, with his ankles fastened together and his wrists bound.

The Englishman stooped over him:

'How much will you take to speak? . . . To tell what you know?'

The man replied with so sarcastic a smile that Shears understood the futility of his question. He contented himself with exploring his captive's pockets, but his investigations produced nothing more than a bunch of keys, a pocket-handkerchief and the little cardboard box used by the fellow and containing a dozen garnets similar to those which Shears had picked up. A poor booty!

Besides, what was he to do with the man? Wait until his friends came to his assistance and hand them all over to the police? What was the good? What advantage could he derive from it against Lupin?

He was hesitating, when a glance at the box made him come to a decision. It bore the address of Léonard, jeweller, Rue de la Paix.

He resolved simply to leave the man where he was. He pushed back the bin, shut the cellar-door and left the house. He went to a post-office and telegraphed to M. Destange that he could not come until the next day. Then he went on to the jeweller and handed him the garnets:

'Madame sent me with these stones. They came off a piece of jewelry which she bought here.'

Shears had hit the nail on the head. The jeweller replied:

'That's right ... The lady telephoned to me. She will call here herself presently.'

★  ★  ★

It was five o'clock before Shears, standing on the pavement, saw a lady arrive, wrapped in a thick veil, whose appearance struck him as suspicious. Through the shop-window he saw her place on the counter an old-fashioned brooch set with garnets.

She went away almost at once, did a few errands on foot, walked up toward Clichy and turned down streets which the Englishman did not know. At nightfall, he followed her, unperceived by the concierge, into a five-storeyed house built on either side of the doorway and therefore containing numberless flats. She stopped at a door on the second floor and went in.

Two minutes later, the Englishman put his luck to the test and, one after the other, carefully tried the keys on the bunch of which he had obtained possession. The fourth key fitted the lock.

Through the darkness that filled them, he saw rooms which were absolutely empty, like those of an unoccupied flat, with all the doors standing open. But the light of a lamp filtered through from the end of a passage; and, approaching on tip-toe, through the glass door that separated the drawing-room from an adjoining bedroom he saw the veiled lady take off her dress and hat, lay them on the one chair which the room contained and slip on a velvet tea-gown.

And he also saw her walk up to the chimney-piece and push an electric bell. And one-half of the panel to the right of the chimney moved from its position and slipped along the wall into the thickness of the next panel. As soon as the gap was wide enough, the lady passed through . . . and disappeared, taking the lamp with her.

The system was a simple one. Shears employed it. He found himself walking in the dark, groping his way; but suddenly his face came upon something soft. By the light of a match, he saw that he was in a little closet filled with dresses and clothes hanging from metal bars. He thrust his way through and stopped before the embrasure of a door closed by a tapestry hanging or, at least, by the back of a hanging. And, his match being now burnt out, he saw light piercing through the loose and worn woof of the old stuff.

Then he looked.

The blonde lady was there, before his eyes, within reach of his hand.

She put out the lamp and turned on the electric switch. For the first time, Shears saw her face in the full light. He gave a start. The woman whom he had ended by overtaking after so many shifts and turns was none other than Clotilde Destange.

★   ★   ★

Clotilde Destange, the murderess of Baron d'Hautrec and the purloiner of the blue diamond! Clotilde Destange the mysterious friend of Arsène Lupin! The blonde lady, in short!

'Why, of course,' he thought, 'I'm the biggest blockhead that ever lived! Just because Lupin's friend is fair and Clotilde dark, I never thought of connecting the two women! As though the blonde lady could afford to continue fair after the murder of the baron and the theft of the diamond!'

Shears saw part of the room, an elegant lady's boudoir, adorned with light hangings and valuable knick-knacks. A mahogany settee stood on a slightly-raised platform. Clotilde had sat down on it and remained motionless, with her head between her hands. And soon he noticed that she was crying. Great tears flowed down her pale cheeks, trickled by her mouth, fell drop by drop on the velvet of her bodice. And more tears followed indefinitely, as though springing from an inexhaustible source. And no sadder sight was ever seen than that dull and resigned despair, which expressed itself in the slow flowing of the tears.

But a door opened behind her. Arsène Lupin entered.

They looked at each other for a long time, without exchanging a word. Then he knelt down beside her, pressed his head to her breast, put his arms round her; and there was infinite tenderness and great pity in the gesture with which he embraced the girl. They did not move. A soft silence united them, and her tears flowed less abundantly.

'I so much wanted to make you happy!' he whispered.

'I am happy.'

'No, for you're crying. And your tears break my heart, Clotilde.'

Yielding, in spite of herself, to the sound of his coaxing voice, she listened, greedy of hope and happiness. A smile softened her face, but, oh, so sad a smile! He entreated her:

'Don't be sad, Clotilde; you have no reason, you have no right to be sad.'

She showed him her white, delicate, lissom hands, and said, gravely:

'As long as these hands are mine, Maxime, I shall be sad.'

'But why?'

'They have taken life.'

Maxime cried:

'Hush, you must not think of that! The past is dead; the past does not count.'

And he kissed her long white hands and she looked at him with a brighter smile, as though each kiss had wiped out a little of that hideous memory:

'You must love me, Maxime, you must, because no woman will ever love you as I do. To please you, I have acted, I am still acting not only according to your orders, but according to your unspoken wishes. I do things against which all my instincts and all my conscience revolt; but I am unable to resist . . . All that I do I do mechanically, because it is of use to you and you wish it . . . and I am ready to begin again to-morrow . . . and always.'

He said, bitterly:

'Ah, Clotilde, why did I ever mix you up in my adventurous life? I ought to have remained the Maxime Bermond whom you loved five years ago and not have let you know . . . the other man that I am.'

She whispered very low!

'I love that other man too; and I regret nothing.'

'Yes, you regret your past life, your life in the light of day.'

'I regret nothing, when you are there!' she said, passionately. 'There is no such thing as guilt, no such thing as crime, when my eyes see you. What do I care if I am unhappy away from you and if I suffer and cry and loathe all that I do! Your love wipes out everything . . . I accept everything . . . But you must love me!'

'I do not love you because I must, Clotilde, but simply because I love you.'

'Are you sure?' she asked, trustingly.

'I am as sure of myself as I am of you. Only, Clotilde, my life is a violent and feverish one and I cannot always give you as much time as I should wish.'

She at once grew terrified.

'What is it? A fresh danger? Tell me, quick!'

'Oh, nothing serious as yet. Still . . . '

'Still what . . . ?'

'Well, he is on our track.'

'Shears?'

'Yes. It was he who set Ganimard at me at the Restaurant Hongrois. It was he who posted the two policemen in the Rue Chalgrin last night. The proof is that Ganimard searched the house this morning and Shears was with him. Besides . . . '

'Besides what?'

'Well, there is something more: one of our men is missing, Jeanniot.'

'The concierge?'

'Yes.'

'Why, I sent him to the Rue Chalgrin this morning to pick up some garnets which had fallen from my brooch.'

'There is no doubt about it, Shears has caught him in a trap.'

'Not at all. The garnets were brought to the jeweller in the Rue de la Paix.'

'Then what has become of Jeanniot since?'

'Oh, Maxime, I'm so frightened!'

'There's no cause for alarm. But I admit that the position is very serious. How much does he know? Where is he hiding? His strength lies in his isolation. There is nothing to betray him.'

'Then what have you decided on?'

'Extreme prudence, Clotilde. Some time ago I made up my mind to move my things to the refuge you know of, the safe refuge. The intervention of Shears hastens the need.

167

When a man like Shears is on a trail, we may take it that he is bound to follow that trail to the end. So I have made all my preparations. The removal will take place on the day after to-morrow, Wednesday. It will be finished by midday. By two o'clock I shall be able myself to leave, after getting rid of the last vestige of our occupation, which is no small matter. Until then . . . '

'Yes . . . ?'

'We must not see each other and no one must see you, Clotilde. Don't go out. I fear nothing for myself. But I fear everything where you're concerned.'

'It is impossible for that Englishman to get at me.'

'Everything is possible to him and I am not easy in my mind. Yesterday, when I was nearly caught by your father, I had come to search the cupboard which contains M. Destange's old ledgers. There is danger there. There is danger everywhere. I feel that the enemy is prowling in the shade and drawing nearer and nearer. I know that he is watching us . . . that he is laying his nets around us. It is one of those intuitions which never fail me.'

'In that case,' said she, 'go, Maxime, and think no more about my tears. I shall be brave and I will wait until the danger is over. Good-bye, Maxime.'

168

She gave him a long kiss. And she herself pushed him outside. Shears heard the sound of their voices grow fainter in the distance.

Boldly, excited by the need of action, toward and against everything, which had been stimulating him since the day before, he made his way to a passage, at the end of which was a staircase. But, just as he was going down, he heard the sound of a conversation below and thought it better to follow a circular corridor which brought him to another staircase. At the foot of this staircase, he was greatly surprised to see furniture the shape and position of which he already knew. A door stood half open. He entered a large round room. It was M. Destange's library.

'Capital! Splendid!' he muttered. 'I understand everything now. The boudoir of Clotilde, that is to say, the blonde lady, communicates with one of the flats in the next house and the door of that house is not in the Place Malesherbes, but in an adjoining street, the Rue Montchanin, if I remember right . . . Admirable! And now I see how Clotilde Destange slips out to meet her sweetheart while keeping up the reputation of a person who never leaves the house. And I also see how Arsène Lupin popped out close to me, yesterday evening, in the gallery: there must be another communication between the flat next door and this library . . . ' And he concluded, 'Another faked house. Once again, no doubt, 'Destange, architect!' And what I must now do is to take advantage of my presence here to examine the contents of the cupboard . . . and obtain all the information I can about the other faked houses.'

Shears went up to the gallery and hid behind the hangings of the rail. He stayed there till the end of the evening. A man-servant came to put out the electric lights. An hour later, the Englishman pressed the spring of his lantern and went down to the cupboard. As he knew, it contained the architect's old papers, files, plans, estimates and account-books. At the back stood a row of ledgers, arranged in chronological order.

He took down the more recent volumes one by one and at once looked through the index-pages, more particularly under the letter H. At last, finding the word 'Harmingeat' followed by the number 63, he turned up page 63 and read:

*Harmingeat, 40, Rue Chalgrin.*

There followed a detailed statement of works executed for this customer, with a view to the installation of a central heating-apparatus in his property. And in the margin was this note:

'I knew it,' muttered Shears. 'File M. B. is the one I want. When I have been through that, I shall know the whereabouts of M. Lupin's present abode.'

The small hours had struck before he found file M. B. It consisted of fifteen pages. One was a copy of the page concerning M. Harmingeat of the Rue Chalgrin. Another contained a detailed account of works executed for M. Vatinel, the owner of 25, Rue Clapeyron. A third was devoted to Baron d'Hautrec, 134, Avenue Henri-Martin; a fourth to the Château de Crozon; and the eleven others to different Paris landlords.

Shears took down the list of eleven names and addresses and then restored the papers to their place, opened a window and jumped out into the deserted square, taking care to close the shutters behind him.

On reaching his room at the hotel, he lit his pipe with the gravity which he always applied to that ceremony and, enveloped in clouds of smoke, studied the conclusions to be drawn from file M. B., or, to be more exact, the file devoted to Maxime Bermond, *alias* Arsène Lupin.

At eight o'clock, he sent Ganimard an express letter:

*I shall probably call on you in the Rue Pergolèse this morning and place in your charge a person whose capture is of the highest importance. In any case, stay at home to-night and until twelve o'clock to-morrow, Wednesday, morning; and arrange to have thirty men at your disposal.'*

Then he went down the boulevard, picked out a motor-cab with a driver whose good-humoured but unintelligent face took his fancy and drove to the Place Malesherbes, fifty yards beyond the Maison Destange.

'Close the hood, my man,' he said, to the driver, 'turn up the collar of your fur, for it's a cold wind, and wait for me patiently. Start your engine in an hour and a half from now. The moment I get in again, drive straight to the Rue Pergolèse.'

With his foot on the doorstep of the house, he had a last moment of hesitation. Was it not a mistake to take so much trouble about the blonde lady, when Lupin was completing his preparations for departure? And would he not have done better, with the aid of his list of houses, to begin by finding out where his adversary lived?

'Pooh!' he said. 'When the blonde lady is my prisoner, I shall be master of the situation.'

And he rang the bell.

He found M. Destange waiting in the library. They worked together for a little while and Shears was seeking a pretext to go up to Clotilde's room, when the girl entered, said good-morning to her father, sat down in the little drawing-room and began to write letters.

From where he was sitting, Shears could see her as she bent over the table and, from time to time, meditated with poised pen and a thoughtful face. He waited and then, taking up a volume, said to M. Destange:

'Oh, this is the book which Mlle. Destange asked me to give her when I found it.'

He went into the little room, stood in front of Clotilde, in such a way that her father could not see her, and said:

'I am M. Stickmann, M. Destange's new secretary.'

'Oh?' she said, without moving. 'Has my father changed his secretary?'

'Yes, mademoiselle, and I should like to speak to you.'

'Take a seat, monsieur; I have just finished.'

She added a few words to her letter, signed it, sealed the envelope, pushed back her papers, took up the telephone, asked to be put on to her dressmaker, begged her to hurry on a travelling-cloak which she needed urgently and then, turning to Shears:

'I am at your service, monsieur. But cannot our conversation take place before my father?'

'No, mademoiselle, and I will even entreat you not to raise your voice. It would be better that M. Destange should not hear us.'

'Better for whom?'

'For you, mademoiselle.'

'I will not permit a conversation which my father cannot hear.'

'And yet you must permit this one.'

They both rose, with their eyes fixed on each other. And she said:

'Speak, monsieur.'

Still standing, he began:

'You must forgive me if I am inaccurate in a few less important particulars. I will vouch for the general correctness of what I am going to say.'

'No speeches, I beg. Facts.'

He felt, from this abrupt interruption, that the girl was on her guard and he continued:

'Very well, I will come straight to the point. Five years ago, your father happened to meet a M. Maxime Bermond, who introduced himself as a contractor . . . or an architect, I am not sure which. In any case, M. Destange took a liking to this young man and, as the state of his health no longer allowed him to attend to his business, he entrusted to M. Bermond the execution of a few orders which he had accepted to please some old customers and which appeared to him to come within the scope of his assistant's capacity.'

Shears stopped. It seemed to him that the girl had grown paler. Still, she answered with the greatest calmness.

'I know nothing of the things about which you are talking, monsieur, and I am quite unable to see how they can interest me.'

'They interest you in so far, mademoiselle, that M. Maxime Bermond's real name, which you know as well as I do, is Arsène Lupin.'

She burst out laughing:

'Nonsense! Arsène Lupin? M. Maxime Bermond's name is Arsène Lupin?'

'As I have the honour to inform you, mademoiselle, and, since you refuse to understand me unless I speak plainly, I will add that Arsène Lupin, to accomplish his designs, has found in this house a friend, more than a friend, a blind and . . . passionately devoted accomplice.'

She rose and, betraying no emotion or, at least, so little emotion that Shears was impressed by her extraordinary self-control, said:

'I do not know the reason for your behaviour, monsieur, and I have no wish to know it. I will ask you, therefore, not to add another word and to leave the room.'

'I had no intention, mademoiselle, of imposing my presence upon you indefinitely,' said Shears, as calmly as herself. 'Only I have resolved not to leave this house alone.'

'And who is going with you, monsieur?'

'You!'

'I?'

'Yes, mademoiselle, we shall leave this house together, and you will accompany me without a word, without a protest.'

The strange feature of this scene was the absolute coolness of the two adversaries. To judge by their attitudes and the tone of their voices, it might have been a courteous discussion between two people who differ in opinion, rather than an implacable duel between two powerful wills.

Through the great open recess, M. Destange could be seen in the round library, handling his books with leisurely movements.

Clotilde sat down again with a slight shrug of the shoulders. Holmlock Shears took out his watch:

'It is now half-past ten. We will start in five minutes.'

'And, if I refuse?'

'If you refuse, I shall go to M. Destange and tell him . . . '

'What?'

'The truth. I shall describe to him the false life led by Maxime Bermond and the double life of his accomplice.'

'Of his accomplice?'

'Yes, of the one known as the blonde lady, the lady whose hair was once fair.'

'And what proofs will you give him?'

'I shall take him to the Rue Chalgrin and show him the passage which Arsène Lupin, when managing the works, made his men construct between Nos. 40 and 42, the passage employed by the two of you on the night before last.'

'Next?'

'Next, I shall take M. Destange to Maître Detinan's. We will go down the servants' staircase which you ran down, with Arsène Lupin, to escape Ganimard. And we will both look for the doubtless similar means of communication with the next house, which has its entrance on the Boulevard des Batignolles and not in the Rue Clapeyron.'

'Next?'

'Next, I shall take M. Destange to the Château de Crozon and it will be easy for him, who knows the nature of the works executed by Arsène Lupin at the time of the restoration of the Château, to discover the secret passages which Arsène Lupin made his men construct. He will find that these passages enabled the blonde lady to enter Madame de Crozon's room at night and take the blue diamond from the chimney and, a fortnight later, to enter Herr Bleichen's room and hide the blue diamond at the bottom of a flask . . . a rather queer thing to do, I admit: perhaps it was a woman's petty vengeance; I do not know and it makes no difference.'

'Next?'

'Next,' said Holmlock Shears, in a more serious voice, 'I shall take M. Destange to 134, Avenue Henri-Martin, and together we will try to discover how Baron d'Hautrec . . . '

'Hush, hush!' stammered the girl, in sudden dismay. 'You must not . . . Do you dare to say it was I . . . ? Do you accuse me . . . ?'

'I accuse you of killing Baron d'Hautrec.'

'No, no; this is monstrous!'

'You killed Baron d'Hautrec, mademoiselle. You entered his service under the name of Antoinette Bréhat, with the intention of robbing him of the blue diamond, and you killed him.'

Again she murmured, breaking down and reduced to entreaties:

'Hush, monsieur, I beg . . . As you know so much, you must also know that I did not murder the baron.'

'I did not say that you murdered him, mademoiselle. Baron d'Hautrec was subject

178

to fits of insanity which only Sœur Auguste was able to check. She has told me this herself. He must have thrown himself upon you in her absence; and it was in the course of the ensuing struggle that you struck at him, in self-defence. Appalled by what you had done, you rang the bell and fled, without even taking from his finger the blue diamond which you had come to secure. A moment later, you returned with one of Lupin's accomplices, a man-servant in the next house, lifted the baron on to his bed and arranged the room ... but still without daring to take the blue diamond. That's what happened. Therefore, I repeat, you did not murder the baron. And yet it was your hands that killed him.'

She was holding them clasped before her forehead, her slim, white, delicate hands, and she kept them long like that, motionless. Then, uncrossing her fingers, she showed her sorrow-stricken face and said:

'And you mean to tell all this to my father?'

'Yes; and I shall tell him that I have as witnesses Mlle. Gerbois, who will recognize the blonde lady, Sœur Auguste, who will recognize Antoinette Bréhat, the Comtesse de Crozon, who will recognize Mme. de Réal. That is what I shall tell him.'

'You will not dare!' she said, recovering her

presence of mind, in the face of immediate danger.

He rose and took a step toward the library. Clotilde stopped him:

'One moment, monsieur.'

She reflected and, now fully mistress of herself, asked, very calmly:

'You are Holmlock Shears, are you not?'

'Yes.'

'What do you want with me?'

'What do I want? I have entered upon a contest with Arsène Lupin from which I must emerge the winner. Pending a result which cannot be far distant, I am of opinion that a hostage as valuable as yourself will give me a considerable advantage over my adversary. You shall go with me, therefore, mademoiselle, and I will place you under the care of a friend of mine. As soon as my object is attained, you shall be set free.'

'Is that all?'

'That is all. I do not belong to the police of your country and consequently I claim no . . . no justiciary rights.'

Her mind appeared made up. However, she asked for a moment's delay. Her eyelids closed and Shears stood watching her, suddenly grown calm, almost indifferent to the perils that threatened her.

'I wonder,' thought the Englishman, 'if she

believes herself to be in danger? Probably not, with Lupin to protect her. With Lupin there, nothing can happen to her, she thinks: Lupin is omnipotent, Lupin is infallible . . . Mademoiselle,' he said aloud, 'I spoke of five minutes: it is now more than thirty.'

'May I go to my room, monsieur, and fetch my things?'

'If you like, mademoiselle, I will go and wait for you in the Rue Montchanin. I am a great friend of Jeanniot, the concierge.'

'Ah, so you know . . . ' she said, with visible dismay.

'I know a great many things.'

'Very well. Then I will ring.'

The servant brought her hat and cloak and Shears said:

'You must give M. Destange some reason to explain our departure and the reason must be enough, in case of need, to explain your absence for two or three days.'

'That is unnecessary. I shall be back presently.'

Again, they exchanged a defiant glance, skeptical, both of them, and smiling.

'How you trust him!' said Shears.

'Blindly.'

'Whatever he does is right, is it not? Whatever he wishes is realized. And you approve of everything and are prepared to do everything for his sake.'

'I love him,' she said, with a tremor of passion.

'And you believe that he will save you?' She shrugged her shoulders and, going up to her father, told him:

'I am robbing you of M. Stickmann. We are going to the National Library.'

'Will you be back to lunch?'

'Perhaps . . . or more likely not . . . but don't worry about me, in any case . . . '

And, in a firm voice, she said to Shears:

'I am ready, monsieur.'

'Without reserve?' he whispered.

'With my eyes closed.'

'If you try to escape, I shall shout and call for help, you will be arrested and it will mean prison. Don't forget that there is a warrant out against the blonde lady.'

'I swear to you on my honour that I will make no attempt to escape.'

'I believe you. Let us go.'

They left the house together, as he had foretold.

★　★　★

The motor-cab had turned round and was waiting in the square. They could see the driver's back and his cap, which was almost covered by the upturned collar of his fur. As they approached, Shears heard the humming of the engine. He opened the door, asked Clotilde to step in and sat down beside her.

The car started with a jerk and soon reached the outer boulevards, the Avenue Hoche, the Avenue de la Grande-Armée.

Shears was thinking out his plans:

'Ganimard is at home . . . I shall leave the girl with him . . . Shall I tell him who she is? No, he would take her straight to the police-station, which would put everything out. As soon as I am alone, I will consult the M. B. list and set out on my chase. And, to-night, or to-morrow morning at latest, I shall go to Ganimard, as arranged, and deliver Arsène Lupin and his gang to him.'

He rubbed his hands, glad to feel that his object was at last within his reach and to see that there was no serious obstacle in the way. And, yielding to a need for expansion, which was not in keeping with his usual nature, he said:

'Forgive me, mademoiselle, for displaying so much satisfaction. It was a difficult fight and I find my success particularly agreeable.'

'A legitimate success, monsieur, in which you have every right to rejoice.'

'Thank you. But what a funny way we are going! Didn't the man understand?'

At that moment, they were leaving Paris by

the Porte de Neuilly. What on earth! . . . After all, the Rue Pergolèse was not outside the fortifications!

Shears let down the glass:

'I say, driver, you're going wrong . . . Rue Pergolèse! . . . '

The man made no reply. Shears repeated, in a louder voice:

'I'm telling you to go to the Rue Pergolèse.'

The man took no notice.

'Look here, my man, are you deaf? Or are you doing it on purpose? . . . This isn't where I told you to go . . . Rue Pergolèse, do you hear! . . . Turn round at once and look sharp about it!'

Still no reply. The Englishman began to be alarmed. He looked at Clotilde: a queer smile was playing on the girl's lips.

'What are you laughing at?' he stormed. 'This doesn't affect . . . it has nothing to say to . . . '

'Nothing in the very least,' she replied.

Suddenly, he was taken aback by an idea. Half rising from his seat, he attentively scrutinized the man on the box. His shoulders were slimmer, his movements easier . . . A cold sweat broke out on Shears's forehead, his hands contracted, while the most hideous conviction forced itself upon his mind: the man was Arsène Lupin.

* ★ ★

'Well, Mr. Shears, what do you think of this little drive?'

'It's delightful, my dear sir, really delightful,' replied Shears.

Perhaps he had never in his life made a more tremendous effort than it cost him to utter those words without a tremor in his voice, without anything that could betray the exasperation that filled his whole being. But, the minute after, he was carried away by a sort of formidable reaction; and a torrent of rage and hatred burst its banks, overcame his will, and made him suddenly draw his revolver and point it at Mlle. Destange.

'Lupin, if you don't stop this minute, this second, I fire at mademoiselle!'

'I advise you to aim at the cheek if you want to hit the temple,' said Lupin, without turning his head.

Clotilde called out:

'Don't go too fast, Maxime! The pavement is very slippery, and you know how timid I am!'

She was still smiling, with her eyes fixed on the cobbles with which the road bristled in front of the car.

'Stop him, tell him to stop!' shouted Shears beside himself with fury. 'You can see for yourself that I am capable of anything!'

The muzzle of the revolver grazed her hair.

'How reckless Maxime is!' she murmured. 'We are sure to skid, at this rate.'

Shears replaced the revolver in his pocket and seized the handle of the door, preparing to jump out, in spite of the absurdity of the act.

'Take care, Mr. Shears,' said Clotilde. 'There's a motor-car behind us.'

He leant out. A car was following them, an enormous car, fierce-looking, with its pointed bonnet, blood-red in colour, and the four men in furs inside it.

'Ah,' he said, 'I'm well guarded! We must have patience!'

He crossed his arms on his chest, with the proud submission of those who bow and wait when fate turns against them. And while they crossed the Seine and tore through Suresnes, Rueil and Chatou, motionless and resigned, without anger or bitterness, he thought only of discovering by what miracle Arsène Lupin had put himself in the driver's place. That the decent fellow whom he had picked out that morning on the boulevard could be an accomplice, posted there of set purpose, he refused to admit. And yet Arsène Lupin must have received a warning and that only after the moment when he, Shears, had threatened

Clotilde, for no one suspected his plan before. Now from that moment Clotilde and he had not left each other's presence.

Suddenly, he remembered the girl's telephoning to her dressmaker. And, all at once, he understood. Even before he spoke, at the very moment when he asked for an interview as M. Destange's new secretary, she had scented danger, guessed the visitor's name and object and, coolly, naturally, as though she were really doing what she appeared to do, had summoned Lupin to her aid, under the pretence of speaking to one of her tradespeople and by means of a formula known to themselves alone.

How Arsène Lupin had come, how that motor-cab in waiting, with its throbbing engine, had aroused his suspicion, how he had bribed the driver: all this mattered little. What interested Shears almost to the point of calming his rage was the recollection of that moment in which a mere woman, a woman in love, it is true, mastering her nerves, suppressing her instinct, controlling the features of her face and the expression of her eyes, had humbugged old Holmlock Shears.

What was he to do against a man served by such allies, a man who, by the sheer ascendancy of his authority, inspired a woman with such a stock of daring and energy?

They re-crossed the Seine and climbed the slope of Saint-Germain; but, five hundred yards beyond the town, the cab slowed down. The other car came up with it and the two stopped alongside. There was no one about.

'Mr. Shears,' said Lupin, 'may I trouble you to change cars? Ours is really so very slow! . . .'

'Certainly,' said Shears, all the more politely, as he had no choice.

'Will you also permit me to lend you this fur, for we shall be going pretty fast, and to offer you a couple of sandwiches? . . . Yes, yes, take them: there's no telling when you will get any dinner.'

The four men had alighted. One of them came up and, as he had taken off the goggles which disguised him, Shears recognized the gentleman in the frock-coat whom he had seen at the Restaurant Hongrois. Lupin gave him his instructions:

'Take the cab back to the driver from whom I hired it. You will find him waiting in the first wine-shop on the right in the Rue Legendre. Pay him the second thousand francs I promised him. Oh, I was forgetting: you might give Mr. Shears your goggles!'

He spoke a few words to Mlle. Destange, then took his seat at the wheel and drove off, with Shears beside him and one of his men behind.

Lupin had not exaggerated when saying that they would go 'pretty fast.' They travelled at a giddy pace from the first. The horizon rushed toward them, as though attracted by a mysterious force, and disappeared at the same moment, as though swallowed up by an abyss into which other things — trees, houses, plains and forests — plunged with the tumultuous speed of a torrent rushing down to the pool below.

Shears and Lupin did not exchange a word. Above their heads, the leaves of the poplars made a great noise as of waves, punctuated by the regular spacing of the trees. And town after town vanished from sight: Mantes, Vernon, Gaillon. From hill to hill, from Bon-Secours to Canteleu, Rouen, with her suburbs, her harbour, her miles upon miles of quays, Rouen seemed no more than the high-street of a market-town. And they rushed through Duclair, through Caudebec, through the Pays de Caux, skimming over its hills and plains in their powerful flight, through Lillebonne, through Quille-beuf. And, suddenly, they were on the bank of the Seine, at the end of a small quay, alongside which lay a steam-yacht, built on sober and powerful lines, with black smoke curling up from her funnel.

The car stopped. They had covered over a hundred miles in two hours.

A man dressed in a blue pea-jacket came forward and touched his gold-laced cap.

'Well done, captain!' said Lupin. 'Did you get my telegram?'

'Yes, sir.'

'Is the *Hirondelle* ready?'

'Quite ready, sir.'

'In that case, Mr. Shears . . . ?'

The Englishman looked around him, saw a group of people seated outside a café, another a little nearer, hesitated for a moment and then, realizing that, before any one could interfere, he would be seized, forced on board and packed off at the bottom of the hold, he crossed the foot-plank and followed Lupin into the captain's cabin.

It was roomy, specklessly clean and shone brightly with its varnished wainscoting and gleaming brass.

Lupin closed the door and, without beating about the bush, said to Shears, almost brutally:

'Tell me exactly how much you know.'

'Everything.'

'Everything? I want details.'

His voice had lost the tone of politeness, tinged with irony, which he adopted toward the Englishman. Instead, it rang with the imperious accent of the master who is accustomed to command and accustomed to see every one bow before his will, even though it be a Holmlock Shears.

They eyed each other now from head to foot as enemies, declared and passionate enemies.

Lupin resumed, with a touch of nervousness:

'You have crossed my path, sir, on several occasions. Each occasion has been one too many; and I am tired of wasting my time avoiding the traps you lay for me. I warn you, therefore, that my conduct toward you will depend upon your answer. How much exactly do you know?'

'Everything, I tell you.'

Arsène Lupin mastered his annoyance and jerked out:

'I will tell you what you know. You know that, under the name of Maxime Bermond, I . . . 'touched up' fifteen houses built by M. Destange.'

'Yes.'

'Of those fifteen houses, you know four.'

'Yes.'

'And you have a list of the eleven others.'

'Yes.'

'You made out the list at M. Destange's, last night, no doubt.'

'Yes.'

'And, as you presume that, among those eleven properties, there must inevitably be one which I keep for my own needs and those of my friends, you have instructed Ganimard to take the field and discover my retreat.'

'No.'

'What do you mean?'

'I mean that I am acting alone and that I intended to take the field alone.'

'So I have nothing to fear, seeing that I have you in my hands.'

'You have nothing to fear so long as I *remain* in your hands.'

'You mean to say that you will not remain?'

'I do.'

Arsène Lupin went up to Holmlock Shears and placed his hand very gently on the Englishman's shoulder:

'Listen to me, sir. I am not in the mood for argument and you, unfortunately for yourself, are not in a position to check me. Let us put an end to this.'

'Yes, let us.'

'You shall give me your word of honour not to attempt to escape from this boat until she reaches English waters.'

'I give you my word of honour that I shall attempt to escape by every means in my power,' said Shears, nothing daunted.

'But, dash it all, you know I have only to speak a word to reduce you to helplessness! All these men obey me blindly. At a sign from me, they will put a chain round your neck . . . '

'Chains can be broken.'

'And throw you overboard at ten miles from the coast.'

'I can swim.'

'Well said,' cried Lupin, laughing. 'Heaven forgive me, but I lost my temper! Accept my apology, maître . . . and let us conclude. Will you allow me to seek the necessary measures for my safety and that of my friends?'

'Any measures you like. But they are useless.'

'Agreed. Still, you will not mind if I take them?'

'It's your duty.'

'To work, then.'

Lupin opened the door and called the captain and two of the crew. The latter seized the Englishman and, after searching him, bound his legs together and tied him down in the captain's berth.

'That will do,' ordered Lupin. 'Really, sir, nothing short of your obstinancy and the exceptional gravity of the circumstances would have allowed me to venture . . . '

The sailors withdrew. Lupin said to the captain:

'Captain, one of the crew must remain in the cabin to wait on Mr. Shears and you yourself must keep him company as much as you can. Let him be treated with every consideration. He is not a prisoner, but a guest. What is the time by your watch, captain?'

'Five minutes past two.'

Lupin looked at his own watch and at a clock which hung on the cabin-wall:

'Five minutes past two? . . . Our watches agree. How long will it take you to reach Southampton?'

'Nine hours, without hurrying.'

'Make it eleven. You must not touch land before the departure of the steamer which leaves Southampton at midnight and is due at the Havre at eight in the morning. You understand, captain, do you not? I repeat: it would be exceedingly dangerous for us all if this gentleman returned to France by the steamer; and you must not arrive at Southampton before one o'clock in the morning.'

'Very well, sir.'

'Good-bye, maître,' said Lupin, turning to Shears. 'We shall meet next year, in this world or another.'

'Let's say to-morrow.'

A few minutes later, Shears heard the car drive away and the engines of the *Hirondelle* at once began to throb with increased force. The yacht threw off her moorings. By three o'clock they had left the estuary of the Seine and entered the Channel. At that moment, Holmlock Shears lay sound asleep in the berth to which he was fastened down.

★  ★  ★

On the following morning, the tenth and last day of the war between the two great rivals, the *Écho de France* published this delicious paragraph:

> *A decree of expulsion was pronounced by Arsène Lupin yesterday against Holmlock Shears, the English detective. The decree was published at noon and executed on the same day. Shears was landed at Southampton at one o'clock this morning.*

# 6

## The Second Arrest of Arsène Lupin

By eight o'clock on Wednesday morning, a dozen pantechnicon vans were blocking the Rue Crevaux from the Avenue du Bois de Boulogne to the Avenue Bougeaud. M. Félix Davey was leaving the flat which he occupied on the fourth floor of No. 8. And, by a sheer coincidence — for the two gentlemen were not acquainted — M. Dubreuil, the expert, who had knocked into one the fifth-floor flat of No. 8 and the fifth-floor flats of the two adjoining houses, had selected the same day on which to send off the collection of furniture and antiques which used to be visited daily by one or other of his many foreign correspondents.

A peculiarity which attracted notice in the neighbourhood, but which was not mentioned until later, was that none of the twelve vans bore the name and address of the firm of removers and that none of the men in charge of them loitered in the wine-shops round about. They worked to such good purpose that all was over by eleven o'clock. Nothing remained but those piles of old papers and rags which are always left behind in the corners of empty rooms.

M. Félix Davey was a young man of smart appearance, dressed in the latest fashion, but carrying a heavily-weighted cane which seemed to indicate unusual muscular strength on the part of its owner. He walked away quietly and sat down on a bench in the cross alley which intersects the Avenue du Bois, opposite the Rue Pergolèse. Beside him sat a young woman, clad in the costume of the lower middle-class and reading her paper, while a child played with its spade in the sand beside her.

Presently, Félix Davey said to the woman, without turning his head:

'Ganimard?'

'Went out at nine o'clock this morning.'

'Where to?'

'Police headquarters.'

'Alone?'

'Yes.'

'No telegram last night?'

'No.'

'Do they still trust you at the house?'

'Yes. I do odd work for Madame Ganimard and she tells me all her husband does . . . We spent the morning together.'

'Good. Continue to come here at eleven every morning, until further orders.'

He rose and walked to the Pavillon Chinois, near the Porte Dauphine, where he took a frugal meal: two eggs, some vegetables and a little fruit. Then he returned to the Rue Crevaux and said to the concierge:

'I am going to have a look round upstairs and then I'll give you the keys.'

He finished his inspection with the room which he used as a study. There he took hold of the end of a jointed gas-bracket which was fixed beside the chimney, unscrewed the brass nozzle, fitted a little funnel-shaped instrument to it and blew up the pipe.

A faint whistle sounded in reply. Putting the pipe to his mouth, he whispered:

'Any one there, Dubreuil?'

'No.'

'Can I come up?'

'Yes.'

He replaced the bracket, saying, as he did so:

'Where will progress stop? Our age teems with little inventions that make life really charming and picturesque. And so amusing too ... especially when a man knows the game of life as I know it!'

He touched one of the marble mouldings of the mantelpiece and made it swing round on a pivot. The marble slab itself moved and the mirror above it slid between invisible grooves, revealing a yawning gap which contained the lower steps of a staircase built in the body of the chimney itself. It was all very clean, in carefully-polished iron and white porcelain tiles.

He climbed up to the fifth floor, which had a similar opening over the mantelpiece, and found M. Dubreuil awaiting him:

'Is everything finished here?'

'Everything.'

'All cleared up?'

'Quite.'

'The staff?'

'All gone, except the three men keeping watch.'

'Let's go up.'

They climbed by the same way to the servants' floor and emerged in a garret where they found three men, one of whom was looking out of the window.

'Any news?'

'No, governor.'

'Is the street quiet?'

'Absolutely.'

'I shall leave for good in ten minutes . . . You will go too. In the meantime, if you notice the least suspicious movement in the street, let me know.'

'I've got my finger on the alarm-bell, governor.'

'Dubreuil, did you remember to tell the removers not to touch the bell-wires?'

'Yes. They work perfectly.'

'That's all right, then.'

The two gentlemen returned to Félix Davey's flat. And Davey, after readjusting the marble moulding, exclaimed, gaily:

'Dubreuil, I should love to see the faces of those who discover all these wonderful contrivances: alarm-bells, a network of electric wires and speaking-tubes, invisible passages, sliding floor-boards, secret staircases! . . . regular pantomime machinery!'

'What an advertisement for Arsène Lupin!'

'We could very well have done without the advertisement. It seems a pity to leave so fine an installation. We shall have to begin all over again, Dubreuil . . . and upon a new plan, of course, for it never does to repeat one's self. Confound that Shears!'

'He's not come back, I suppose?'

'How could he? There's only one boat from Southampton, which leaves at midnight. From the Havre, there's only one train, which leaves at eight in the morning and arrives at eleven three. Once he has not taken the midnight steamer — and he has not, for my orders to the captain were formal — he can't reach France till this evening, *via* Newhaven and Dieppe.'

'If he comes back!'

'Shears never throws up the game. He will come back, but it will be too late. We shall be far away.'

'And Mlle. Destange?'

'I am to meet her in an hour.'

'At her house?'

'No, she won't go home for a few days, until the storm has blown over . . . and I am able to look after her more thoroughly . . . But you must hurry, Dubreuil. It will take a long time to ship all the cases and you will be wanted on the wharf.'

'You're sure we are not being watched?'

'Whom by? I was never afraid of any one but Shears.'

Dubreuil went away. Félix Davey took a last walk round the flat, picked up a torn letter or two and then, seeing a piece of chalk, he took it, drew a large circle on the dark wall-paper of the dining room, and wrote, after the style of a commemorative tablet:

ARSÈNE LUPIN,
GENTLEMAN BURGLAR,
LIVED HERE
FOR 5 YEARS
AT THE COMMENCEMENT
OF
THE TWENTIETH CENTURY

This little joke seemed to cause him a lively satisfaction. He whistled gaily as he looked at it and cried:

'Now that I have put myself right with the historians of the future generations, let's be off! Hurry up, Maître Holmlock Shears! In three minutes I shall have left my lair, and your defeat will be absolute . . . Two minutes more! You're keeping me waiting, maître! . . . One minute more! Aren't you coming? Very well, I proclaim your downfall and my apotheosis . . . With which last words I proceed to make myself scarce. Farewell, O Kingdom of Arsène Lupin! I shall not look upon you again. Farewell, ye five-and-fifty rooms of the six flats over which I reigned! Farewell, austere and humble dwelling!'

A bell cut short his lyrical effusion, a short, shrill, strident bell, twice interrupted, twice resumed and then ceasing. It was the alarm-bell.

What could it mean? Some unexpected danger? Ganimard? Surely not! . . .

He was on the point of making for his study and escaping. But first he turned to the window. There was no one in the street. Was the enemy already in the house, then? He listened and seemed to distinguish confused sounds. Without further hesitation he ran to his study and, as he crossed the threshold, heard the sound of a latchkey fumbling at the lock of the hall-door.

'By Jove!' he muttered. 'I have only just time. The house may be surrounded ... No use trying the servants' staircase ... Fortunately, the chimney ... '

He pushed the moulding smartly: it did not move. He exerted greater force: it did not move.

At the same moment, he received the impression that the outer door was opening and that steps sounded.

'Curse it all!' he swore. 'I'm lost, if this confounded spring ... '

His fingers clutched the moulding; he bore upon it with all his weight. Nothing moved, nothing! By some incredible bad luck, by a really bewildering piece of malice on the part of fate, the spring, which was working only a moment before, now refused to work!

He persisted madly, convulsively. The block of marble remained inert, motionless. Curse it! Was it conceivable that this stupid obstacle should bar his way? He struck the marble, struck it furious blows with his fists, hammered it, insulted it ...

'Why, M. Lupin, is something not going as you wish?'

Lupin turned round, terror-stricken. Holmlock Shears stood before him.

Holmlock Shears! Lupin gazed at him, blinking his eyes, as though smarting under a cruel vision. Holmlock Shears in Paris! Holmlock Shears, whom he had packed off to England the day before, as he might a compromising parcel, stood there before him, triumphant and free! Ah, for this impossible miracle to be performed in despite of Arsène Lupin's will there must have been a revolution of the laws of nature, a victory of all that is illogical and abnormal! Holmlock Shears standing opposite him!

And the Englishman, resorting to irony in his turn, said, with that supercilious politeness with which his adversary had so often lashed him:

'M. Lupin, believe me, from this minute I shall cease to remember the night you made me spend in Baron d'Hautrec's house, cease to remember my friend Wilson's mishaps, cease to remember how I was kidnapped by motor-car, cease to remember the sea-voyage which I have just taken, fastened down, by your orders, to an uncomfortable berth. This minute wipes out all. I forget everything. I am rewarded, amply rewarded.'

Lupin did not speak. The Englishman added:

'Don't you think so yourself?'

He appeared to be insisting, as though demanding an assent, a sort of receipt with regard to the past.

After a moment's reflection, during which the Englishman felt himself searched and fathomed to the very bottom of his soul, Lupin said:

'I presume, sir, that your present action rests upon serious motives?'

'Extremely serious motives.'

'The fact of your escaping from my captain and his crew is only a secondary incident in our struggle. But the fact of your being here, before me, alone, do you understand, *alone* in the presence of Arsène Lupin, makes me believe that your revenge is as complete as possible.'

'It is as complete as possible.'

'This house . . . ?'

'Surrounded.'

'The two next houses . . . ?'

'Surrounded.'

'The flat above this . . . ?'

'The three flats on the fifth floor which were occupied by M. Dubreuil are invested.'

'So that . . . ?'

'So that you are caught, M. Lupin, irredeemably caught.'

Lupin now experienced the same feelings

that had stirred Shears during his motor-car drive: the same concentrated rage, the same rebellion; but also, when all was said and done, the same sense of loyalty which compelled him to bow before the force of circumstances. Both were equally strong: both alike were bound to accept defeat as a temporary evil, to be received with resignation.

'We are quits, sir,' he said, bluntly.

*   *   *

The Englishman seemed delighted at this confession. The two men were silent. Then Lupin, already master of himself, resumed with a smile:

'And I am not sorry. It was becoming wearisome to win every thrust. I had only to put out my arm to hit you full in the chest. This time, you score one. Well, hit, maître!' He laughed whole-heartedly. 'At last we shall have some fun! Lupin is caught in the trap. How will he get out? . . . Caught in the trap! . . . What an adventure! . . . Ah, maître, I have to thank you for a grand emotion. This is what I call life!'

He pressed his clenched fists to his temples as though to restrain the ungovernable joy that was bubbling up within him; and he also had gestures like those of a child amusing itself beyond its power of endurance.

At last, he went up to the Englishman:

'And now, what are you here for?'

'What am I here for?'

'Yes. Ganimard is outside, with his men. Why does he not come in?'

'I asked him not to.'

'And he consented?'

'I called in his services only on the express condition that he would be led by me. Besides, he believes that M. Félix Davey is merely an accomplice of Lupin's.'

'Then I will repeat my question under another form. Why did you come in alone?'

'I wanted to speak to you first.'

'Aha! You want to speak to me!'

The idea seemed to please Lupin greatly. There are circumstances in life in which we much prefer words to deeds.

'Mr. Shears, I am sorry not to have a chair to offer you. Does this broken box suit you? Or the window-ledge? I am sure a glass of beer would be acceptable . . . Do you like it light or dark? . . . But do sit down, I beg . . . '

'Never mind that: let us talk.'

'I am listening.'

'I shall not be long. The object of my stay in France was not to effect your arrest. I was obliged to pursue you, because no other means offered of attaining my real object.'

'Which was?'

'To recover the blue diamond.'

'The blue diamond!'

'Certainly; because the one discovered in Herr Bleichen's tooth-powder flask was not the real one.'

'Just so. The real one was posted by the blonde lady. I had an exact copy made; and as, at that time, I had designs upon the Comtesse de Crozon's other jewels and as the Austrian consul was already under suspicion, the aforesaid blonde lady, lest she should be suspected in her turn, slipped the imitation diamond into the aforesaid consul's luggage.'

'While you kept the real one.'

'Quite right.'

'I want that diamond.'

'Impossible. I'm sorry.'

'I have promised it to the Comtesse de Crozon. I mean to have it.'

'How can you have it, seeing that it's in my possession?'

'I mean to have it just because it is in your possession.'

'You mean that I shall give it back to you?'

'Yes.'

'Voluntarily?'

'I will buy it of you.'

Lupin had a fit of merriment:

'Any one can tell what country *you* come from! You treat this as a matter of business.'

'It is a matter of business.'

'And what price do you offer?'

'The liberty of Mlle. Destange.'

'Her liberty? But I am not aware that she is under arrest.'

'I shall give M. Ganimard the necessary information. Once deprived of your protection, she will be taken also.'

Lupin burst out laughing again:

'My dear sir, you are offering me what you do not possess. Mlle. Destange is safe and fears nothing. I want something else.'

The Englishman hesitated, obviously embarrassed and flushing slightly. Then he put his hand brusquely on his adversary's shoulder:

'And, if I offered you . . . ?'

'My liberty?'

'No . . . but, still, I might leave the room, to arrange with M. Ganimard . . . '

'And leave me to think things over?'

'Yes.'

'Well, what on earth would be the good of that? This confounded spring won't work,' said Lupin, irritably pushing the moulding of the mantel.

He stifled an exclamation of surprise: this time, freakish chance had willed that the block of marble should move under his fingers! Safety, flight became possible. In that case, why submit to Holmlock Shears's conditions?

He walked to and fro, as though reflecting upon his answer. Then he, in his turn, put his hand on the Englishman's shoulder:

'After due consideration, Mr. Shears, I prefer to settle my little affairs alone.'

'Still . . . '

'No, I don't want anybody's help.'

'When Ganimard has you, it will be up with you. They won't let you go again.'

'Who knows?'

'Come, this is madness. Every outlet is watched.'

'One remains.'

'Which one?'

'The one I shall select.'

'Words! Your arrest may be looked upon as effected.'

'It is not effected.'

'So . . . ?'

'So I shall keep the blue diamond.'

Shears took out his watch:

'It is ten minutes to three. At three o'clock, I call Ganimard.'

'That gives us ten minutes to chat in. Let us make the most of our time, Mr. Shears, and tell me, to satisfy the curiosity by which I am devoured: how did you procure my address and my name of Félix Davey?'

Keeping a watchful eye on Lupin, whose good-humour made him feel uneasy, Shears gladly consented to give this little explanation, which flattered his vanity, and said:

'I had your address from the blonde lady.'

'Clotilde?'

'Yes. You remember . . . yesterday morning . . . when I meant to carry her off in the motor-cab, she telephoned to her dressmaker.'

'So she did.'

'Well, I understood later that the dressmaker was yourself. And, last night, in the boat, thanks to an effort of memory which is perhaps one of the things of which I am most proud, I succeeded in recollecting the last two figures of your telephone number: 73. In this way, as I possessed the list of the houses which you had 'touched up,' it was easy for me, on my arrival in Paris at eleven o'clock this morning, to look through the telephone directory until I discovered the name and address of M. Félix Davey. The name and address once known, I called in the aid of M. Ganimard.'

'Admirable! First-rate! I make you my bow! But what I can't quite grasp is that you took the train at the Havre. How did you manage to escape from the *Hirondelle*?'

'I did not escape.'

'But . . .'

'You gave the captain orders not to reach Southampton until one o'clock. Well, they landed me at twelve and I caught the Havre boat.'

'The captain played me false? Impossible.'

'He did not play you false.'

'What then . . . ?'

'It was his watch.'

'His watch?'

'Yes, I put his watch on an hour.'

'How?'

'The only way in which one can put a watch on, by turning the winder. We were sitting together chatting and I told him things that interested him . . . By Jove, he noticed nothing!'

'Well done; well done! It's a good trick and I must remember it. But what about the cabin clock?'

'Oh, the clock was more difficult, for my legs were bound: but the sailor who was put in charge of me whenever the captain went on deck kindly consented to give the hands a push.'

'The sailor? Nonsense! Do you mean to say, he consented . . . ?'

'Oh, he did not know the importance of what he was doing! I told him I must, at all costs, catch the first train to London and . . . he allowed himself to be persuaded . . . '

'In consideration . . . '

'In consideration of a little present . . . which the decent fellow, however, intends faithfully to send to you.'

'What present?'

'A mere nothing.'

'Well, but what?'

'The blue diamond.'

'The blue diamond!'

'Yes, the imitation one, which you substituted for the countess's diamond and which she left in my hands . . . '

Arsène Lupin gave a sudden and tumultuous burst of laughter. He seemed ready to die: his eyes were wet with tears:

'Oh, what a joke! My faked diamond handed back to the sailor! And the captain's watch! And the hands of the clock! . . . '

Never before had Holmlock Shears felt the struggle between Arsène Lupin and himself grow so intense as now. With his prodigious intuition, he guessed that, under this excessive gaiety, Lupin was concentrating his formidable mind and collecting all his faculties.

Lupin had gradually drawn closer. The Englishman stepped back and slipped his fingers, as though absent-mindedly, into his pocket:

'It's three o'clock, M. Lupin.'

'Three o'clock already? What a pity! . . . We

were having such fun!'

'I am waiting for your answer.'

'My answer? Goodness me, what a lot you want! So this finishes the game. With my liberty for the stakes!'

'Or the blue diamond.'

'Very well . . . It's your lead. What do you do?'

'I mark the king,' said Shears, firing a shot with his revolver.

'And here's *my hand*,' retorted Arsène, hurling his fist at the Englishman.

Shears had fired at the ceiling, to summon Ganimard, the need for whose intervention now seemed urgent. But Arsène's fist caught him full in the wind and he turned pale and staggered back. Lupin gave one bound toward the chimney and the marble slab moved . . . Too late! The door opened.

'Surrender, Lupin! If not . . . '

Ganimard, who had doubtless been posted nearer than Lupin thought, stood there, with his revolver aimed at him. And, behind Ganimard, ten men, twenty men crowded upon one another's heels, powerful, ruthless fellows, prepared to beat Lupin down like a dog at the least sign of resistance.

He made a quiet gesture:

'Hands off there! I surrender.'

And he crossed his arms over his chest.

A sort of stupor followed. In the room stripped of its furniture and hangings, Arsène Lupin's words seemed drawn-out like an echo:

'I surrender!'

The words sounded incredible. The others were expecting to see him vanish suddenly down a trap or a panel of the wall to fall back and once more to hide him from his assailants. And he surrendered!

Ganimard stepped forward and, greatly excited, with all the gravity that the act demanded, brought his hand slowly down upon his adversary's shoulder and enjoyed the infinite satisfaction of saying:

'Lupin, I arrest you.'

'Brrrrr!' shivered Lupin. 'You make me feel quite overcome, my dear Ganimard. What a solemn face! One would think you were making a speech over a friend's grave. Come, drop these funereal airs!'

'I arrest you.'

'You seem quite flabbergasted! In the name of the law, of which he is a faithful limb, Chief-Inspector Ganimard arrests wicked Arsène Lupin. It is an historic moment and you grasp its full importance . . . And this is the second time a similar fact occurs. Bravo,

Ganimard; you will do well in your career!'

And he held out his wrists for the handcuffs . . .

They were fastened on almost solemnly. The detectives, in spite of their usual roughness and the bitterness of their resentment against Lupin, acted with reserve and discretion, astounded as they were at being allowed to touch that intangible being.

'My poor Lupin,' he sighed, 'what would your smart friends say if they saw you humbled like this!'

He separated his wrists with a growing and continuous effort of every muscle. The veins on his forehead swelled. The links of the chain dug into his skin.

'Now then!' he said.

The chain snapped and broke in two.

'Another, mates: this one's no good.'

They put two pairs on him. He approved:

'That's better. You can't be too careful.'

Then, counting the detectives, he continued:

'How many of you are there, my friends? Twenty-five? Thirty? That's a lot . . . I can't do anything against thirty. Ah, if there had been only fifteen of you!'

★　★　★

He really had a manner about him, the manner of a great actor playing his instinctive, spirited part impertinently and frivolously. Shears watched him as a man watches a fine sight of which he is able to appreciate every beauty and every shade. And he absolutely received the strange impression that the struggle was an equal one between those thirty men on the one hand, backed up by all the formidable machinery of the law, and that single being on the other, fettered and unarmed. The two sides were evenly matched.

'Well, maître,' said Lupin, 'this is your work. Thanks to you, Lupin is going to rot on the damp straw of the cells. Confess that your conscience is not quite easy and that you feel the pangs of remorse.'

The Englishman gave an involuntary shrug, as though to say:

'You had the chance . . . '

'Never! Never!' exclaimed Lupin. 'Give you back the blue diamond? Ah, no, it has cost me too much trouble already! I value it, you see. At the first visit I have the honour of paying you in London, next month, I daresay, I will tell you why . . . But shall you be in London next month? Would you rather I met you in Vienna? Or St. Petersburg?'

He started. Suddenly, an electric bell rang just below the ceiling. And, this time, it was not the alarm-bell, but the bell of the telephone, which had not been removed and which stood between the two windows.

The telephone! Ah, who was going to fall into the trap laid by an odious chance? Arsène Lupin made a furious move toward the instrument, as though he would have smashed it to atoms and, in so doing, stifled the unknown voice that wished to speak to him. But Ganimard took the receiver from its hook and bent down:

'Hullo! . . . Hullo! . . . 64873 . . . Yes, that's right.'

With a brisk gesture of authority, Shears pushed him aside, took the two receivers and put his handkerchief over the mouthpiece to make the sound of his voice less distinct.

At that moment, he glanced at Lupin. And the look which they exchanged showed them that the same thought had struck them both and that they both foresaw to the end the consequences of that possible, probable, almost certain supposition: it was the blonde lady telephoning. She thought that she was telephoning to Félix Davey, or, rather, Maxime Bermond; and she was about to confide in Holmlock Shears!

And the Englishman repeated:

'Hullo! . . . Hullo! . . . '

A pause and Shears:

'Yes, it's I; Maxime.'

The drama took shape forthwith, with tragic precision. Lupin, the mocking, indomitable Lupin, no longer even thought of concealing his anxiety and, with features pale as death, strove to hear, to guess. And Shears continued, in reply to the mysterious voice:

'Yes, yes, it's all finished and I was just getting ready to come on to you, as arranged . . . Where? Why, where you are . . . Isn't that best?'

He hesitated, seeking his words, and then stopped. It was evident that he was trying to draw out the girl without saying too much himself and that he had not the least idea where she was. Besides, Ganimard's presence seemed to hinder him . . . Oh, if some miracle could have cut the thread of that diabolical conversation! Lupin called for it with all his might, with all his strained nerves!

And Shears went on:

'Hullo! . . . Hullo! . . . Can't you hear? . . . It's very bad at this end too . . . and I can hardly make out . . . Can you hear me now? Well . . . on second thoughts . . . you had better go home . . . Oh, no, there's no danger at all . . . Why, he's in England! I've had a telegram from Southampton!'

The irony of the words! Shears uttered them with an inexpressible sense of satisfaction. And he added.

'So go at once, dear, and I shall be with you soon.'

He hung up the receivers.

'M. Ganimard, I propose to borrow three of your men.'

'It's for the blonde lady, I suppose?'

'Yes.'

'Do you know who she is, where she is?'

'Yes.'

'By Jove! A fine capture! She and Lupin . . . that completes the day's work. Folenfant, take two men and go with Mr. Shears.'

The Englishman walked away, followed by the three detectives.

The end had come. The blonde lady also was about to fall into Shears's hands. Thanks to his wonderful persistency, thanks to the aid of fortunate events, the battle was turning to victory for him and irreparable disaster for Lupin.

'Mr. Shears!'

The Englishman stopped:

'Yes, M. Lupin?'

Lupin seemed completely crushed by this last blow. His forehead was wrinkled; he was worn-out and gloomy. Yet he drew himself up, with a revival of energy; and, in spite of all, exclaimed, in a voice of glad unconcern:

'You must admit that fate is dead against me. Just now, it prevented me from escaping by the chimney and delivered me into your hands. This moment, it has made use of the telephone to make you a present of the blonde lady. I bow before its decrees.'

'Meaning . . . ?'

'Meaning that I am prepared to reopen negotiations.'

Shears took the inspector aside and begged permission, but in a tone that allowed of no refusal, to exchange a few words with Lupin. Then he walked across to him. The momentous conversation took place. It opened in short, nervous phrases:

'What do you want?'

'Mlle. Destange's liberty.'

'You know the price?'

'Yes.'

'And you agree?'

'I agree to all your conditions.'

'Ah!' exclaimed the astonished Englishman. 'But . . . you refused just now . . . for yourself . . . '

'It was a question of myself, Mr. Shears. Now it involves a woman . . . and a woman whom I love. You see, we have very peculiar ideas about these things in France, and it does not follow that, because a man's name is Lupin, he will act differently: on the contrary!'

He said this quite simply. Shears gave him an imperceptible nod and whispered:

'Where is the blue diamond?'

'Take my cane, over there, in the chimney corner. Hold the knob in one hand and turn the iron ferrule with the other.'

Shears took the cane, turned the ferrule and, as he turned it, perceived that the knob became unscrewed. Inside the knob was a ball of putty. Inside the putty a diamond.

He examined it. It was the blue diamond.

'Mlle. Destange is free, M. Lupin.'

'Free in the future as in the present? She has nothing to fear from you?'

'Nor from any one else.'

'Whatever happens?'

'Whatever happens. I have forgotten her name and where she lives.'

'Thank you. And *au revoir*. For we shall meet again, Mr. Shears, shall we not?'

'I have no doubt we shall.'

A more or less heated explanation followed between the Englishman and Ganimard and was cut short by Shears with a certain roughness:

'I am very sorry, M. Ganimard, that I can't agree with you. But I have no time to persuade you now. I leave for England in an hour.'

'But . . . the blonde lady?'

'I know no such person.'

'Only a moment ago . . .'

'You must take it or leave it. I have already

caught Lupin for you. Here is the blue diamond . . . which you may have the pleasure of handing to the countess yourself. I can't see that you have anything to complain of.'

'But the blonde lady?'

'Find her.'

He settled his hat on his head and walked away with a brisk step, like a gentleman who has no time to loiter once his business is done.

★   ★   ★

'Good-bye, maître!' cried Lupin. 'And a pleasant journey! I shall always remember the cordial relations between us. My kind regards to Mr. Wilson!'

He received no reply and chuckled:

'That's what we call taking English leave. Ah, those worthy islanders do not possess that elegant courtesy which distinguishes us. Just think, Ganimard, of the exit which a Frenchman would have made in similar circumstances! Under what exquisite politeness would he not have concealed his triumph! . . . But, Lord bless my soul, Ganimard, what are you doing? Well, I never: a search! But there's nothing left, my poor friend, not a scrap of paper! My archives have been moved to a place of safety.'

'One can never tell.'

Lupin looked on in resignation. Held by two inspectors and surrounded by all the rest, he patiently watched the various operations. But, after twenty minutes, he sighed:

'Come along, Ganimard; you'll never be finished, at this rate.'

'Are you in a great hurry?'

'Yes, I should think I was! I have an important engagement!'

'At the police-station?'

'No, in town.'

'Tut, tut! At what time?'

'At two o'clock.'

'It's past three.'

'Exactly: I shall be late; and there's nothing I detest so much as being late.'

'Will you give me five minutes?'

'Not a minute longer.'

'You're too good . . . I'll try . . . '

'Don't talk so much . . . What, that cupboard too? Why, it's empty!'

'There are some letters, for all that.'

'Old bills.'

'No, a bundle done up in ribbon.'

'A pink ribbon, is it? Oh, Ganimard, don't untie it, for heaven's sake!'

'Are they from a woman?'

'Yes.'

'A lady?'

'Rather!'

'What's her name?'

'Mme. Ganimard.'

'Very witty! Oh, very witty!' cried the inspector, in an affected tone.

At that moment, the men returned from the other rooms and declared that their search had led to nothing. Lupin began to laugh:

'Of course not! Did you expect to find a list of my friends, or a proof of my relations with the German Emperor? What you ought to have looked for, Ganimard, are the little mysteries of this flat. For instance, that gas-pipe is a speaking tube. The chimney contains a staircase. This wall here is hollow. And such a tangle of bell-wires! Look here, Ganimard: just press that button.'

Ganimard did as he was asked.

'Did you hear anything?'

'No.'

'Nor I. And yet you have instructed the captain of my balloon-park to get ready the airship which is soon to carry us up to the sky.'

'Come,' said Ganimard, who had finished his inspection. 'Enough of this nonsense. Let us start.'

He took a few steps, followed by his men.

Lupin did not budge a foot's breadth.

His custodians pushed him. In vain.

'Well,' said Ganimard, 'do you refuse to come?'

'Not at all.'

'Then . . . '

'It all depends.'

'Depends on what?'

'On where you're taking me.'

'To the police-station, of course.'

'Then I shan't come. I have nothing to do at the station.'

'You're mad!'

'Didn't I tell you I had an important engagement?'

'Lupin!'

'Come, Ganimard, the blonde lady must be getting quite anxious about me; and do you think I could have the rudeness to keep her waiting? It would not be the conduct of a gentleman!'

'Listen to me, Lupin,' said the inspector, who was beginning to lose his temper under all this chaff. 'So far, I have treated you with excessive consideration. But there are limits. Follow me.'

'Impossible. I have an engagement and that engagement I mean to keep.'

'For the last time?'

'Impossible!'

Ganimard made a sign. Two men seized Lupin under the arms and lifted him from the floor. But they dropped him at once with howls of pain: with his two hands, Arsène Lupin had dug two long needles into their flesh.

Maddened with rage, the others rushed upon him, wreaking their hatred at last, burning to avenge their comrades and themselves for the numberless affronts put upon them, and they rained a shower of blows upon his body. One blow, more violent than the rest, struck him on the temple. He fell to the floor.

'If you hurt him,' growled Ganimard, angrily, 'you'll have me to deal with.'

He bent over Lupin, prepared to assist him. But, finding that he was breathing freely, he told the men to take Lupin by the head and feet, while he himself supported his hips.

'Slowly, now, gently! . . . Don't jolt him! . . . Why, you brutes, you might have killed him. Well, Lupin, how do you feel?'

Lupin opened his eyes and stammered:

'Not up to much, Ganimard . . . You shouldn't have let them knock me about.'

'Dash it, it's your own fault . . . with your obstinacy!' replied Ganimard, in real distress. 'But you're not hurt?'

They reached the landing. Lupin moaned:

'Ganimard . . . the lift . . . they'll break my bones.'

'Good idea, capital idea!' agreed the inspector. 'Besides, the stairs are so narrow . . . it would be impossible . . . '

He got the lift up. They laid Lupin on the seat with every imaginable precaution. Ganimard sat down beside him and said to his men:

'Go down the stairs at once. Wait for me by the porter's lodge. Do you understand?'

He shut the door. But it was hardly closed when shouts arose. The lift had shot up, like a balloon with its rope cut. A sardonic laugh rang out.

'Damnation!' roared Ganimard, feeling frantically in the dark for the lever. And failing to find it, he shouted, 'The fifth floor! Watch the door on the fifth floor!'

The detectives rushed upstairs, four steps at a time. But a strange thing happened: the lift seemed to shoot right through the ceiling of the top floor, disappeared before the detectives' eyes and suddenly emerged on the upper story, where the servants' bedrooms were, and stopped.

Three men were in waiting and opened the door. Two of them overpowered Ganimard, who, hampered in his movements and completely bewildered, hardly thought of defending himself. The third helped Lupin out.

'I told you, Ganimard! . . . Carried off by

balloon . . . and thanks to you! . . . Next time, you must show less compassion. And, above all, remember that Arsène Lupin does not allow himself to be bashed and mauled about without good reasons. Good-bye . . . '

The lift-door was already closed and the lift, with Ganimard inside, sent back on its journey toward the ground floor. And all this was done so expeditiously that the old detective caught up his subordinates at the door of the porter's lodge.

Without a word, they hurried across the courtyard and up the servants' staircase, the only means of communication with the floor by which the escape had been effected.

A long passage, with many windings, lined with small, numbered rooms, led to a door, which had been simply left ajar. Beyond this door and, consequently, in another house, was another passage, also with a number of turns and lined with similar rooms. Right at the end was a servants' staircase. Ganimard went down it, crossed a yard, a hall and rushed into a street: the Rue Picot. Then he understood: the two houses were built back to back and their fronts faced two streets, running not at right angles, but parallel, with a distance of over sixty yards between them.

He entered the porter's lodge and showed his card:

'Have four men just gone out?'

'Yes, the two servants of the fourth and fifth floors, with two friends.'

'Who lives on the fourth and fifth floors?'

'Two gentlemen of the name of Fauvel and their cousins, the Provosts . . . They moved this morning. Only the two servants remained . . . They have just gone.'

'Ah,' thought Ganimard, sinking on to a sofa in the lodge, 'what a fine stroke we have missed! The whole gang occupied this rabbit-warren! . . . '

★　★　★

Forty minutes later, two gentlemen drove up in a cab to the Gare du Nord and hurried toward the Calais express, followed by a porter carrying their bags.

One of them had his arm in a sling and his face was pale and drawn. The other seemed in great spirits:

'Come along, Wilson; it won't do to miss the train! . . . Oh, Wilson, I shall never forget these ten days!'

'No more shall I.'

'What a fine series of battles!'

'Magnificent!'

'A regrettable incident, here and there, but of very slight importance.'

230

'Very slight, as you say.'

'And, lastly, victory all along the line. Lupin arrested! The blue diamond recovered!'

'My arm broken!'

'With a success of this kind, what does a broken arm matter?'

'Especially mine.'

'Especially yours. Remember, Wilson, it was at the very moment when you were at the chemist's, suffering like a hero, that I discovered the clue that guided me through the darkness.'

'What a piece of luck!'

The doors were being locked.

'Take your seats, please. Hurry up, gentlemen!'

The porter climbed into an empty compartment and placed the bags in the rack, while Shears hoisted the unfortunate Wilson in:

'What are you doing, Wilson? Hurry up, old chap! . . . Pull yourself together, do!'

'It's not for want of pulling myself together.'

'What then?'

'I can only use one hand.'

'Well?' cried Shears, gaily. 'What a fuss you make! One would think you were the only man in your plight. What about the fellows who have really lost an arm? Well, are you settled? Thank goodness for that!'

He gave the porter a half-franc piece.

'Here, my man. That's for you.'

'Thank you, Mr. Shears.'

The Englishman raised his eyes: Arsène Lupin!

'You! . . . You!' he blurted in his bewilderment.

And Wilson stammered, waving his one hand with the gestures of a man proving a fact:

'You! . . . You! . . . But you're arrested! Shears told me so. When he left you, Ganimard and his thirty detectives had you surrounded!'

Lupin crossed his arms with an air of indignation:

'So you thought I would let you go without coming to see you off? After the excellent friendly relations which we never ceased to keep up? Why, it would have been unspeakably rude. What do you take me for?'

The engine whistled.

'However, I forgive you . . . Have you all you want? Tobacco, matches? . . . That's right . . . And the evening papers? You will find the details of my arrest in them: your last exploit, maître! And now, *au revoir*; and delighted to have made your acquaintance . . . delighted, I mean it! . . . And, if ever I can do anything for you, I shall be only too pleased.'

He jumped down to the platform and closed the door.

'Good-bye!' he cried again, waving his

handkerchief. 'Good-bye . . . I'll write to you! . . . Mind you write too; let me know how the broken arm is, Mr. Wilson! I shall expect to hear from both of you . . . Just a picture postcard, now and again . . . 'Lupin, Paris' will always find me . . . It's quite enough . . . Never mind about stamping the letters . . . Good-bye! . . . See you soon, I hope!'

# SECOND EPISODE

# The Jewish Lamp

# 1

Holmlock Shears and Wilson were seated on either side of the fireplace in Shears's sitting-room. The great detective's pipe had gone out. He knocked the ashes into the grate, re-filled his briar, lit it, gathered the skirts of his dressing-gown around his knees, puffed away and devoted all his attention to sending rings of smoke curling gracefully up to the ceiling.

Wilson watched him. He watched him as a dog, rolled up on the hearth-rug, watches its master, with wide-open eyes and unblinking lids, eyes which have no other hope than to reflect the expected movement on the master's part. Would Shears break silence? Would he reveal the secret of his present dreams and admit Wilson to the realm of meditation into which he felt that he was not allowed to enter uninvited?

Shears continued silent.

Wilson ventured upon a remark:

'Things are very quiet. There's not a single case for us to nibble at.'

Shears was more and more fiercely silent; but the rings of tobacco-smoke became more and more successful and any one but Wilson would have observed that Shears obtained from this the profound content which we derive from the minor achievements of our vanity, at times when our brain is completely void of thought.

Disheartened, Wilson rose and walked to the window. The melancholy street lay stretched between the gloomy fronts of the houses, under a dark sky whence fell an angry and pouring rain. A cab drove past; another cab. Wilson jotted down their numbers in his notebook. One can never tell!

The postman came down the street, gave a treble knock at the door; and, presently, the servant entered with two registered letters.

'You look remarkably pleased,' said Wilson, when Shears had unsealed and glanced through the first.

'This letter contains a very attractive proposal. You were worrying about a case: here is one. Read it.'

Wilson took the letter and read:

*18, Rue Murillo,*
*Paris.*

*Sir:*
*I am writing to ask for the benefit of your assistance and experience. I have been the*

*victim of a serious theft and all the investigations attempted up to the present would seem to lead to nothing.*

*I am sending you by this post a number of newspapers which will give you all the details of the case; and, if you are inclined to take it up, I shall be pleased if you will accept the hospitality of my house and if you will fill in the enclosed signed check for any amount which you like to name for your expenses.*

*Pray, telegraph to inform me if I may expect you and believe me to be, sir,*

*Yours very truly,*

*Baron Victor d'Imblevalle.*

'Well,' said Shears, 'this comes just at the right time: why shouldn't I take a little run to Paris? I haven't been there since my famous duel with Arsène Lupin and I shan't be sorry to re-visit it under rather more peaceful conditions.'

He tore the cheque into four pieces and, while Wilson, whose arm had not yet recovered from the injury received in the course of the aforesaid encounter, was inveighing bitterly against Paris and all its inhabitants, he opened the second envelope.

A movement of irritation at once escaped him; he knitted his brow as he read the letter and, when he had finished, he crumpled it into a ball and threw it angrily on the floor.

'What's the matter?' exclaimed Wilson, in amazement.

He picked up the ball, unfolded it and read, with ever-increasing stupefaction:

'My dear Maître:

'You know my admiration for you and the interest which I take in your reputation. Well, accept my advice and have nothing to do with the case in which you are asked to assist. Your interference would do a great deal of harm, all your efforts would only bring about a pitiable result and you would be obliged publicly to acknowledge your defeat.

'I am exceedingly anxious to spare you this humiliation and I beg you, in the name of our mutual friendship, to remain very quietly by your fireside.

'Give my kind remembrances to Dr. Wilson and accept for yourself the respectful compliments of

'Yours most sincerely,

'Arsène Lupin.

'Arsène Lupin!' repeated Wilson, in bewilderment.

Shears banged the table with his fist:

'Oh, I'm getting sick of the brute! He laughs at me as if I were a schoolboy! I am publicly to acknowledge my defeat, am I?

Didn't I compel him to give up the blue diamond?'

'He's afraid of you,' suggested Wilson.

'You're talking nonsense! Arsène Lupin is never afraid; and the proof is that he challenges me.'

'But how does he come to know of Baron d'Imblevalle's letter?'

'How can I tell? You're asking silly questions, my dear fellow!'

'I thought . . . I imagined . . . '

'What? That I am a sorcerer?'

'No, but I have seen you perform such marvels!'

'No one is able to perform marvels . . . I no more than another. I make reflections, deductions, conclusions, but I don't make guesses. Only fools make guesses.'

Wilson adopted the modest attitude of a beaten dog and did his best, lest he should be a fool, not to guess why Shears was striding angrily up and down the room. But, when Shears rang for the servant and asked for his travelling-bag, Wilson thought himself entitled, since this was a material fact, to reflect, deduce and conclude that his chief was going on a journey.

The same mental operation enabled him to declare, in the tone of a man who has no fear of the possibility of a mistake:

'Holmlock, you are going to Paris.'

'Possibly.'

'And you are going to Paris even more in reply to Lupin's challenge than to oblige Baron d'Imblevalle.'

'Possibly.'

'Holmlock, I will go with you.'

'Aha, old friend!' cried Shears, interrupting his walk. 'Aren't you afraid that your left arm may share the fate of the right?'

'What can happen to me? You will be there.'

'Well said! You're a fine fellow! And we will show this gentleman that he may have made a mistake in defying us so boldly. Quick, Wilson, and meet me at the first train.'

'Won't you wait for the newspapers the baron mentions?'

'What's the good?'

'Shall I send a telegram?'

'No. Arsène Lupin would know I was coming and I don't wish him to. This time, Wilson, we must play a cautious game.'

★　★　★

That afternoon, the two friends stepped on board the boat at Dover. They had a capital crossing. In the express from Calais to Paris, Shears indulged in three hours of the soundest sleep, while Wilson kept a good watch at the door of the compartment and meditated with a wandering eye.

Shears woke up feeling happy and well. The prospect of a new duel with Arsène Lupin delighted him; and he rubbed his hands with the contented air of a man preparing to taste untold joys.

'At last,' exclaimed Wilson, 'we shall feel that we're alive!'

And he rubbed his hands with the same contented air.

At the station, Shears took the rugs, and, followed by Wilson carrying the bags — each his burden! — handed the tickets to the collector and walked gaily into the street.

'A fine day, Wilson . . . Sunshine! . . . Paris is dressed in her best to receive us.'

'What a crowd!'

'So much the better, Wilson: we stand less chance of being noticed. No one will recognize us in the midst of such a multitude.'

'Mr. Shears, I believe?'

He stopped, somewhat taken aback. Who on earth could be addressing him by name?

A woman was walking beside him, or rather a girl whose exceedingly simple dress accentuated her well-bred appearance. Her pretty face wore a sad and anxious expression. She repeated:

'You must be Mr. Shears, surely?'

He was silent, as much from confusion as from the habit of prudence, and she asked for the third time:

'Surely I am speaking to Mr. Shears?'

'What do you want with me?' he asked, crossly, thinking this a questionable meeting. She placed herself in front of him:

'Listen to me, Mr. Shears: it is a very serious matter. I know that you are going to the Rue Murillo.'

'What's that?'

'I know . . . I know . . . Rue Murillo . . . No. 18. Well, you must not . . . no, you must not go . . . I assure you, you will regret it. Because I tell you this, you need not think that I am interested in any way. I have a reason; I know what I am saying.'

He tried to push her aside. She insisted:

'I entreat you; do not be obstinate . . . Oh, if I only knew how to convince you! Look into me, look into the depths of my eyes . . . they are sincere . . . they speak the truth . . . '

Desperately, she raised her eyes, a pair of beautiful, grave and limpid eyes that seemed to reflect her very soul. Wilson nodded his head:

'The young lady seems quite sincere,' he said.

'Indeed I am,' she said beseechingly, 'and you must trust me . . . '

'I do trust you, mademoiselle,' replied Wilson.

'Oh, how happy you make me! And your friend trusts me too, does he not? I feel it . . . I am sure of it! How glad I am! All will be well! . . . Oh, what a good idea I had! Listen, Mr. Shears: there's a train for Calais in twenty minutes . . . Now, you must take it . . . Quick, come with me: it's this way and you have not much time.'

She tried to drag Shears with her. He seized her by the arm and, in a voice which he strove to make as gentle as possible, said: 'Forgive me, mademoiselle, if I am not able to accede to your wish; but I never turn aside from a task which I have undertaken.'

'I entreat you . . . I entreat you . . . Oh, if you only knew!'

He passed on and walked briskly away.

Wilson lingered behind and said to the girl:

'Be of good hope . . . He will see the thing through to the end . . . He has never yet been known to fail . . .'

And he ran after Shears to catch him up.

## HOLMLOCK SHEARS

## VERSUS

## ARSÈNE LUPIN

These words, standing out in great black letters, struck their eyes at the first steps they took. They walked up to them: a procession of sandwich-men was moving along in single file. In their hands they carried heavy ferruled canes, with which they tapped the pavement in unison as they went; and their boards bore the above legend in front and a further huge poster at the back which read:

**THE SHEARS-LUPIN CONTEST**

**ARRIVAL OF
THE ENGLISH CHAMPION**

**THE GREAT DETECTIVE
GRAPPLES WITH
THE RUE MURILLO MYSTERY**

**FULL DETAILS
*ÉCHO DE FRANCE***

Wilson tossed his head:

'I say, Holmlock, I thought we were travelling incognito! I shouldn't be astonished to find the Republican Guard waiting for us in the Rue Murillo, with an official reception and champagne!'

'When you try to be witty, Wilson,' snarled Shears, 'you're witty enough for two!'

He strode up to one of the men with apparent intention of taking him in his powerful hands and tearing him and his advertisement to shreds. Meanwhile, a crowd gathered round the posters, laughing and joking.

Suppressing a furious fit of passion, Shears said to the man:

'When were you hired?'

'This morning.'

'When did you start on your round?'

'An hour ago.'

'But the posters were ready?'

'Lord, yes! They were there when we came to the office this morning.'

So Arsène Lupin had foreseen that Shears would accept the battle! Nay, more, the letter written by Lupin proved that he himself wished for the battle and that it formed part of his intentions to measure swords once more with his rival. Why? What possible motive could urge him to re-commence the contest?

Holmlock Shears showed a momentary hesitation. Lupin must really feel very sure of victory to display such insolence; and was it not falling into a trap to hasten like that in answer to the first call? Then, summoning up all his energy:

'Come along, Wilson! Driver, 18, Rue Murillo!' he shouted.

And, with swollen veins and fists clenched as though for a boxing-match, he leapt into a cab.

★ ★ ★

The Rue Murillo is lined with luxurious private residences, the backs of which look out upon the Parc Monceau. No. 18 is one of the handsomest of these houses; and Baron d'Imblevalle, who occupies it with his wife and children, has furnished it in the most sumptuous style, as befits an artist and millionaire. There is a courtyard in front of the house, skirted on either side by the servants' offices. At the back, a garden mingles the branches of its trees with the trees of the park.

The two Englishmen rang the bell, crossed the courtyard and were admitted by a footman, who showed them into a small drawing-room at the other side of the house.

They sat down and took a rapid survey of the many valuable objects with which the room was filled.

'Very pretty things,' whispered Wilson. 'Taste and fancy . . . One can safely draw the deduction that people who have had the leisure to hunt out these articles are persons of a certain age . . . fifty, perhaps . . .'

He did not have time to finish. The door

opened and M. d'Imblevalle entered, followed by his wife.

Contrary to Wilson's deductions, they were both young, fashionably dressed and very lively in speech and manner. Both were profuse in thanks:

'It is really too good of you! To put yourself out like this! We are almost glad of this trouble since it procures us the pleasure . . . '

'How charming those French people are!' thought Wilson, who never shirked the opportunity of making an original observation.

'But time is money,' cried the baron. 'And yours especially, Mr. Shears. Let us come to the point! What do you think of the case? Do you hope to bring it to a satisfactory result?'

'To bring the case to a satisfactory result, I must first know what the case is.'

'Don't you know?'

'No; and I will ask you to explain the matter fully, omitting nothing. What is it a case of?'

'It is a case of theft.'

'On what day did it take place?'

'On Saturday,' replied the baron. 'On Saturday night or Sunday morning.'

'Six days ago, therefore. Now, pray, go on.'

'I must first tell you that my wife and I, though we lead the life expected of people in our position, go out very little. The education of our children, a few receptions, the beautifying of our home: these make up our existence; and all or nearly all our evenings are spent here, in this room, which is my wife's boudoir and in which we have collected a few pretty things. Well, on Saturday last, at about eleven o'clock, I switched off the electric light and my wife and I retired, as usual, to our bedroom.'

'Where is that?'

'The next room: that door over there. On the following morning, that is to say, Sunday, I rose early. As Suzanne — my wife — was still asleep, I came into this room as gently as possible, so as not to awake her. Imagine my surprise at finding the window open, after we had left it closed the evening before!'

'A servant . . . ?'

'Nobody enters this room in the morning before we ring. Besides, I always take the precaution of bolting that other door, which leads to the hall. Therefore the window must have been opened from the outside. I had a proof of it, besides: the second pane of the right-hand casement, the one next to the latch, had been cut out.'

'And the window?'

'The window, as you perceive, opens on a little balcony surrounded by a stone balustrade. We are on the first floor here and you can see the garden at the back of the house and the railings that separate it from the Parc Monceau. It is certain, therefore, that the man came from the Parc Monceau, climbed the railings by means of a ladder and got up to the balcony.'

'It is certain, you say?'

'On either side of the railings, in the soft earth of the borders, we found holes left by the two uprights of the ladder; and there were two similar holes below the balcony. Lastly, the balustrade shows two slight scratches, evidently caused by the contact of the ladder.'

'Isn't the Parc Monceau closed at night?'

'Closed? No. But, in any case, there is a house building at No. 14. It would have been easy to effect an entrance that way.'

Holmlock Shears reflected for a few moments and resumed:

'Let us come to the theft. You say it was committed in the room where we now are?'

'Yes. Just here, between this twelfth-century Virgin and that chased-silver tabernacle, there was a little Jewish lamp. It has disappeared.'

'And is that all?'

'That is all.'

'Oh! . . . And what do you call a Jewish lamp?'

'It is one of those lamps which they used to employ in the old days, consisting of a stem and of a receiver to contain the oil. This receiver had two or more burners, which held the wicks.'

'When all is said, objects of no great value.'

'Just so. But the one in question formed a hiding-place in which we had made it a practice to keep a magnificent antique jewel, a chimera in gold, set with rubies and emeralds and worth a great deal of money.'

'What was your reason for this practice?'

'Upon my word, Mr. Shears, I should find it difficult to tell you! Perhaps we just thought it amusing to have a hiding-place of this kind.'

'Did nobody know of it?'

'Nobody.'

'Except, of course, the thief,' objected Shears. 'But for that, he would not have taken the trouble to steal the Jewish lamp.'

'Obviously. But how could he know of it, seeing that it was by an accident that we discovered the secret mechanism of the lamp?'

'The same accident may have revealed it to somebody else: a servant . . . a visitor to the house . . . But let us continue: have you informed the police?'

'Certainly. The examining-magistrate has made his inquiry. The journalistic detectives attached to all the big newspapers have made theirs. But, as I wrote to you, it does not seem as though the problem had the least chance of ever being solved.'

Shears rose, went to the window, inspected the casement, the balcony, the balustrade, employed his lens to study the two scratches on the stone and asked M. d'Imblevalle to take him down to the garden.

When they were outside, Shears simply sat down in a wicker chair and contemplated the roof of the house with a dreamy eye. Then he suddenly walked toward two little wooden cases with which, in order to preserve the exact marks, they had covered the holes which the uprights of the ladder had left in the ground, below the balcony. He removed the cases, went down on his knees and, with rounded back and his nose six inches from the ground, searched and took his measurements. He went through the same performance along the railing, but more quickly.

That was all.

★   ★   ★

They both returned to the boudoir, where Madame d'Imblevalle was waiting for them.

Shears was silent for a few minutes longer and then spoke these words:

'Ever since you began your story, monsieur le baron, I was struck by the really too simple side of the offence. To apply a ladder, remove a pane of glass, pick out an object and go away: no, things don't happen so easily as that. It is all too clear, too plain.'

'You mean to say . . . ?'

'I mean to say that the theft of the Jewish lamp was committed under the direction of Arsène Lupin.'

'Arsène Lupin!' exclaimed the baron.

'But it was committed without Arsène Lupin's presence and without anybody's entering the house . . . Perhaps a servant slipped down to the balcony from his garret, along a rain-spout which I saw from the garden.'

'But what evidence have you?'

'Arsène Lupin would not have left the boudoir empty-handed.'

'Empty-handed! And what about the lamp?'

'Taking the lamp would not have prevented him from taking this snuff-box, which, I see, is studded with diamonds, or this necklace of old opals. It would require but two movements more. His only reason for not making those movements was that he was not here to make them.'

'Still, the marks of the ladder?'

'A farce! Mere stage-play to divert suspicions!'

'The scratches on the balustrade?'

'A sham! They were made with sandpaper. Look, here are a few bits of paper which I picked up.'

'The marks left by the uprights of the ladder?'

'Humbug! Examine the two rectangular holes below the balcony and the two holes near the railings. The shape is similar, but, whereas they are parallel here, they are not so over there. Measure the space that separates each hole from its neighbour: it differs in the two cases. Below the balcony, the distance is nine inches. Beside the railings, it is eleven inches.'

'What do you conclude from that?'

'I conclude, since their outline is identical, that the four holes were made with one stump of wood, cut to the right shape.'

'The best argument would be the stump of wood itself.'

'Here it is,' said Shears. 'I picked it up in the garden, behind a laurel-tub.'

★　★　★

The baron gave in. It was only forty minutes since the Englishman had entered by that door; and not a vestige remained of all that had been believed so far on the evidence of the apparent facts themselves. The reality, a different reality, came to light, founded upon something much more solid: the reasoning faculties of a Holmlock Shears.

'It is a very serious accusation to bring against our people, Mr. Shears,' said the baroness. 'They are old family servants and not one of them is capable of deceiving us.'

'If one of them did not deceive you, how do you explain that this letter was able to reach me on the same day and by the same post as the one you sent me?'

And he handed her the letter which Arsène Lupin had written to him.

Madame d'Imblevalle was dumbfounded:

'Arsène Lupin! . . . How did he know?'

'Did you tell no one of your letter?'

'No one,' said the baron. 'The idea occurred to us the other evening, at dinner.'

'Before the servants?'

'There were only our two children. And even then . . . no, Sophie and Henrietta were not at table, were they Suzanne?'

Madame d'Imblevalle reflected and declared:

'No, they had gone up to mademoiselle.'

'Mademoiselle?' asked Shears.

'The governess, Alice Demun.'

'Doesn't she have her meals with you?'

'No, she has them by herself, in her room.'

Wilson had an idea:

'The letter written to my friend Holmlock Shears was posted?'

'Naturally.'

'Who posted it?'

'Dominique, who has been with me as my own man for twenty years,' replied the baron. 'Any search in that direction would be a waste of time.'

'Time employed in searching is never wasted,' stated Wilson, sententiously.

This closed the first inquiries and Shears asked leave to withdraw.

An hour later, at dinner, he saw Sophie and Henrietta, the d'Imblevalles' children, two pretty little girls of eight and six respectively. The conversation languished. Shears replied to the pleasant remarks of the baron and his wife in so surly a tone that they thought it better to keep silence. Coffee was served. Shears swallowed the contents of his cup and rose from his chair.

At that moment, a servant entered with a telephone message for him. Shears opened it and read:

*Accept my enthusiastic admiration. Results obtained by you in so short a time make my head reel. I feel quite giddy.*

*Arsène Lupin.*

He could not suppress a gesture of annoyance and, showing the telegram to the baron:

'Do you begin to believe,' he said, 'that

your walls have eyes and ears?'

'I can't understand it,' murmured M. d'Imblevalle, astounded.

'Nor I. But what I do understand is that not a movement takes place here unperceived by him. Not a word is spoken but he hears it.'

★ ★ ★

That evening, Wilson went to bed with the easy conscience of a man who has done his duty and who has no other business before him than to go to sleep. So he went to sleep very quickly and was visited by beautiful dreams, in which he was hunting down Lupin all by himself and just on the point of arresting him with his own hand; and the feeling of the pursuit was so lifelike that he woke up.

Some one was touching his bed. He seized his revolver:

'Another movement, Lupin, and I shoot!'

'Steady, old chap, steady on!'

'Hullo, is that you, Shears? Do you want me?'

'I want your eyes. Get up . . . '

He led him to the window:

'Look over there . . . beyond the railings . . . '

'In the park?'

'Yes. Do you see anything?'

'No, nothing.'

'Try again; I am sure you see something.'

'Oh, so I do: a shadow . . . no, two!'

'I thought so: against the railings . . . See, they're moving . . . Let's lose no time.'

Groping and holding on to the banister, they made their way down the stairs and came to a room that opened on to the garden steps. Through the glass doors, they could see the two figures still in the same place.

'It's curious,' said Shears. 'I seem to hear noises in the house.'

'In the house? Impossible! Everbody's asleep.'

'Listen, though . . . '

At that moment, a faint whistle sounded from the railings and they perceived an undecided light that seemed to come from the house.

'The d'Imblevalles must have switched on their light,' muttered Shears. 'It's their room above us.'

'Then it's they we heard, no doubt,' said Wilson. 'Perhaps they are watching the railings.'

A second whistle, still fainter than the first.

'I can't understand, I can't understand,' said Shears, in a tone of vexation.

'No more can I,' confessed Wilson.

Shears turned the key of the door, unbolted it and softly pushed it open.

A third whistle, this time a little deeper and in a different note. And, above their heads, the noise grew louder, more hurried.

'It sounds rather as if it were on the balcony of the boudoir,' whispered Shears.

He put his head between the glass doors, but at once drew back with a stifled oath. Wilson looked out in his turn. Close to them, a ladder rose against the wall, leaning against the balustrade of the balcony.

'By Jove!' said Shears. 'There's some one in the boudoir. That's what we heard. Quick, let's take away the ladder!'

But, at that moment, a form slid from the top to the bottom, the ladder was removed and the man who carried it ran swiftly toward the railings, to the place where his accomplices were waiting. Shears and Wilson had darted out. They came up with the man as he was placing the ladder against the railings. Two shots rang out from the other side.

'Wounded?' cried Shears.

'No,' replied Wilson.

He caught the man around the body and tried to throw him. But the man turned, seized him with one hand and, with the other, plunged a knife full into his chest. Wilson gave a sigh, staggered and fell.

'Damnation!' roared Shears. 'If they've done for him, I'll do for them!'

He laid Wilson on the lawn and rushed at the ladder. Too late: the man had run up it and, in company with his accomplices, was fleeing through the shrubs.

'Wilson, Wilson, it's not serious, is it? Say it's only a scratch!'

The doors of the house opened suddenly. M. d'Imblevalle was the first to appear, followed by the men-servants carrying candles.

'What is it?' cried the baron. 'Is Mr. Wilson hurt?'

'Nothing; only a scratch,' repeated Shears, endeavouring to delude himself into the belief.

Wilson was bleeding copiously and his face was deathly pale. Twenty minutes later, the doctor declared that the point of the knife had penetrated to within a quarter of an inch of the heart.

'A quarter of an inch! That Wilson was always a lucky dog!' said Shears, summing up the situation, in an envious tone.

'Lucky . . . lucky . . . ' grunted the doctor.

'Why, with his strong constitution, he'll be all right . . . '

'After six weeks in bed and two months' convalescence.'

'No longer?'

'No, unless complications ensue.'

'Why on earth should there be any complications?'

Fully reassured, Shears returned to M. d'Imblevalle in the boudoir. This time, the mysterious visitor had not shown the same discretion. He had laid hands without shame on the diamond-studded snuff-box, on the opal necklace and, generally, on anything that could find room in the pockets of a self-respecting burglar.

The window was still open, one of the panes had been neatly cut out and a summary inquiry held at daybreak showed that the ladder came from the unfinished house and that the burglars must have come that way.

'In short,' said M. d'Imblevalle, with a touch of irony in his voice, 'it is an exact repetition of the theft of the Jewish lamp.'

'Yes, if we accept the first version favoured by the police.'

'Do you still refuse to adopt it? Doesn't this second theft shake your opinion as regards the first?'

'On the contrary, it confirms it.'

'It seems incredible! You have the undoubted proof that last night's burglary was committed by somebody from the outside and you still maintain that the Jewish lamp was stolen by one of our people?'

'By some one living in the house.'

'Then how do you explain . . . ?'

'I explain nothing, monsieur: I establish two facts, which resemble each other only in appearance, I weigh them separately and I am trying to find the link that connects them.'

His conviction seemed so profound, his actions based upon such powerful motives, that the baron gave way:

'Very well. Let us go and inform the commissary of the police.'

'On no account!' exclaimed the Englishman, eagerly. 'On no account whatever! The police are people whom I apply to only when I want them.'

'Still, the shots . . . ?'

'Never mind the shots!'

'Your friend . . . '

'My friend is only wounded . . . Make the doctor hold his tongue . . . I will take all the responsibility as regards the police.'

★　★　★

Two days elapsed, devoid of all incident, during which Shears pursued his task with a minute care and a conscientiousness that was exasperated by the memory of that daring onslaught, perpetrated under his eyes, despite his presence and without his being able to prevent its success. He searched the house and garden indefatigably, talked to the servants and paid long visits to the kitchen and stables. And, though he gathered no clue that threw any light upon the subject, he did not lose courage.

'I shall find what I am looking for,' he thought, 'and I shall find it here. It is not a question now, as in the case of the blonde lady, of walking at haphazard and of reaching, by roads unknown to me, an equally unknown goal. This time I am on the battlefield itself. The enemy is no longer the invisible, elusive Lupin, but the flesh-and-blood accomplice who moves within the four walls of this house. Give me the least little particular, and I know where I stand.'

This little particular, from which he was to derive such remarkable consequences, with a skill so prodigious that the case of the Jewish Lamp may be looked upon as one in which his detective genius bursts forth most triumphantly, this little particular he was to obtain by accident.

★　★　★

On the third day, entering the room above the boudoir, which was used as a schoolroom for the children, he came upon Henriette, the smaller of the two. She was looking for her scissors.

'You know,' she said to Shears, 'I make papers too, like the one you got the other evening.'

'The other evening?'

'Yes, after dinner. You got a paper with strips on it . . . you know, a telegram . . . Well, I make them too.'

She went out. To any one else, these words would have represented only the insignificant observation of a child; and Shears himself listened without paying much attention and continued his inspection. But, suddenly, he started running after the child, whose last phrase had all at once impressed him. He caught her at the top of the staircase and said:

'So you stick strips on to paper also, do you?'

Henriette, very proudly, declared:

'Yes, I cut out the words and stick them on.'

'And who taught you that pretty game?'

'Mademoiselle . . . my governess . . . I saw her do it. She takes words out of newspapers and sticks them on . . . '

'And what does she do with them?'

'Makes telegrams and letters which she sends off.'

Holmlock Shears returned to the schoolroom, singularly puzzled by this confidence and doing his utmost to extract from it the inferences of which it allowed.

There was a bundle of newspapers on the mantelpiece. He opened them and saw, in fact, that there were groups of words or lines missing, regularly and neatly cut out. But he had only to read the words that came before or after to ascertain that the missing words had been removed with the scissors at random, evidently by Henriette. It was possible that, in the pile of papers, there was one which mademoiselle had cut herself. But how was he to make sure?

Mechanically, Shears turned the pages of the lesson-books heaped up on the table and of some others lying on the shelves of a cupboard. And suddenly a cry of joy escaped him. In a corner of the cupboard, under a pile of old exercise-books, he had found a children's album, a sort of picture alphabet, and, in one of the pages of this album, he had seen a gap.

He examined the page. It gave the names of the days of the week: Sunday, Monday, Tuesday, and so on. The word 'Saturday' was missing. Now the Jewish Lamp was stolen on a Saturday night.

★ ★ ★

Shears felt that little clutch at his heart which always told him, in the plainest manner possible, when he had hit upon the knotty point of a mystery. That grip of truth, that feeling of certainty never deceived him.

He hastened to turn over the pages of the album, feverishly and confidently. A little further on came another surprise.

It was a page consisting of capital letters followed by a row of figures.

Nine of the letters and three of the figures had been carefully removed.

Shears wrote them down in his note-book, in the order which they would have occupied, and obtained the following result:

CDEHNOPRZ — 237

'By Jove!' he muttered. 'There's not much to be made out of that, at first sight.'

Was it possible to rearrange these letters and, employing them all, to form one, two or three complete words?

Shears attempted to do so in vain.

One solution alone suggested itself, returned continually to the point of his pencil and, in the end, appeared to him the right one, because it agreed with the logic of the facts and also corresponded with the general circumstances.

Admitting that the page in the album contained each of the letters of the alphabet once and once only, it was probable, it was certain that he had to do with incomplete words and that these words had been completed with letters taken from other pages.

Given these conditions, and allowing for the possibility of a mistake, the puzzle stood thus:

REPOND.Z — CH — 237

The first word was clear: '*Répondez*, reply.' An E was missing, because the letter E, having been once used, was no longer available.

As for the last, unfinished word, it undoubtedly formed, with the number 237, the address which the sender gave to the receiver of the letter. He was advised to fix the day for Saturday and asked to send a reply to C H 237.

Either C H 237 was the official number of a *poste restante* or else the two letters C H formed part of an incomplete word. Shears turned over the leaves of the album: nothing had been cut from any of the following pages. He must, therefore, until further orders, be content with the explanation hit upon.

★  ★  ★

'Isn't it fun?'

Henriette had returned.

He replied:

'Yes, great fun! Only, haven't you any other papers? . . . Or else some words ready cut out, for me to stick on?'

'Papers? . . . No . . . And then mademoiselle wouldn't like it.'

'Mademoiselle?'

'Yes, mademoiselle has scolded me already.'

'Why?'

'Because I told you things . . . and she says
you must never tell things about people you
are fond of.'

'You were quite right to tell me.'

Henriette seemed delighted with his
approval, so much so that, from a tiny canvas
bag pinned on to her frock, she took a few
strips of stuff, three buttons, two lumps of
sugar and, lastly, a square piece of paper
which she held out to Shears:

'There, I'll give it you all the same.' It was
the number of a cab, No. 8279.

'Where did you get this from?'

'It fell out of her purse.'

'When?'

'On Sunday, at Mass, when she was taking
out some coppers for the collection.'

'Capital! And now I will tell you how not to
get scolded. Don't tell mademoiselle that you
have seen me.'

★ ★ ★

Shears went off in search of M. d'Imblevalle
and asked him straight out about mademoiselle.

269

The baron gave a start:

'Alice Demun! . . . Would you think? . . . Oh, impossible!'

'How long has she been in your service?'

'Only twelve months, but I know no quieter person nor any in whom I place more confidence.'

'How is it that I have not yet seen her?'

'She was away for two days.'

'And at present?'

'Immediately on her return, she took up her position by your friend's bedside. She is a first-rate nurse . . . gentle . . . attentive. Mr. Wilson seems delighted with her.'

'Oh!' said Shears, who had quite omitted to inquire after old chap's progress.

He thought for a moment and asked:

'And did she go out on Sunday morning?'

'The day after the robbery?'

'Yes.'

The baron called his wife and put the question to her. She replied:

'Mademoiselle took the children to the eleven o'clock Mass, as usual.'

'But before that?'

'Before? No . . . Or rather . . . But I was so upset by the theft! . . . Still, I remember that, on the evening before, she asked leave to go out on Sunday morning . . . to see a cousin who was passing through Paris, I think. But surely you don't suspect her?'

'Certainly not. But I should like to see her.'

He went up to Wilson's room. A woman dressed like a hospital nurse, in a long gray linen gown, was stooping over the sick man and giving him a draught. When she turned round, Shears recognized the girl who had spoken to him outside the Gare du Nord.

★   ★   ★

Not the slightest explanation passed between them. Alice Demun smiled gently, with her grave and charming eyes, without a trace of embarrassment. The Englishman wanted to speak, tried to utter a syllable or two and was silent. Then she resumed her task, moved about peacefully before Shears's astonished eyes, shifted bottles, rolled and unrolled linen bandages and again gave him her bright smile.

Shears turned on his heels, went downstairs, saw M. d'Imblevalle's motor in the courtyard, got into it and told the chauffeur to drive him to the yard at Levallois of which the address was marked on the cab-ticket given him by the child. Duprêt, the driver who had taken out No. 8279 on Sunday morning, was not there and Shears sent back the motor-car and waited until he came to change horses.

Duprêt the driver said yes, he had taken up a lady near the Parc Monceau, a young lady in black, with a big veil on her: she seemed very excited.

'Was she carrying a parcel?'

'Yes, a longish parcel.'

'And where did you drive her to?'

'Avenue des Ternes, at the corner of the Place Saint-Ferdinand. She stayed for ten minutes or so; and then we went back to the Parc Monceau.'

'Would you know the house again, in the Avenue des Ternes?'

'Rather! Shall I take you there?'

'Presently. Go first to 36, Quai des Orfèvres.'

At the police headquarters he had the good fortune to come upon Chief-Inspector Ganimard:

'Are you disengaged, M. Ganimard?'

'If it's about Lupin, no.'

'It is about Lupin.'

'Then I shan't stir.'

'What! You give up . . . '

'I give up the impossible. I am tired of this unequal contest of which we are certain to have the worst. It's cowardly, it's ridiculous, it's anything you please . . . I don't care! Lupin is stronger than we are. Consequently, there's nothing to do but give in.'

'I'm not giving in!'

'He'll make you give in like the rest of us.'

'Well, it's a sight that can't fail to please you.'

'That's true enough,' said Ganimard, innocently. 'And, as you seem to want another beating, come along!'

Ganimard and Shears stepped into the cab. They told the driver to stop a little way before he came to the house and on the other side of the avenue, in front of a small café. They sat down outside it, among tubs of laurels and spindle-trees. The light was beginning to wane.

'Waiter!' said Shears. 'Pen and ink!'

He wrote a note and, calling the waiter again, said:

'Take this to the concierge of the house opposite. It's the man in the cap smoking his pipe in the gateway.'

The concierge hurried across and, after Ganimard had announced himself as a chief-inspector, Shears asked if a young lady in black had called at the house on Sunday morning.

'In black? Yes, about nine o'clock: it's the one who goes up to the second floor.'

'Do you see much of her?'

'No, but she's been oftener lately: almost every day during the past fortnight.'

'And since Sunday?'

'Only once . . . without counting to-day.'

'What! Has she been to-day?'

'She's there now.'

'She's there now?'

'Yes, she came about ten minutes ago. Her cab is waiting on the Place Saint-Ferdinand, as usual. I passed her in the gateway.'

'And who is the tenant of the second floor?'

'There are two: a dressmaker, Mademoiselle Langeais, and a gentleman who hired a couple of furnished rooms, a month ago, under the name of Bresson.'

'What makes you say 'under the name'?'

'I have an idea that it's an assumed name. My wife does his rooms: well, he hasn't two articles of clothing marked with the same initials.'

'How does he live?'

'Oh, he's almost always out. Sometimes, he does not come home for three days together.'

'Did he come in on Saturday night?'

'On Saturday night? . . . Wait, while I think . . . Yes, he came in on Saturday night and hasn't stirred out since.'

'And what sort of a man is he?'

'Faith, I couldn't say. He changes so! He's tall, he's short, he's fat, he's thin . . . dark and fair. I don't always recognize him.'

Ganimard and Shears exchanged glances.

'It's he,' muttered Ganimard. 'It must be he.'

For a moment, the old detective experienced a real agitation, which betrayed itself by a deep breath and a clenching of the fists.

Shears too, although more master of himself, felt something clutching at his heart.

'Look out!' said the concierge. 'Here comes the young lady.'

As he spoke, mademoiselle appeared in the gateway and crossed the square.

'And here is M. Bresson.'

'M. Bresson? Which is he?'

'The gentleman with a parcel under his arm.'

'But he's taking no notice of the girl. She is going to her cab alone.'

'Oh, well, I've never seen them together.'

The two detectives rose hurriedly. By the light of the street-lamps, they recognized Lupin's figure, as he walked away in the opposite direction to the square.

'Which will you follow?' asked Ganimard.

' 'Him,' of course. He's big game.'

'Then I'll shadow the young lady,' suggested Ganimard.

'No, no,' said the Englishman quickly, not wishing to reveal any part of the case to Ganimard. 'I know where to find the young lady when I want her . . . Don't leave me.'

★ ★ ★

At a distance and availing themselves of the occasional shelter of the passers-by and the kiosks, Ganimard and Shears set off in pursuit of Lupin. It was an easy enough pursuit, for he did not turn round and walked quickly, with a slight lameness in the right leg, so slight that it needed the eye of a trained observer to perceive it.

'He's pretending to limp!' said Ganimard. And he continued, 'Ah, if we could only pick up two or three policemen and pounce upon the fellow! As it is, here's a chance of our losing him.'

But no policeman appeared in sight before the Porte des Ternes; and, once the fortifications were passed, they could not reckon on the least assistance.

'Let us separate,' said Shears. 'The place is deserted.'

They were on the Boulevard Victor-Hugo. They each took a different pavement and followed the line of the trees.

They walked like this for twenty minutes, until the moment when Lupin turned to the left and along the Seine. Here they saw him go down to the edge of the river. He remained there for a few seconds, during which they were unable to distinguish his movements. Then he climbed up the bank again and returned by the way he had come. They pressed back against the pillars of a gate. Lupin passed in front of them. He no longer carried a parcel.

And, as he moved away, another figure appeared from behind the corner of a house and slipped in between the trees.

Shears said, in a low voice:

'That one seems to be following him too.'

'Yes, I believe I saw him before, as we came.'

The pursuit was resumed, but was now complicated by the presence of this figure. Lupin followed the same road, passed through the Porte des Ternes again, and entered the house on the Place Saint-Ferdinand.

The concierge was closing the door for the night when Ganimard came up:

'You saw him, I suppose?'

'Yes, I was turning off the gas on the stairs. He has bolted his door.'

'Is there no one with him?'

'No one: he doesn't keep a servant . . . he never has his meals here.'

'Is there no back staircase?'

'No.'

Ganimard said to Shears:

'The best thing will be for me to place myself outside Lupin's door, while you go to the Rue Demours and fetch the commissary of police. I'll give you a line for him.'

Shears objected:

'Suppose he escapes meanwhile?'

'But I shall be here! . . . '

'Single-handed, it would be an unequal contest between you and him.'

'Still, I can't break into his rooms. I'm not entitled to, especially at night.'

Shears shrugged his shoulders:

'Once you've arrested Lupin, no one will haul you over the coals for the particular manner in which you effected the arrest. Besides, we may as well ring the bell, what! Then we'll see what happens.'

They went up the stairs. There was a double door on the left of the landing. Ganimard rang the bell.

Not a sound. He rang again. No one stirred.

'Let's go in,' muttered Shears.

'Yes, come along.'

Nevertheless, they remained motionless, irresolute. Like people who hesitate before taking a decisive step, they were afraid to act; and it suddenly seemed to them impossible that Arsène Lupin should be there, so near to them, behind that frail partition, which they could smash with a blow of their fists. They both of them knew him too well, demon that he was, to admit that he would allow himself to be nabbed so stupidly. No, no, a thousand times no; he was not there. He must have escaped, by the adjoining houses, by the roofs, by some suitably prepared outlet; and, once again, the shadow of Arsène Lupin was all that they could hope to lay hands upon.

They shuddered. An imperceptible sound, coming from the other side of the door, had, as it were, grazed the silence. And they received the impression, the certainty that he was there after all, separated from them by that thin wooden partition, and that he was listening to them, that he heard them.

What were they to do? It was a tragic situation. For all their coolness as old stagers of the police, they were overcome by so great an excitement that they imagined they could hear the beating of their own hearts.

Ganimard consulted Shears with a silent glance and then struck the door violently with his fist.

A sound of footsteps was now heard, a sound which there was no longer any attempt to conceal.

Ganimard shook the door. Shears gave an irresistible thrust with his shoulder and burst it open; and they both rushed in.

Then they stopped short. A shot resounded in the next room. And another, followed by the thud of a falling body.

When they entered, they saw the man lying with his face against the marble of the mantel-piece. He gave a convulsive movement. His revolver slipped from his hand.

Ganimard stooped and turned the dead man's head, it was covered with blood, which trickled from two large wounds in the cheek and temple.

'There's no recognizing him,' he whispered.

'One thing is certain,' said Shears. 'It's not 'he.''

'How do you know? You haven't even examined him.'

The Englishman sneered:

'Do you think Arsène Lupin is the man to kill himself?'

'Still, we believed we knew him outside.'

'We believed, because we *wanted* to believe. The fellow besets our minds.'

'Then it's one of his accomplices.'

'Arsène Lupin's accomplices do not kill themselves.'

'Then who is it?'

They searched the body. In one pocket, Holmlock Shears found an empty note-case; in another, Ganimard found a few louis. There were no marks on his linen or on his clothes.

The trunks — a big box and two bags — contained nothing but personal effects. There was a bundle of newspapers on the mantelpiece. Ganimard opened them. They all spoke of the theft of the Jewish lamp.

An hour later, when Ganimard and Shears left the house, they knew no more about the strange individual whom their intervention had driven to suicide.

Who was he? Why had he taken his life? What link connected him with the disappearance of the Jewish lamp? Who was it that dogged his steps during his walk? These were all complicated questions ... so many mysteries.

★　★　★

Holmlock Shears went to bed in a very bad temper. When he woke, he received an express letter couched in these words:

*Arsène Lupin begs to inform you of his tragic decease in the person of one Bresson and requests the honour of your company at his funeral, which will take place, at the public expense, on Thursday, the 25th of June.*

# 2

'You see, old chap,' said Holmlock Shears to Wilson, waving Arsène Lupin's letter in his hand, 'the worst of this business is that I feel the confounded fellow's eye constantly fixed upon me. Not one of my most secret thoughts escape him. I am behaving like an actor, whose steps are ruled by the strictest stage-directions, who moves here or there and says this or that because a superior will has so determined it. Do you understand, Wilson?'

Wilson would no doubt have understood had he not been sleeping the sound sleep of a man whose temperature is fluctuating between 102 and 104 degrees. But whether he heard or not made no difference to Shears, who continued:

'It will need all my energy and all my resources not to be discouraged. Fortunately, with me, these little gibes are only so many pin-pricks which stimulate me to further exertions. Once the sting is allayed and the wound in my self-respect closed, I always end by saying: 'Laugh away, my lad. Sooner or later, you will be betrayed by your own hand.' For, when all is said, Wilson, wasn't it Lupin himself who, with his first telegram and the reflection which it suggested to that little Henriette, revealed to me the secret of his correspondence with Alice Demun? You forget that detail, old chap.'

He walked up and down the room, with resounding strides, at the risk of waking old chap:

'However, things might be worse; and, though the paths which I am following appear a little dark, I am beginning to see my way. To start with, I shall soon know all about Master Bresson. Ganimard and I have an appointment on the bank of the Seine, at the spot where Bresson flung his parcel, and we shall find out who he was and what he wanted. As regards the rest, it's a game to be played out between Alice Demun and me. Not a very powerful adversary, eh, Wilson? And don't you think I shall soon know the sentence in the album and what those two single letters mean, the C and the H? For the whole mystery lies in that, Wilson.'

At this moment, mademoiselle entered the room and, seeing Shears wave his arms about, said: 'Mr. Shears, I shall be very angry with you if you wake my patient. It's not nice of you to disturb him. The doctor insists upon absolute calm.'

He looked at her without a word,

astonished, as on the first day, at her inexplicable composure.

'Why do you look at me like that, Mr. Shears? ... You always seem to have something at the back of your mind ... What is it? Tell me, please.'

She questioned him with all her bright face, with her guileless eyes, her smiling lips and with her attitude too, her hands joined together, her body bent slightly forward. And so great was her candour that it roused the Englishman's anger. He came up to her and said, in a low voice:

'Bresson committed suicide yesterday.'

She repeated, without appearing to understand:

'Bresson committed suicide yesterday?'

As a matter of fact, her features underwent no change whatever; nothing revealed the effort of a lie.

'You have been told,' he said, irritably. 'If not, you would at least have started ... Ah, you are cleverer than I thought! But why pretend?'

He took the picture-book, which he had placed on a table close at hand, and, opening it at the cut page:

'Can you tell me,' he asked, 'in what order I am to arrange the letters missing here, so that I may understand the exact purport of

284

the note which you sent to Bresson four days before the theft of the Jewish Lamp?'

'In what order? . . . Bresson? . . . The theft of the Jewish Lamp?'

She repeated the words, slowly, as though to make out their meaning.

He insisted:

'Yes, here are the letters you used . . . on this scrap of paper. What were you saying to Bresson?'

'The letters I used . . . ? What was I saying to . . . ?'

Suddenly she burst out laughing:

'I see! I understand! I am an accomplice in the theft! There is a M. Bresson who stole the Jewish Lamp and killed himself. And I am the gentleman's friend! Oh, how amusing!'

'Then whom did you go to see yesterday evening, on the second floor of a house in the Avenue des Ternes?'

'Whom? Why, my dressmaker, Mlle. Langeais! Do you mean to imply that my dressmaker and my friend M. Bresson are one and the same person?'

Shears began to doubt, in spite of all. It is possible to counterfeit almost any feeling in such a way as to put another person off: terror, joy, anxiety; but not indifference, not happy and careless laughter.

However, he said:

'One last word. Why did you accost me at the Gare du Nord the other evening? And why did you beg me to go back at once without busying myself about the robbery?'

'Oh, you're much too curious, Mr. Shears,' she replied, still laughing in the most natural way. 'To punish you, I will tell you nothing and, in addition, you shall watch the patient while I go to the chemist . . . There's an urgent prescription to be made up . . . I must hurry!'

She left the room.

'I have been tricked,' muttered Shears. 'I've not only got nothing out of her, but I have given myself away.'

And he remembered the case of the blue diamond and the cross-examination to which he had subjected Clotilde Destange. Mademoiselle had encountered him with the same serenity as the blonde lady and he felt that he was again face to face with one of those creatures who, protected by Arsène Lupin and under the direct action of his influence, preserved the most inscrutable calmness amid the very agony of danger.

'Shears . . . Shears . . .'

It was Wilson calling him. He went to the bed and bent over him:

'What is it, old chap? Feeling bad?'

Wilson moved his lips, but was unable to

speak. At last, after many efforts, he stammered out:

'No . . . Shears . . . it wasn't she . . . it can't have been . . . '

'What nonsense are you talking now? I tell you that it was she! It's only when I'm in the presence of a creature of Lupin's, trained and drilled by him, that I lose my head and behave so foolishly . . . She now knows the whole story of the album . . . I bet you that Lupin will be told in less than an hour. Less than an hour? What am I talking about? This moment, most likely! The chemist, the urgent prescription: humbug!'

Without a further thought of Wilson, he rushed from the room, went down the Avenue de Messine and saw Mademoiselle enter a chemist's shop. She came out, ten minutes later, carrying two or three medicine-bottles wrapped up in white paper. But, when she returned up the avenue, she was accosted by a man who followed her, cap in hand and with an obsequious air, as though he were begging.

She stopped, gave him an alms and then continued on her way.

'She spoke to him,' said the Englishman to himself.

It was an intuition rather than a certainty, but strong enough to induce him to alter his tactics. Leaving the girl, he set off on the track of the sham beggar.

They arrived in this way, one behind the other, on the Place Saint-Ferdinand; and the man hovered long round Bresson's house, sometimes raising his eyes to the second-floor windows and watching the people who entered the house.

At the end of an hour's time, he climbed to the top of a tram-car that was starting for Neuilly. Shears climbed up also and sat down behind the fellow, at some little distance, beside a gentleman whose features were concealed by the newspaper which he was reading. When they reached the fortifications, the newspaper was lowered, Shears recognized Ganimard and Ganimard, pointing to the fellow, said in his ear:

'It's our man of last night, the one who followed Bresson. He's been hanging round the square for an hour.'

'Nothing new about Bresson?'

'Yes, a letter arrived this morning addressed to him.'

'This morning? Then it must have been posted yesterday, before the writer knew of Bresson's death.'

'Just so. It is with the examining magistrate, but I can tell you the exact words: 'He accepts no compromise. He wants everything, the first thing as well as those of the second business. If not, he will take steps.' And no signature,' added Ganimard. 'As you can see, those few lines won't be of much use to us.'

'I don't agree with you at all, M. Ganimard: on the contrary, I consider them very interesting.'

'And why, bless my soul?'

'For reasons personal to myself,' said Shears, with the absence of ceremony with which he was accustomed to treat his colleague.

The tram stopped at the terminus in the Rue du Château. The man climbed down and walked away quietly. Shears followed so closely on his heels that Ganimard took alarm:

'If he turns round, we are done.'

'He won't turn round now.'

'What do you know about it?'

'He is an accomplice of Arsène Lupin's and the fact that an accomplice of Lupin's walks away like that, with his hands in his pockets, proves, in the first place, that he knows he's followed, and in the second, that he's not afraid.'

'Still, we're running him pretty hard!'

'No matter, he can slip through our fingers in a minute, if he wants. He's too sure of himself.'

'Come, come; you're getting at me! There are two cyclist police at the door of that café over there. If I decide to call on them and to tackle our friend, I should like to know how he's going to slip through our fingers.'

'Our friend does not seem much put out by that contingency. And he's calling on them himself!'

'By Jupiter!' said Ganimard. 'The cheek of the fellow!'

The man, in fact, had walked up to the two policemen just as these were preparing to mount their bicycles. He spoke a few words to them and then, suddenly, sprang upon a third bicycle, which was leaning against the wall of the café, and rode away quickly with the two policemen.

The Englishman burst with laughter:

'There, what did I tell you? Off before we knew where we were; and with two of your colleagues, M. Ganimard! Ah, he looks after himself, does Arsène Lupin! With cyclist policemen in his pay! Didn't I tell you our friend was a great deal too calm!'

'What then?' cried Ganimard, angrily. 'What could I do? It's very easy to laugh!'

'Come, come, don't be cross. We'll have our revenge. For the moment, what we want is reinforcements.'

'Folenfant is waiting for me at the end of the Avenue de Neuilly.'

'All right, pick him up and join me, both of you.'

Ganimard went away, while Shears followed the tracks of the bicycles, which were easily visible on the dust of the road because two of the machines were fitted with grooved tires. And he soon saw that these tracks were leading him to the bank of the Seine and that the three men had turned in the same direction as Bresson on the previous evening. He thus came to the gate against which he himself had hidden with Ganimard and, a little farther on, he saw a tangle of grooved lines which showed that they had stopped there. Just opposite, a little neck of land jutted into the river and, at the end of it, an old boat lay fastened.

This was where Bresson must have flung his parcel, or, rather, dropped it. Shears went down the incline and saw that, as the bank sloped very gently, and the water was low, he would easily find the parcel . . . unless the three men had been there first.

'No, no,' he said to himself, 'they have not had time . . . a quarter of an hour at most . . . And, yet, why did they come this way?'

A man was sitting in the boat, fishing. Shears asked him:

'Have you seen three men on bicycles?'

The angler shook his head.

The Englishman insisted:

'Yes, yes . . . Three men . . . They stopped

only a few yards from where you are.'

The angler put his rod under his arm, took a note-book from his pocket, wrote something on one of the pages, tore it out and handed it to Shears.

A great thrill shook the Englishman. At a glance, in the middle of the page which he held in his hand, he recognized the letters torn from the picture-book:

CDEHNOPRZEO — 237

The sun hung heavily over the river. The angler had resumed his work, sheltered under the huge brim of his straw hat; his jacket and waistcoat lay folded by his side. He fished attentively, while the float of his line rocked idly on the current.

Quite a minute elapsed, a minute of solemn and awful silence.

'Is it he?' thought Shears, with an almost painful anxiety.

And then the truth burst upon him:

'It is he! It is he! He alone is capable of sitting like that, without a tremor of uneasiness, without the least fear as to what will happen . . . And who else could know the story of the picture-book? Alice must have told him by her messenger.'

Suddenly, the Englishman felt that his hand,

that his own hand, had seized the butt-end of his revolver and that his eyes were fixed on the man's back, just below the neck. One movement and the whole play was finished; a touch of the trigger and the life of the strange adventurer had come to a miserable end.

The angler did not stir.

Shears nervously gripped his weapon with a fierce longing to fire and have done with it and, at the same time, with horror of a deed against which his nature revolted. Death was certain. It would be over.

'Oh,' he thought, 'let him get up, let him defend himself . . . If not, he will have only himself to blame . . . Another second . . . and I fire.'

But a sound of footsteps made him turn his head and he saw Ganimard arrive, accompanied by the inspectors.

Then, changing his idea, he leapt forward, sprang at one bound into the boat, breaking the painter with the force of the jump, fell upon the man and held him in a close embrace. They both rolled to the bottom of the boat.

'Well?' cried Lupin, struggling. 'And then? What does this prove? Suppose one of us reduces the other to impotence: what will he have gained? You will not know what to do with me nor I with you. We shall stay here like a couple of fools!'

The two oars slipped into the water. The boat began to drift. Mingled exclamations resounded along the bank and Lupin continued:

'Lord, what a business! Have you lost all sense of things? . . . Fancy being so silly at your age! You great schoolboy! You ought to be ashamed!'

He succeeded in releasing himself.

Exasperated, resolved to stick at nothing, Shears put his hand in his pocket. An oath escaped him. Lupin had taken his revolver.

Then he threw himself on his knees and tried to catch hold of one of the oars, in order to pull to the shore, while Lupin made desperate efforts after the other, in order to pull out to mid-stream.

'Got it! . . . Missed it!' said Lupin. 'However, it makes no difference . . . If you get your oar, I'll prevent your using it . . . And you'll do as much for me . . . But there, in life, we strive to act . . . without the least reason, for it's always fate that decides . . . There, you see, fate . . . well, she's deciding for her old friend Lupin! . . . Victory! The current's favouring me!'

The boat, in fact, was drifting away.

'Look out!' cried Lupin.

Some one, on the bank, pointed a revolver. Lupin ducked his head; a shot rang out; a little water spurted up around them. He burst out laughing:

'Heaven help us, it's friend Ganimard! . . . Now that's very wrong of you, Ganimard. You have no right to fire except in self-defence . . . Does poor Arsène make you so furious that you forget your duties? . . . Hullo, he's starting again! . . . But, wretched man, be careful: you'll hit my dear maître here!'

He made a bulwark of his body for Shears and, standing up in the boat, facing Ganimard:

'There, now I don't mind! . . . Aim here, Ganimard, straight at my heart! . . . Higher . . . to the left . . . Missed again . . . you clumsy beggar! . . . Another shot? . . . But you're trembling, Ganimard! . . . At the word of command, eh? And steady now . . . one, two, three, fire! . . . Missed! Dash it all, does the Government give you toys for pistols?'

He produced a long, massive, flat revolver and fired without taking aim.

The inspector lifted his hand to his hat: a bullet had made a hole through it.

'What do you say to that, Ganimard? Ah, this is a better make! Hats off, gentlemen: this is the revolver of my noble friend, Maître Holmlock Shears!'

And he tossed the weapon to the bank, right at the inspector's feet.

Shears could not help giving a smile of

admiration. What superabundant life! What young and spontaneous gladness! And how he seemed to enjoy himself! It was as though the sense of danger gave him a physical delight, as though life had no other object for this extraordinary man than the search of dangers which he amused himself afterward by averting.

Meantime, crowds had gathered on either side of the river and Ganimard and his men were following the craft, which swung down the stream, carried very slowly by the current. It meant inevitable, mathematical capture.

'Confess, maître,' cried Lupin, turning to the Englishman, 'that you would not give up your seat for all the gold in the Transvaal! You are in the first row of the stalls! But, first and before all, the prologue . . . after which we will skip straight to the fifth act, the capture or the escape of Arsène Lupin. Therefore, my dear maître, I have one request to make of you and I beg you to answer yes or no, to save all ambiguity. Cease interesting yourself in this business. There is yet time and I am still able to repair the harm which you have done. Later on, I shall not be. Do you agree?'

'No.'

Lupin's features contracted. This obstinacy was causing him visible annoyance. He resumed:

'I insist. I insist even more for your sake

than my own, for I am certain that you will be the first to regret your interference. Once more, yes or no?'

'No.'

Lupin squatted on his heels, shifted one of the planks at the bottom of the boat and, for a few minutes, worked at something which Shears could not see. Then he rose, sat down beside the Englishman and spoke to him in these words:

'I believe, maître, that you and I came to the river-bank with the same purpose, that of fishing up the object which Bresson got rid of, did we not? I, for my part, had made an appointment to meet a few friends and I was on the point, as my scanty costume shows, of effecting a little exploration in the depths of the Seine when my friends gave me notice of your approach. I am bound to confess that I was not surprised, having been kept informed, I venture to say, hourly, of the progress of your inquiry. It is so easy! As soon as the least thing likely to interest me occurs in the Rue Murillo, quick, they ring me up and I know all about it! You can understand that, in these conditions . . . '

He stopped. The plank which he had removed now rose a trifle and water was filtering in, all around, in driblets.

'The deuce! I don't know how I managed

it, but I have every reason to think that there's a leak in this old boat. You're not afraid, maître?'

Shears shrugged his shoulders. Lupin continued:

'You can understand, therefore, that, in these conditions and knowing beforehand that you would seek the contest all the more greedily the more I strove to avoid it, I was rather pleased at the idea of playing a rubber with you the result of which is certain, seeing that I hold all the trumps. And I wished to give our meeting the greatest possible publicity, so that your defeat might be universally known and no new Comtesse de Crozon nor Baron d'Imblevalle be tempted to solicit your aid against me. And, in all this, my dear maître, you must not see . . . '

He interrupted himself again, and, using his half-closed hands as a field-glass, he watched the banks:

'By Jove! They've freighted a splendid cutter, a regular man-of-war's boat, and they're rowing like anything! In five minutes they will board us and I shall be lost. Mr. Shears, let me give you one piece of advice: throw yourself upon me, tie me hand and foot and deliver me to the law of my country . . . Does that suit you? . . . Unless we suffer shipwreck meanwhile, in which case there will be nothing for us to do but make our wills. What do you say?'

Their eyes met. This time, Shears understood Lupin's operations: he had made a hole in the bottom of the boat.

And the water was rising. It reached the soles of their boots. It covered their feet; they did not move.

It came above their ankles: the Englishman took his tobacco-pouch, rolled a cigarette and lit it.

Lupin continued:

'And, in all this, my dear maître, you must not see anything more than the humble confession of my powerlessness in face of you. It is tantamount to yielding to you, when I accept only those contests in which my victory is assured, in order to avoid those of which I shall not have selected the field. It is tantamount to recognizing that Holmlock Shears is the only enemy whom I fear and proclaiming my anxiety as long as Shears is not removed from my path. This, my dear maître, is what I wished to tell you, on this one occasion when fate has allowed me the honour of a conversation with you. I regret only one thing, which is that this conversation should take place while we are having a foot-bath . . . a position lacking in dignity, I must confess . . . And what was I saying? . . . A foot-bath! . . . A hip-bath rather!'

The water, in fact, had reached the seat on which they were sitting and the boat sank lower and lower in the water.

Shears sat imperturbable, his cigarette at his lips, apparently wrapped in contemplation of the sky. For nothing in the world, in the face of that man surrounded by dangers, hemmed in by the crowd, hunted down by a posse of police and yet always retaining his good humour, for nothing in the world would he have consented to display the least sign of agitation.

'What!' they both seemed to be saying. 'Do people get excited about such trifles? Is it not a daily occurrence to get drowned in a river? Is this the sort of event that deserves to be noticed?'

And the one chattered and the other mused, while both concealed under the same mask of indifference the formidable clash of their respective prides.

Another minute and they would sink.

'The essential thing,' said Lupin, 'is to know if we shall sink before or after the arrival of the champions of the law! All depends upon that. For the question of shipwreck is no longer in doubt. Maître, the solemn moment has come to make our wills. I leave all my real and personal estate to

Holmlock Shears, a citizen of the British Empire ... But, by Jove, how fast they are coming, those champions of the law! Oh, the dear people! It's a pleasure to watch them! What precision of stroke! Ah, is that you, Sergeant Folenfant? Well done! That idea of the man-of-war's cutter was capital. I shall recommend you to your superiors, Sergeant Folenfant ... And weren't you hoping for a medal? Right you are! Consider it yours! ... and where's your friend Dieuzy? On the left bank, I suppose, in the midst of a hundred natives ... So that, if I escape shipwreck, I shall be picked up on the left by Dieuzy and his natives or else on the right by Ganimard and the Neuilly tribes. A nasty dilemma ... '

There was an eddy. The boat swung round and Shears was obliged to cling to the rowlocks.

'Maître,' said Lupin, 'I beg of you to take off your jacket. You will be more comfortable for swimming. You won't? Then I shall put on mine again.'

He slipped on his jacket, buttoned it tightly like Shears's and sighed:

'What a fine fellow you are! And what a pity that you should persist in a business ... in which you are certainly doing the very best you can, but all in vain! Really, you are

301

throwing away your distinguished talent.'

'M. Lupin,' said Shears, at last abandoning his silence, 'you talk a great deal too much and you often err through excessive confidence and frivolity.'

'That's a serious reproach.'

'It was in this way that, without knowing it, you supplied me, a moment ago, with the information I wanted.'

'What! You wanted some information, and you never told me!'

'I don't require you or anybody. In three hours' time I shall hand the solution of the puzzle to M. and reply . . . '

He did not finish his sentence. The boat had suddenly foundered, dragging them both with her. She rose to the surface at once, overturned, with her keel in the air. Loud shouts came from the two banks, followed by an anxious silence and, suddenly, fresh cries: one of the shipwrecked men had reappeared.

It was Holmlock Shears.

An excellent swimmer, he struck out boldly for Folenfant's boat.

'Cheerly, Mr. Shears!' roared the detective-sergeant. 'You're all right! . . . Keep on . . . we'll see about him afterward . . . We've got him right enough . . . one more effort, Mr. Shears . . . catch hold . . . '

The Englishman seized a rope which they

threw to him. But, while they were dragging him on board, a voice behind him called out:

'Yes, my dear maître, you shall have the solution. I am even surprised that you have not hit upon it already . . . And then? What use will it be to you? It's just then that you will have lost the battle . . . '

Seated comfortably astride the hulk, of which he had scaled the sides while talking, Arsène Lupin continued his speech with solemn gestures and as though he hoped to convince his hearers:

'Do you understand, my dear maître, that there is nothing to be done, absolutely nothing . . . You are in the deplorable position of a gentleman who . . . '

Folenfant took aim at him:

'Lupin, surrender!'

'You're an ill-bred person, Sergeant Folenfant; you've interrupted me in the middle of a sentence. I was saying . . . '

'Lupin, surrender!'

'But, dash it all, Sergeant Folenfant, one only surrenders when in danger! Now surely you have not the face to believe that I am running the least danger!'

'For the last time, Lupin, I call on you to surrender!'

'Sergeant Folenfant, you have not the smallest intention of killing me; at the most you mean to wound me, you're so afraid of my escaping! And supposing that, by accident, the wound should be mortal? Oh, think of your remorse, wretched man, of your blighted old age . . . '

The shot went off.

Lupin staggered, clung for a moment to the overturned boat, then let go and disappeared.

★   ★   ★

It was just three o'clock when these events happened. At six o'clock precisely, as he had declared, Holmlock Shears, clad in a pair of trousers too short and a jacket too tight for him, which he had borrowed from an inn-keeper at Neuilly, and wearing a cap and a flannel shirt with a silk cord and tassels, entered the boudoir in the Rue Murillo, after sending word to M. and Mme. d'Imblevalle to ask for an interview.

They found him walking up and down. And he looked to them so comical in his queer costume that they had a difficulty in suppressing their inclination to laugh. With a pensive air and a bent back, he walked, like an automaton, from the window to the door and the door to the window, taking each time the same number of steps and turning each time in the same direction.

He stopped, took up a knick-knack, examined it mechanically and then resumed his walk.

At last, planting himself in front of them, he asked:

'Is mademoiselle here?'

'Yes, in the garden, with the children.'

'Monsieur le baron, as this will be our final conversation, I should like Mlle. Demun to be present at it.'

'So you decidedly . . . ?'

'Have a little patience, monsieur. The truth will emerge plainly from the facts which I propose to lay before you with the greatest possible precision.'

'Very well. Suzanne, do you mind . . . ?'

Mme. d'Imblevalle rose and returned almost at once, accompanied by Alice Demun. Mademoiselle, looking a little paler than usual, remained standing, leaning against a table and without even asking to know why she had been sent for.

Shears appeared not to see her and, turning abruptly toward M. d'Imblevalle, made his statement in a tone that admitted of no reply:

'After an inquiry extending over several days, and although certain events for a moment altered my view, I will repeat what I said from the first, that the Jewish lamp was stolen by some one living in this house.'

'The name?'

'I know it.'

'Your evidence?'

'The evidence which I have is enough to confound the culprit.'

'It is not enough that the culprit should be confounded. He must restore . . . '

'The Jewish lamp? It is in my possession!'

'The opal necklace? The snuff-box? . . . '

'The opal necklace, the snuff-box, in short everything that was stolen on the second occasion is in my possession.'

Shears loved this dry, claptrap way of announcing his triumphs.

As a matter of fact, the baron and his wife seemed stupefied and looked at him with a silent curiosity which was, in itself, the highest praise.

He next summed up in detail all that he had done during those three days. He told how he had discovered the picture-book, wrote down on a sheet of paper the sentence formed by the letters which had been cut out, then described Bresson's expedition to the bank of the Seine and his suicide and, lastly, the struggle in which he, Shears, had just been engaged with Lupin, the wreck of the boat and Lupin's disappearance.

When he had finished, the baron said, in a low voice:

'Nothing remains but that you should reveal the name of the thief. Whom do you accuse?'

'I accuse the person who cut out the letters from this alphabet and communicated, by means of those letters, with Arsène Lupin.'

'How do you know that this person's correspondent was Arsène Lupin?'

'From Lupin himself.'

He held out a scrap of moist and crumpled paper. It was the page which Lupin had torn from his note-book in the boat, and on which he had written the sentence.

'And observe,' said Shears, in a gratified voice, 'that there was nothing to compel him to give me this paper and thus make himself known. It was a mere schoolboy prank on his part, which gave me the information I wanted.'

'What information?' asked the baron. 'I don't see . . . '

Shears copied out the letters and figures in pencil:

CDEHNOPRZEO — 237

'Well?' said M. d'Imblevalle. 'That's the formula which you have just shown us yourself.'

'No. If you had turned this formula over and over, as I have done, you would have seen at once that it contains two more letters than the first, an E and an O.'

307

'As a matter of fact, I did not notice . . . '

'Place these two letters beside the C and H which remained over from the word *Répondez*, and you will see that the only possible word is 'ÉCHO.''

'Which means . . . ?'

'Which means the *Écho de France*, Lupin's newspaper, his own organ, the one for which he reserves his official communications. 'Send reply to the *Écho de France*, agony column, No. 237.' That was the key for which I had hunted so long and with which Lupin was kind enough to supply me. I have just come from the office of the *Écho de France*.'

'And what have you found?'

'I have found the whole detailed story of the relations between Arsène Lupin and . . . his accomplice.'

And Shears spread out seven newspapers, opened at the fourth page, and picked out the following lines:

1. *ARS. LUP. Lady impl. protect. 540.*
2. *540. Awaiting explanations. A. L.*
3. *A. L. Under dominion of enemy. Lost.*
4. *540. Write address. Will make enq.*
5. *A. L. Murillo.*
6. *540. Park 3 p. m. Violets.*
7. *237. Agreed Sat. Shall be park. Sun. morn.*

'And you call that a detailed story!' exclaimed M. d'Imblevalle.

'Why, of course; and, if you will pay attention, you will think the same. First of all, a lady, signing herself 540, implores the protection of Arsène Lupin. To this Lupin replies with a request for explanations. The lady answers that she is under the dominion of an enemy, Bresson, no doubt, and that she is lost unless some one comes to her assistance. Lupin, who is suspicious and dares not yet have an interview with the stranger, asks for the address and suggests an inquiry. The lady hesitates for four days — see the dates — and, at last, under the pressure of events and the influence of Bresson's threats, gives the name of her street, the Rue Murillo. The next day, Arsène Lupin advertises that he will be in the Parc Monceau at three o'clock and asks the stranger to wear a bunch of violets as a token. Here follows an interruption of eight days in the correspondence. Arsène Lupin and the lady no longer need write through the medium of the paper: they see each other or correspond direct. The plot is contrived: to satisfy Bresson's requirements, the lady will take the Jewish lamp. It remains to fix the day. The lady, who, from motives of prudence, corresponds by means of words cut out and stuck together, decides upon Saturday, and adds, 'Send reply

*Écho* 237.' Lupin replies that it is agreed and that, moreover, he will be in the park on Sunday morning. On Sunday morning, the theft took place.'

'Yes, everything fits in,' said the baron, approvingly, 'and the story is complete.'

Shears continued:

'So the theft took place. The lady goes out on Sunday morning, tells Lupin what she has done and carries the Jewish lamp to Bresson. Things then happen as Lupin foresaw. The police, misled by an open window, four holes in the ground and two scratches on a balcony, at once accept the burglary suggestion. The lady is easy in her mind.'

'Very well,' said the baron. 'I accept this explanation as perfectly logical. But the second theft . . . '

'The second theft was provoked by the first. After the newspapers had told how the Jewish lamp had disappeared, some one thought of returning to the attack and seizing hold of everything that had not been carried away. And, this time, it was not a pretended theft, but a real theft, with a genuine burglary, ladders, and so on.'

'Lupin, of course . . . ?'

'No, Lupin does not act so stupidly. Lupin does not fire at people without very good reason.'

310

'Then who was it?'

'Bresson, no doubt, unknown to the lady whom he had been blackmailing. It was Bresson who broke in here, whom I pursued, who wounded my poor Wilson.'

'Are you quite sure?'

'Absolutely. One of Bresson's accomplices wrote him a letter yesterday, before his suicide, which shows that this accomplice and Lupin had entered upon a parley for the restitution of all the articles stolen from your house. Lupin demanded everything, 'the first thing,' that is to say, the Jewish lamp, 'as well as those of the second business.' Moreover, he watched Bresson. When Bresson went to the bank of the Seine yesterday evening, one of Lupin's associates was dogging him at the same time as ourselves.'

'What was Bresson doing at the bank of the Seine?'

'Warned of the progress of my inquiry . . .'

'Warned by whom?'

'By the same lady, who very rightly feared lest the discovery of the Jewish lamp should entail the discovery of her adventure . . . Bresson, therefore, warned, collected into one parcel all that might compromise him and dropped it in a place where it would be possible for him to recover it, once the danger was past. It was on his return that, hunted down by Ganimard and me and doubtless having other crimes on his conscience, he lost his head and shot himself.'

'But what did the parcel contain?'

'The Jewish lamp and your other things.'

'Then they are not in your possession?'

'Immediately after Lupin's disappearance, I took advantage of the bath which he had compelled me to take to drive to the spot chosen by Bresson; and I found your stolen property wrapped up in linen and oil-skin. Here it is, on the table.'

Without a word, the baron cut the string, tore through the pieces of wet linen, took out the lamp, turned a screw under the foot, pressed with both hands on the receiver, opened it into two equal parts and revealed the golden chimera, set with rubies and emeralds. It was untouched.

★   ★   ★

In all this scene, apparently so natural and consisting of a simple statement of facts, there was something that made it terribly tragic, which was the formal, direct, irrefutable accusation which Shears hurled at mademoiselle with every word he uttered. And there was also Alice Demun's impressive silence.

During that long, that cruel accumulation of small super-added proofs, not a muscle of her face had moved, not a gleam of rebellion or fear had disturbed the serenity of her limpid glance. What was she thinking? And, still more, what would she say at the solemn moment when she must reply, when she must defend herself and break the iron circle in which the Englishman had so cleverly imprisoned her?

The moment had struck, and the girl was silent.

'Speak! speak!' cried M. d'Imblevalle.

She did not speak.

He insisted:

'One word will clear you . . . One word of protest and I will believe you.'

That word she did not utter.

The baron stepped briskly across the room, returned, went back again and then, addressing Shears:

'Well, no, sir! I refuse to believe it true! There are some crimes which are impossible! And this is opposed to all that I know, all that I have seen for a year.' He put his hand on the Englishman's shoulder. 'But are you yourself, sir, absolutely and definitely sure that you are not mistaken?'

Shears hesitated, like a man attacked unawares, who does not defend himself at once. However, he smiled and said:

'No one but the person whom I accuse could, thanks to the position which she fills in your house, know that the Jewish lamp contained that magnificent jewel.'

'I refuse to believe it,' muttered the baron.

'Ask her.'

It was, in fact, the one thing which he had not tried, in the blind confidence which he felt in the girl. But it was no longer permissible to deny the evidence.

He went up to her and, looking her straight in the eyes:

'Was it you, mademoiselle? Did you take the jewel? Did you correspond with Arsène Lupin and sham the burglary?'

She replied:

'Yes, monsieur.'

She did not lower her head. Her face expressed neither shame nor embarrassment.

'Is it possible?' stammered M. d'Imblevalle. 'I would never have believed . . . you are the last person I should have suspected . . . How did you do it, unhappy girl?'

She said:

'I did as Mr. Shears has said. On Saturday night, I came down here to the boudoir, took the lamp and, in the morning, carried it . . . to that man.'

'But no,' objected the baron; 'what you say is impossible.'

'Impossible! Why?'

'Because I found the door of the boudoir locked in the morning.'

She coloured, lost countenance and looked at Shears as though to ask his advice.

The Englishman seemed struck by Alice's embarrassment even more than by the baron's objection. Had she, then, no reply to make? Did the confession that confirmed the explanation which he, Shears, had given of the theft of the Jewish lamp conceal a lie which an examination of the facts at once laid bare?

The baron continued:

'The door was locked, I repeat. I declare that I found the bolt as I left it at night. If you had come that way, as you pretend, someone must have opened the door to you from the inside — that is to say, from the boudoir or from our bedroom. Now there was no one in these two rooms . . . no one except my wife and myself.'

Shears bent down quickly and covered his face with his two hands to hide it. He had flushed scarlet. Something resembling too sudden a light had struck him and left him dazed and ill at ease. The whole stood revealed to him like a dim landscape from which the darkness was suddenly lifting.

Alice Demun was innocent.

Alice Demun was innocent. That was a

certain, blinding fact and, at the same time, explained the sort of embarrassment which he had felt since the first day at directing the terrible accusation against this young girl. He saw clearly now. He knew. It needed but a movement and, then and there, the irrefutable proof would stand forth before him.

He raised his head and, after a few seconds, as naturally as he could, turned his eyes toward Mme. d'Imblevalle.

She was pale, with that unaccustomed pallor that overcomes us at the relentless hours of life. Her hands, which she strove to hide, trembled imperceptibly.

'Another second,' thought Shears, 'and she will have betrayed herself.'

He placed himself between her and her husband, with the imperious longing to ward off the terrible danger which, through his fault, threatened this man and this woman. But, at the sight of the baron, he shuddered to the very depths of his being. The same sudden revelation which had dazzled him with its brilliancy was now enlightening M. d'Imblevalle. The same thought was working in the husband's brain. He understood in his turn! He saw!

Desperately, Alice Demun strove to resist the implacable truth:

'You are right, monsieur; I made a mistake.

As a matter of fact, I did not come in this way. I went through the hall and the garden and, with the help of a ladder . . . '

It was a supreme effort of devotion . . . but a useless effort! The words did not ring true. The voice had lost its assurance and the sweet girl was no longer able to retain her limpid glance and her great air of sincerity. She hung her head, defeated.

*   *   *

The silence was frightful. Mme. d'Imblevalle waited, her features livid and drawn with anguish and fear. The baron seemed to be still struggling, as though refusing to believe in the downfall of his happiness.

At last he stammered:

'Speak! Explain yourself!'

'I have nothing to say, my poor friend,' she said, in a very low voice her features wrung with despair.

'Then . . . mademoiselle . . . ?'

'Mademoiselle saved me . . . through devotion . . . through affection . . . and accused herself . . . '

'Saved you from what? From whom?'

'From that man.'

'Bresson?'

'Yes, he held me by his threats . . . I met

317

him at a friend's house . . . and I had the madness to listen to him. Oh, there was nothing that you cannot forgive! . . . But I wrote him two letters . . . you shall see them . . . I bought them back . . . you know how . . . Oh, have pity on me . . . I have been so unhappy!'

'You! You! Suzanne!'

He raised his clenched fists to her, ready to beat her, ready to kill her. But his arms fell to his sides and he murmured again:

'You, Suzanne! . . . You! . . . Is it possible?'

In short, abrupt sentences, she told the heartbreaking and commonplace story: her terrified awakening in the face of the man's infamy, her remorse, her madness; and she also described Alice's admirable conduct: the girl suspecting her mistress's despair, forcing a confession from her, writing to Lupin and contriving this story of a robbery to save her from Bresson's clutches.

'You, Suzanne, you!' repeated M. d'Imblevalle, bent double, overwhelmed. 'How could you . . . ?'

★　★　★

On the evening of the same day, the steamer *Ville de Londres*, from Calais to Dover, was gliding slowly over the motionless water. The night was dark and calm. Peaceful clouds were suggested rather than seen above the boat and, all around, light veils of mist separated her from the infinite space in which the moon and stars were shedding their cold, but invisible radiance.

Most of the passengers had gone to the cabins and saloons. A few of them, however, bolder than the rest, were walking up and down the deck or else dozing under thick rugs in the big rocking-chairs. Here and there the gleam showed of a cigar; and, mingling with the gentle breath of the wind, came the murmur of voices that dared not rise high in the great solemn silence.

One of the passengers, who was walking to and fro with even strides, stopped beside a person stretched out on a bench, looked at her and, when she moved slightly, said:

'I thought you were asleep, Mlle. Alice.'

'No, Mr. Shears, I do not feel sleepy. I was thinking.'

'What of? Is it indiscreet to ask?'

'I was thinking of Mme. d'Imblevalle. How sad she must be! Her life is ruined.'

'Not at all, not at all,' he said, eagerly. 'Her fault is not one of those which can never be forgiven. M. d'Imblevalle will forget that lapse. Already, when we left, he was looking at her less harshly.'

'Perhaps . . . but it will take long to forget . . . and she is suffering.'

'Are you very fond of her?'

'Very. That gave me such strength to smile when I was trembling with fear, to look you in the face when I wanted to avoid your glance.'

'And are you unhappy at leaving her?'

'Most unhappy. I have no relations or friends . . . I had only her . . . '

'You shall have friends,' said the Englishman, whom this grief was upsetting, 'I promise you that . . . I have connections . . . I have much influence . . . I assure you that you will not regret your position . . . '

'Perhaps, but Mme. d'Imblevalle will not be there . . . '

They exchanged no more words. Holmlock Shears took two or three more turns along the deck and then came back and settled down near his travelling-companion.

The misty curtain lifted and the clouds seemed to part in the sky. Stars twinkled up above.

Shears took his pipe from the pocket of his Inverness cape, filled it and struck four matches, one after the other, without succeeding in lighting it. As he had none left, he rose and said to a gentleman seated a few steps off:

'Could you oblige me with a light, please?'

The gentleman opened a box of fusees and struck one. A flame blazed up. By its light, Shears saw Arsène Lupin.

If the Englishman had not given a tiny movement, an almost imperceptible movement of recoil, Lupin might have thought that his presence on board was known to him, so great was the mastery which Shears retained over himself and so natural the ease with which he held out his hand to his adversary:

'Keeping well, M. Lupin?'

'Bravo!' exclaimed Lupin, from whom this self-command drew a cry of admiration.

'Bravo? . . . What for?'

'What for? You see me reappear before you like a ghost, after witnessing my dive into the Seine, and, from pride, from a miraculous pride which I will call essentially British, you give not a movement of astonishment, you utter not a word of surprise! Upon my word, I repeat, bravo! It's admirable!'

'There's nothing admirable about it. From the way you fell off the boat, I could see that you fell of your own accord and that you had not been struck by the sergeant's shot.'

'And you went away without knowing what became of me?'

'What became of you? I knew. Five hundred people were commanding the two banks over a distance of three-quarters of a mile. Once you escaped death, your capture was certain.'

'And yet I'm here!'

'M. Lupin, there are two men in the world of whom nothing can astonish me: myself first and you next.'

★  ★  ★

Peace was concluded.

If Shears had failed in his undertakings against Arsène Lupin, if Lupin remained the exceptional enemy whom he must definitely renounce all attempts to capture, if, in the course of the engagements, Lupin always preserved his superiority, the Englishman had, nevertheless, thanks to his formidable tenacity, recovered the Jewish lamp, just as he had recovered the blue diamond. Perhaps, this time, the result was less brilliant, especially from the point of view of the public, since Shears was obliged to suppress the circumstances in which the Jewish lamp had been discovered and to proclaim that he did not know the culprit's name. But, as between man and man, between Lupin and Shears, between burglar and detective, there was, in all fairness, neither victor nor vanquished. Each of them could lay claim to equal triumphs.

They talked, therefore, like courteous adversaries who have laid down their arms and who esteem each other at their true worth.

At Shears's request, Lupin described his escape.

'If, indeed,' he said, 'you can call it an escape. It was so simple! My friends were on the watch, since we had arranged to meet in order to fish up the Jewish lamp. And so, after remaining a good half-hour under the overturned keel of the boat, I took advantage of a moment when Folenfant and his men were looking for my corpse along the banks and I climbed on to the wreck again. My friends had only to pick me up in their motor-boat and to dash off before the astounded eyes of the five hundred sightseers, Ganimard and Folenfant.'

'Very pretty!' cried Shears. 'Most successful! And now have you business in England?'

'Yes, a few accounts to settle . . . But I was forgetting . . . M. d'Imblevalle . . . ?'

'He knows all.'

'Ah, my dear maître, what did I tell you? The harm's done now, beyond repair. Would it not have been better to let me go to work in my own way? A day or two more and I should have recovered the Jewish lamp and the other things from Bresson and sent them back to the d'Imblevalles; and those two good people would have gone on living peacefully together. Instead of which . . . '

'Instead of which,' snarled Shears, 'I have

muddled everything up and brought discord into a family which you were protecting.'

'Well, yes, if you like, protecting! Is it indispensable that one should always steal, cheat and do harm?'

'So you do good also?'

'When I have time. Besides, it amuses me. I think it extremely funny that, in the present adventure, I should be the good genius who rescues and saves and you the wicked genius who brings despair and tears.'

'Certainly! The d'Imblevalle home is broken up and Alice Demun is weeping.'

'She could not have remained . . . Ganimard would have ended by discovering her . . . and through her they would have worked back to Mme. d'Imblevalle.'

'Quite of your opinion, maître; but whose fault was it?'

★ ★ ★

Two men passed in front of them. Shears said to Lupin, in a voice the tone of which seemed a little altered:

'Do you know who those two gentlemen are?'

'I think one was the captain of the boat.'

'And the other?'

'I don't know.'

'It is Mr. Austin Gilett. And Mr. Austin Gilett occupies in England a post which corresponds with that of your M. Dudouis.'

'Oh, what luck! Would you have the kindness to introduce me? M. Dudouis is a great friend of mine and I should like to be able to say as much of Mr. Austin Gilett.'

The two gentlemen reappeared.

'And, suppose I were to take you at your word, M. Lupin . . . ?' said Shears, rising.

He had seized Arsène Lupin's wrist and held it in a grip of steel.

'Why grip me so hard, maître? I am quite ready to go with you.'

He allowed himself, in fact, to be dragged along, without the least resistance. The two gentlemen were walking away from them.

Shears increased his pace. His nails dug into Lupin's very flesh.

'Come along, come along!' he said, under his breath, in a sort of fevered haste to settle everything as quickly as possible. 'Come along! Quick!'

But he stopped short: Alice Demun had followed them.

'What are you doing, mademoiselle? You need not trouble to come!'

It was Lupin who replied:

'I beg you to observe, maître, that mademoiselle is not coming of her own free will. I am holding her wrist with an energy similar to that which you are applying to mine.'

'And why?'

'Why? Well, I am bent upon introducing her also. Her part in the story of the Jewish Lamp is even more important than mine. As an accomplice of Arsène Lupin, and of Bresson as well, she too must tell the adventure of the Baronne d'Imblevalle . . . which is sure to interest the police immensely. And in this way you will have pushed your kind interference to its last limits, O generous Shears!'

The Englishman had released his prisoner's wrist. Lupin let go of mademoiselle's.

They stood, for a few seconds, without moving, looking at one another. Then Shears went back to his bench and sat down. Lupin and the girl resumed their places.

*  *  *

A long silence divided them. Then Lupin said:

'You see, maître, do what we may, we shall never be in the same camp. You will always be on one side of the ditch, I on the other. We can nod, shake hands, exchange a word or two; but the ditch is always there. You will always be, Holmlock Shears, detective, and I Arsène Lupin, burglar. And Holmlock Shears will always, more or less spontaneously, more or less seasonably, obey his instinct as a detective, which is to hound down the burglar and 'run him in' if possible. And Arsène Lupin will always be consistent with his burglar's soul in avoiding the grasp of the detective and laughing at him if he can. And, this time, he can! Ha, ha, ha!'

He burst into a cunning, cruel and detestable laugh . . . Then, suddenly becoming serious, he leaned toward the girl:

'Be sure, mademoiselle, that, though reduced to the last extremity, I would not have betrayed you. Arsène Lupin never betrays, especially those whom he likes and admires. And you must permit me to say that I like and admire the dear, plucky creature that you are.'

He took a visiting-card from his pocket-book, tore it in two, gave one-half to the girl and, in a touched and respectful voice:

'If Mr. Shears does not succeed in his steps, mademoiselle, pray go to Lady Strongborough, whose address you can easily find out, hand her this half-card and say, 'Faithful memories!' Lady Strongborough will show you the devotion of a sister.'

'Thank you,' said the girl, 'I will go to her to-morrow.'

'And now, maître,' cried Lupin, in the satisfied tone of a man who has done his duty, 'let me bid you good night. The mist has delayed us and there is still time to take forty winks.' He stretched himself at full length and crossed his hands behind his head.

★ ★ ★

The sky had opened before the moon. She shed her radiant brightness around the stars and over the sea. It floated upon the water; and space, in which the last mists were dissolving, seemed to belong to it.

The line of the coast stood out against the dark horizon. Passengers came up on deck, which was now covered with people. Mr. Austin Gilett passed in the company of two men whom Shears recognized as members of the English detective-force.

On his bench, Lupin slept . . .